HOME FREE

Books by Fern Michaels:

Sins of the Flesh
Sins of Omission
Return to Sender
Mr. and Miss Anonymous
Up Close and Personal
Fool Me Once
Picture Perfect
About Face
The Future Scrolls
Kentucky Sunrise
Kentucky Heat
Kentucky Rich
Plain Jane
Charming Lily
What You Wish For
The Guest List
Listen to Your Heart
Celebration
Yesterday
Finders Keepers
Annie's Rainbow
Sara's Song
Vegas Sunrise
Vegas Heat
Vegas Rich
Whitefire
Wish List
Dear Emily

The Godmothers Series:

Exclusive
The Scoop

The Sisterhood Novels:

Home Free
Déjà Vu
Cross Roads
Game Over
Deadly Deals
Vanishing Act
Razor Sharp
Under the Radar
Final Justice
Collateral Damage
Fast Track
Hokus Pokus
Hide and Seek
Free Fall
Lethal Justice
Sweet Revenge
The Jury
Vendetta
Payback
Weekend Warriors

Anthologies:

Holiday Magic √
Snow Angels
Silver Bells ⁓
Comfort and Joy
Sugar and Spice
Let It Snow
A Gift of Joy
Five Golden Rings
Deck the Halls
Jingle All the Way

FERN MICHAELS

HOME FREE

KENSINGTON PUBLISHING CORP.
http://www.kensingtonbooks.com

KENSINGTON BOOKS are published by

Kensington Publishing Corp.
119 West 40th Street
New York, NY 10018

Library of Congress Control Number: 2010937903

ISBN-13: 978-0-7582-4694-3
ISBN-10: 0-7582-4694-3

First Hardcover Printing: January 2011
10 9 8 7 6 5 4 3 2 1

Printed in the United States of America

I'd like to dedicate this book to my dear friend,
Sister Julienne Brandt SOSF.
—FM

Prologue

Martine Connor hung up the phone. Her eyes burned with unshed tears. She slid off her chair onto her knees and hugged the dog, which was looking at her expectantly. She had come to love this dog more than anything in the whole world, more than her absentee brother and sister, more than her job as president. And the dog loved her; she was sure of it. She was at her side twenty-four/seven, even in security meetings. She slept at the foot of her bed. Cleo was the first thing she saw in the morning when she opened her eyes and the last thing she saw at night when she closed them.

The tears she'd been trying to hold in check trickled down her cheeks and fell onto the big dog's shoulder as the president cupped Cleo's head in her two hands. She wanted to say something, but the words just wouldn't come.

The big dog suddenly stiffened. She looked around, turning her head this way and that, then ran to the door. The president sighed and got to her feet and walked over to the door. She opened it, and Cleo moved like lightning, shrill, happy barks filling the halls of 1600 Pennsylvania Avenue. The president swiped at her tears a second time. She waited as she remembered all she knew about Master Sergeant Gus Sullivan. A remarkable man in all ways according to what she'd read. A career soldier. He'd called himself a foot soldier. When she met him, he'd already put in twenty-six years, which made him forty-six years of age, and now, a year later, he was looking at retirement, something that hadn't been in his plans. What was it he'd said? "My life is the military. It's the only home I've ever known." How was a wounded soldier, possibly handicapped for life, going to make it when he was suddenly thrust into a world he hadn't lived in for twenty-seven years? The president shook her head to clear her thoughts.

Master Sergeant Gus Sullivan could be seen guiding his wheelchair down the hall, with a marine on each side of him, Cleo frolicking and dancing ahead of the trio.

"Welcome home, Gus," the president said as she held out her hand.

"Thank you, Madam President! And thank you for seeing me on such short notice. They let me out of Walter Reed to come and see Cleo. I hope that was okay. You did say when I got back to stop by *anytime.*"

The president struggled to make her words light even though her heart was breaking in a million pieces. How could she keep this returning hero's dog? She couldn't, and she knew it. "I did say that, and I meant it. Please, come in and make yourself at home. Looks to me like Cleo needs a few hugs and some Gus Sullivan love."

The moment the door closed, Gus rolled his chair to the center of the room. The president gingerly sat down across from him. A second later, Cleo was in his lap. The president fought her tears again. Not so, Gus Sullivan. Fat tears rolled down his cheeks as he nuzzled the huge dog. "I missed you, girl," he said in a choked voice. Cleo whimpered.

The president looked on. She didn't know what to do. So she did nothing. She rang for a steward to bring coffee. God, she wanted a cigarette.

It took a good ten minutes for man and dog to calm down. "It looks like it worked out for the two of you. I knew it would. And thank you so much, Madam President, for sending me all those pictures over the Internet."

The president swallowed and nodded. "Everyone loves her. She visits all the offices, and I think it's safe to say that everyone here is her friend. She loves romping on the South Lawn. She likes Air Force One, and she absolutely loves the helicopter. She adjusted well, but she did miss you. We talk . . . talked about you every single day. I promised you I wouldn't let her forget you, and it looks to me like you're front and center." Her eyes started to burn again.

Gus finished his coffee, motioned for the dog to jump off his lap, which she did. "I have to get back. My nurses are waiting for me outside. I promised I wouldn't . . . they just let me out because I . . . Never mind, it's not important."

"You're not taking Cleo with you?" the president blurted.

"Oh, no, ma'am. Is that why you thought I came here? I'd cut off my right arm to take her, but I can't. I've got two more operations to go, then months and months of therapy ahead of me. Right now, I am so full of pain pills that I can hardly see straight. There's no way I could take care of Cleo and these are her retirement years. She certainly doesn't need to be taking care of me. I have way too much on my plate right now. The doctors told me that if there was a way for you to bring her by from time to time, they would allow it."

The president's insides turned to mush. "Consider it done. Would three times a week work for you?"

"Yessireee, that would work for me, Madam President. Lord, I can't thank you enough for that."

"Listen, Gus, how about if I leave you two alone for a few minutes? I think you might want to explain the situation to Cleo, although I think she already knows." The president literally ran to the small powder room off the sitting room and closed the door. Her shoulders heaved as she tried to stifle her sobs of gratitude now that Cleo was going to stay with her. She dropped to her knees and offered up a prayer, a very short one but straight from her heart. Though her eyes were dry when she walked back into the room, they still burned.

"Gus, I know this is short notice, and I don't know what kind of restrictions your doctors have you on, but I'd like to invite you to Camp David for Thanksgiving. Since this is August, I'm hoping you will be well on the road to recovery by then. If, for whatever reason, we can't make that work, how about we plan for you to join Cleo and me over the Christmas holidays at Camp David?"

Cleo pranced and danced around Gus, urging him to comment. "I'll see what I can do, Madam President, and I thank you for the invitation. Thanks . . . thanks for everything," he said, suddenly shy.

"Don't mention it. In here we're just two people who love this dog. I'll have my secretary make arrangements for Cleo to visit. You take care of yourself, you hear?"

Gus nodded.

"Cleo, I want you to give Gus a presidential escort out of this glorious building. Can you do that?" She hated seeing the look of pain on her guest's face. She wondered if his medication was beginning to wear off.

Cleo looked first at the president, then at Gus before she dropped her head and her two front legs and bowed. Gus laughed. "I taught her that little trick in Iraq."

"And she remembered." The president opened the door. The two marines who had escorted Gus to her quarters fell into line until the president said, "No, Cleo will do the honors, gentlemen. She can find her way back."

The president waited in the open doorway for a full ten minutes, until she saw her best friend trotting down the hall. Cleo let loose with a joyous bark and bounded into the room. She stopped in the middle of the sitting room, threw her head back, let out a loud howl, and flopped down and rolled over. She was on her feet in an instant as she waited for the treat she'd just earned. The president laughed and handed it over.

"Time to go to work, Cleo. We've got some serious business to deal with this morning. I think we're going to be able to make it work. I am the president, so it better work."

Cleo made a short, high-pitched barking sound that said she understood perfectly, and it was time to get their respective shows on the road.

Martine Connor wondered if she'd made a mistake in holding this meeting in the Oval Office instead of the Situation Room. She could still change her mind. Actually, if it hadn't been November, she could have held the meeting outdoors, under one of the arbors. While it was brisk outside, the temperature, according to the weatherman, was in the high fifties. Definitely not too cold for a stroll around the grounds with no prying eyes and ears. And,

Cleo needed to be walked. The more she thought about it, the more she liked the idea of an outdoor meeting. She hated recording devices. No matter how many she dismantled, there would still be that one that would somehow find a way to come back and bite her.

Okay. She was going to switch plans. A nice brisk outside walk. Then a nice warm early lunch to take the edge off a meeting that wasn't going to be recorded in any logs. She rang for her secretary, issued clipped orders in her best presidential voice, then broke the connection.

Fifteen minutes later, the president's chief of staff escorted nine people, four men and five women, into the Oval Office. Martine was already wearing a lightweight jacket, her guests carrying either coats or jackets over their arms.

The formal greeting over, the president looked at the curious faces as they wondered what this unorthodox summons out of the blue was all about. She smiled. "I thought a nice brisk walk in the fresh air would do wonders for us all. Then, when we come back in, we'll all have lunch." She almost laughed aloud at the startled expressions she was seeing. "Follow me, please."

As they walked along, the president began to rethink her plans yet again. Maybe this little meeting outside wasn't such a good idea, after all. How could she talk to nine people unless she rounded them all up in a circle and stood in the middle? Cleo, sensing her dilemma, headed to the president's own personal gazebo, which was lined with benches and contained a round wooden table. Weather permitting, she often had her meals served out there. She patted the big dog's head as she stood aside to usher her guests into the gazebo. How did this magnificent dog know instinctively what she was thinking and wanting? She wondered if she would ever figure it out.

The president's thoughts wandered for a few moments as she tried to figure out why she hadn't told Gus Sullivan she'd agreed to mate Cleo next week. Did she forget on purpose? Or did she feel she'd overstepped her bounds and should never have done it without Gus's permission? Regardless, it wasn't going to work. The vet said that Cleo, in his opinion, was too old to have pups. So there was no need even to bring the subject up. If it wasn't good for Cleo, then it wasn't good for Martine, either.

Someone coughed, feet were shuffling. Her guests were getting antsy.

In a very unladylike, unpresidential move, the president perched on the table and looked around at her guests. "Ladies and gentlemen, I want to thank you for coming to this meeting that never took place. What we are going to discuss here today never happened, either. To show you how serious I am about this, I am going to ask you to put your hands on this little Bible that I carry with me at all times. It was given to me when I was seven years old by my mother. It belonged to her and to her mother. As you can see, it is tattered and well worn, to the point that some of the pages are loose and held together with tape and a rubber band. I cherish this above all else in my life.

"Having said that, I now want you each to place a hand on my Bible and swear to me, the president of the United States, that not one word of what is spoken here will ever pass your lips. Anyone who can't see her or his way to doing this is free to leave."

No one moved to leave. One by one, hands reached out to touch the small, tattered white Bible.

Twenty-seven minutes into the meeting, much of it heated, all of it loud and angry at times, the assembled guests finally agreed to the president's demands to form a new agency among the many others in Alphabet City.

"Taxpayers will not be funding this agency. There will be neither a temporary nor a permanent address for this agency on record anywhere, because this agency does not exist. The new agency is to have carte blanche. It will report directly to me. And I want to personally assure all of you that the *Post,* which has been the White House's nemesis, is on board with all of this. By four o'clock this afternoon I want the twelve special gold shields, which I believe are in your care, Director Yantzy, on my desk. Do we understand each other, Director Yantzy?"

The director of the FBI nodded. "There are only eleven shields, Madam President. One went missing. There is no proof. Well, actually there is proof, but we thought, as a matter of discretion, not to make an issue of it. The *Post* would have gone nuclear with that information if it got out the way they threatened to make it public. Jack Emery and that thug, Harry Wong, confiscated it from our agent."

The president looked Yantzy in the eye and said, "I heard about your agent, who beat reporter Ted Robinson within an inch of his life, and Mr. Emery and Mr. Wong felt duty bound to protect their colleague. Harry Wong is not a thug. Bear that in mind, Director. Seems like a fair trade to me, the gold shield for Mr. Robinson's missing spleen. You will have all eleven shields on my desk by four o'clock this afternoon. And make arrangements to have the twelfth one made up."

"Why?" the national security advisor asked.

"Do you want the long or the short version, Mr. NSA?"

The national security advisor looked sheepish. "The short version, Madam President."

Martine Connor slipped off her perch and went to stand behind him. She clamped her hands hard on his shoulders,

Cleo at her side, looked around at the group as she said, so quietly the others had to strain to hear the words, "Because when the FBI, the CIA, and the entire Secret Service—not to mention the DOJ—on their own couldn't find the head of the Secret Service when he was kidnapped, I had to ask seven very talented ladies, also known as the vigilantes, to step in and do your damn job for you. Which, by the way, they succeeded in doing with absolutely no fanfare and no publicity. No one but me, my chief of staff, and all of you here know about it. Not one word leaked out. I also ask you to recall, Mr. National Security Advisor, what happened to your predecessor, Karl Woodley, when he went up against the vigilantes. Unless you're totally stupid, I think you will all agree that we would rather have the vigilantes working for us than against us.

"I want to see a show of hands."

Cleo stood on her hind legs and let loose with a blood-curdling bark.

Nine hands instantly shot upward.

Cleo offered a more subdued bark.

"I think our business here is finished and we should adjourn for lunch."

The president then did something else that was totally unprecedented and oh so unpresidential. She looked down at Cleo and said, "I'll race you!"

The huge dog sprinted off with the president hot on her heels. At the door to the White House, she stopped, gasping for breath. "Are you ever going to let me win?"

A sharp bark said absolutely not.

"Would you look at those slugs back there!"

Cleo barked again. The president swore the huge dog was laughing at her and the circumstances.

"I think we did good, Cleo. I really do."

Cleo barked, then did her favorite trick: she lay down, rolled over, then leaped to her feet and waited. The president handed over a treat before she walked sedately into the White House, where she stood waiting for her guests, all of whom wore sour expressions.

Just another day at 1600 Pennsylvania Avenue.

Chapter 1

It was an ugly, cold November day, with rain sluicing down in torrents. It wasn't just the ugliness of the day, Jack Emery thought. It was everything going haywire at the dojo, where he and Bert Navarro were trying to keep things going while Harry Wong trained for the martial-arts trials that would, if he was successful, enable him to capture the gold medal in the field of martial arts.

It wasn't that he and Bert weren't capable of handling and training the classes that flowed into the dojo, compliments of the FBI and the CIA and a few other lettered agencies. They were. That they were exhausted at the end of the day was true. It was also true that there had been no complaints apart from a little whining now and then. Once in a while there was even a compliment tossed their way by the agents' superiors.

All in all, both he and Bert were content with their performance and handling of the dojo, along with twice as many classes as Harry had before he went into training mode. Money by way of government flowed into the dojo like clockwork. Chunks of money. Lots of money. The United States government loved Harry Wong.

And on top of all that, his married life was now rock solid, as was Bert's relationship with Kathryn. Win! Win!

Jack felt Bert's presence before he clapped a hand on his shoulder and said, "Crappy day out there. Doesn't look like it's going to let up anytime soon, either. Since George-town floods with rains like these, you might want to bunk in with me tonight or hang out here. Your call. But first we have to Clorox these mats and clean up the training room. Jesus, there's nothing worse than a hundred men's sweat swirling around."

When Jack continued to stare out the window at the driving rain without responding, Bert poked him in the arm.

"Earth to Jack! What's wrong?"

Jack whirled around, his tone fierce when he said, "You know damn well what's wrong, Bert. Didn't you see Yoko's face when she came home at lunchtime? How much longer are we going to stand still for this? And don't tell me you don't know what *this* is. It's been three months, Bert! Three months!"

Bert yanked at Jack's arm and pulled him over to a slat-ted bench. "Listen, Jack, Harry . . . Harry will not appreci-ate us sticking our noses into his business. We both know that. Yoko . . . well, don't you think Yoko would at the very least talk to us, ask for our help?"

"It's not their way, Bert. You know that. I've done a lot of thinking on this, just as you have, and I can't think of a way to do a sneaky intervention. Harry would see right through anything we tried. Unless we hog-tie him and make him listen."

Bert's eyes almost popped out of his head at Jack's suggestion. "Hog-tie Harry! That's never going to happen. What planet are you living on, Jack?"

"Okay, okay. So we drug him by putting something in that shitty green tea he drinks. That way we can hog-tie him. With steel cables."

Bert actually pondered Jack's suggestion for a moment. Then he shook his head. "I think we're going about this all wrong. Let's try going through Yoko first. She should be home soon. She can't be blind to what's going on. Hell, she knows Harry better than anyone, and she just might have some ideas. It's worth a try, don't you think?"

"I'm willing to try anything right now. He's already wasted three months. What's really weird is, he has not come into the workout rooms once since he started his training."

"That's because he trusts us, Jack. He knows he can depend on us, so why waste time railing at us when there's nothing to rail at. Harry's Harry. We should both be proud that he has that much confidence in us."

"Yeah, I know, but I miss that cranky son of a bitch! Watching him through the windows isn't doing it for me. I can't even imagine what Yoko is going through."

"Come on, let's get this place cleaned up, and by that time Yoko should be home. Let's agree that we both talk to her. Not that we're ganging up on her, but she might pay more attention to what we're going to say if we both say it."

"Okay. I'll do the blue and red rooms. You do the yellow and green ones." The colors of the rooms referred to the level of the class the agents were taking. The brown and black rooms had yet to be used because the students hadn't progressed to that level of achievement.

An hour later, with the smell of Clorox overpowering even with the AC going full blast to drive out the fumes,

Jack and Bert stood outside the back door, under the overhang. Jack fired up a cigarette and waited for Bert to chastise him, and when he didn't, Jack just tossed the cigarette into the soaking bushes.

"I hate the smell of Clorox," Bert mumbled.

"Yeah, it does stink," Jack mumbled in return. He fired up another cigarette just to have something to do.

"How do you think she'll take it? Her meaning Yoko."

"I know who you mean. Who the hell knows? She isn't spending much time here, that's for sure. Last night was our late night, and by the time we cleaned up at nine thirty, she still wasn't here. Plant nurseries close at six as a rule, especially in the winter months. We are in the winter months."

"Yeah. I noticed that, too."

"So, things are going good with you and Kathryn?"

"Yeah, pretty good. We might even get married someday. She said that. Someday might never happen, but I'm hopeful. We had this . . . really, really good talk. I understand her better now than I ever did. I don't push anymore. I even came to understand how she likes going on the road. And here is something even stranger that you might find hard to believe, but I now know and realize there is a part of her life that she will never really share with me. I'm okay with it now. Sometimes, Jack, you have to actually *hear* the words to make them penetrate. So, in summary, Kathryn and I are okay. Things good with you and Nikki?"

"Yeah, they are. Once Jellicoe was out of our lives, it was like someone waved a magic wand, and we got back to where we were before all that bullshit went down. The firm is doing great. Of course, she's rarely home before nine or ten most weeknights. Weekends, and when she does manage to get home early, she makes dinner, and we just do what married couples do, hang out, get comfortable with each other. I only wish the press of work would ease up some. I'm looking forward to after Thanksgiving, when things usually get quieter until after New Year's. I know this sounds corny, but I feel blessed. Do you ever feel that way, Bert?"

"Every damn day! I really like this life. Every so often I think about the FBI and how I loved being the director, but I do not miss the politics of it at all. I just keep telling myself that we're the good guys, and now I believe it a hundred percent."

"Wonder what happened to that deal the president presented to the girls in Vegas, at Kathryn's birthday party? The girls were talking about it last weekend out at the farm," Jack said.

Bert barked a laugh. At least Jack thought it was a laugh. "Annie said the president was fine-tuning the offer, whatever that means. By the way, I hear Thanksgiving this year is going to be at Annie's new house. Kathryn told me last night that it's all done now except for some minor things. She called it a punch list. New furniture is being delivered, and they're hanging drapes, all that kind of stuff. Twelve bedrooms in that farmhouse! Annie had the girls each pick a room, then decorate it so when we all stay overnight, it will be like home."

"That's Annie for you. Where the hell is Yoko?" Jack asked.

"Speaking of the lady of the manor, I do believe I hear the sound of her chariot approaching," Bert replied.

"Thank God! I'm freezing my ass off out here. You know what? I think I will bunk with you tonight. I'll text Nikki now and tell her. We can pick up some Chinese or Italian. I'll buy."

"Sounds like a plan to me," Bert said as he watched Yoko park the car and run through the rain.

"Is something wrong?" Yoko asked as she hit the over-hang and started to wipe her face with the sleeve of her jacket.

"Yeah, Yoko, something is wrong," Jack said. "We need to talk. Do you want to talk in your apartment upstairs or in one of the classrooms?"

"Let's go upstairs so I can make some hot tea. It's cold and damp. Aren't you freezing out here?"

"We are, but we were waiting for you, and the smell of Clorox was especially strong today."

"I understand. Come along. It won't take long to make the tea, and yes, Jack, I know you only like Lipton. I keep some just for you. Bert?"

"I'll go with the Lipton, too."

Yoko made a sound that could have been laughter. Bert looked at Jack and rolled his eyes as they followed the tiny woman through the dojo to the stairs that led to her and Harry's apartment on the second floor.

Within ten minutes, the tea was ready, and the three of them were seated at a tiled kitchen table. "Talk to me," Yoko said after the tea was served.

Jack took the lead. "Listen to me, Yoko. We, Bert and I, wouldn't be Harry's friends if we didn't . . . What I mean is . . . Harry is like a brother to both of us. You know that. It's not working for him. Surely you can see that. That . . . that guy in there, his so-called master, has to be at least one hundred fifty years old. He sleeps through Harry's training. Harry is training himself. He is still at the same level he was at when he started three months ago. He has not gained one bit of ground. There's no way he can be ready or even hope to win at the trials if he doesn't switch gears. Can't he get a new master or something?"

"Master Choy is one hundred three years of age. He is

full of wisdom, as all the ancients are," Yoko said softly. "It would be disrespectful for Harry to say otherwise."

"With all due respect, Yoko, what good is he to Harry if he sleeps all day? Didn't you hear me? Harry is essentially training himself, and he is not advancing beyond his own level. Can't you do something? If you can't or won't, will you tell us what to do?"

"Harry is my husband. I cannot interfere. It must be Harry's decision. I can tell you this. He is not sleeping. He has lost weight, and he is not eating properly. All I can do is be supportive of his endeavors."

Bert's eyebrows shot upward. "Even if it means he will go to the trials and lose face? There must be something we can do."

"How much are you paying that master?" Jack snarled.

"A fortune," Yoko said sadly. "We have had to tap into our nest egg. It is a complicated monetary situation, one neither of you would understand. I have been staying late at the nursery and doing most of the work myself to cut back on expenses. We pay all the expenses for the dojo out of the nursery profits. My money is dwindling."

"That doesn't make sense, Yoko. Those old ways don't work here in the United States. You pay for something, you expect a return on that money. The guy just *sleeps*. Two days ago, I turned the surveillance cameras on and the old guy did not move a muscle for seven hours. And he damn well snores."

"What do you want me to do, Jack?" Tears sparkled in Yoko's eyes.

"I want you to fire the son of a bitch. Bert and I will train Harry. We're qualified."

"You aren't a master, Jack, and neither is Bert. One must have a master to go to the exhibition. It does not matter how qualified you are. And it won't look good for

Harry if his master quits in the middle or bows out for whatever reason."

"So what you're saying is, we're between a rock and a hard place?" Jack fumed.

Yoko nodded.

"No, no, no, that doesn't work for me," Bert snapped. "I refuse to accept that. I say we try to talk to Harry. If that doesn't work, we'll go to Plan B."

"And Plan B would be what?" Jack thundered. "Plan Bs for some reason don't work all that well for us, or haven't you noticed?"

"The *vigilantes*!" Bert exploded.

Yoko's teacup shattered on the floor.

"Well, hot damn! Why didn't I think of that?" Jack said, excitement ringing in his voice. "I do think, Mr. Navarro, you just might be onto something here. Yoko, what do you think?"

"I . . . I can't be part of . . . I just can't, Jack," Yoko said, tears streaming down her cheeks.

"You won't have a choice. You are one of *them*. You have to follow the oath you all swore. This is for Harry, for his lifelong dream. We can make it happen for him but only if we have help. Harry will understand. At least I hope Harry will understand," Jack mumbled.

"Let's call it a night now and attack this first thing in the morning," Bert said. "We'll call the girls when we get home. Then we'll try and talk to Harry about it in the morning."

Her eyes wet with tears, Yoko led the way downstairs and through the dojo. She allowed herself to be hugged and her tears to be wiped away by Jack.

"It's all going to work out, Yoko. Trust us, okay?"

Yoko's head bobbed up and down, but fresh tears trailed down her cheeks.

Chapter 2

Jack Emery leaned back and sighed. "I'm stuffed. We should have just gone with the Chinese instead of doubling up on the Italian. I guess the good thing is, you're going to be eating all of this food for the rest of the week, unless Kathryn cooks when she comes over."

"Kathryn does not cook. She's on the road and won't be back till the weekend. You're right, though. One or the other would have been enough. C'mon, we've danced around this long enough. What are we going to do about Harry?"

At that very moment, the doorbell decided to ring. Bert's eyebrows shot upward as he walked through the living room to the foyer and front door. "It's Maggie!" he shouted to Jack. "Bet she couldn't get through the streets of Georgetown, either. That takes care of what to do with all this food. Set another place, Jack!"

Bert opened the door with a flourish and bowed low. "Welcome to my abode, my soaking wet friend."

"Eat me," Maggie snapped as she sloshed her way into Bert's house. "I need some dry clothes and I am not fussy. Oh, food. Warm some up for me."

"Hello to you, too, Miss Cranky Curmudgeon," Jack said.

"Can you turn up the heat, Jack? I'm freezing," Maggie said as she followed Bert to the bathroom and waited while he brought her a pile of clothes.

"Absolutely I can turn up the heat. I'm here to serve you, Miss EIC of the *Post*." Not for the world would Jack ever admit he was glad to see Maggie. Three heads, or even four if one counted Yoko, were better than one.

Jack slammed the door of the microwave oven and pressed the buttons that would warm up all the leftover food. He knew it would all be gone by the end of the evening and Bert would be back to eating out for the rest of the week.

Maggie walked into the kitchen, dressed in a pair of Bert's sweats, which were only a dozen sizes too big and made her look like something out of a traveling circus. The arms and legs were rolled up six or seven times, and they still hung like a sack on her slim frame. "Ah, Chinese and Italian, my two favorites." She crunched down on a garlic stick and sighed happily. "Everything is flooded. Can I sleep on your couch? Did you put my clothes in the dryer? Paper plates, plastic silverware. How gross," Maggie said as she dived into the food Jack had put in front of her.

"Can you eat and listen while we talk?" Bert asked.

Maggie nodded.

Both men rattled on, one or the other jostling the other's memory with something forgotten or left unsaid.

"You getting all of this?" Jack asked.

Maggie nodded again as she stuffed the last of a shrimp roll into her mouth.

"Yoko isn't going to be any help," Bert said. "You got any ideas?"

Maggie swallowed hard and reached for her tea. "With Harry? You have to be kidding. You've already said that the guy doesn't move. Are you sure he isn't dead?" Reaching for a wonton, she crammed it into her mouth.

Jack grimaced. "Now, why didn't we think of that? He's not dead, but we didn't really check. We think he's just sleeping. That's all he does is sleep. For hours and hours and hours. And his sect, his clan, or whatever you call his people, the ones who set this all up, are charging a fortune for his services. From what Yoko said, you can't piss them off. I think that means if you piss them off, they kill you."

Maggie burped and apologized. "Aren't you being overly melodramatic? I think your original idea of calling in the vigilantes is a good one. Did you run it by any of the girls?"

"Not yet," Bert said. "Kathryn's on the road, for one thing. She'll be back by the weekend."

"There's no real urgency, right? Like a few more days isn't going to matter, is it? Time enough to talk to everyone and make a plan. Think about this. Can we find a way to maybe have someone else hire that particular master for even more money? Then Harry would have to be assigned a new master, hopefully one who is more . . . alive and with it."

"You mean a bogus trainee?" Jack asked, hope written all over his face.

"Exactly," Maggie said as she commenced her attack on the plate of baked ziti.

"You know what, Maggie? I think you just earned all that food you've been scarfing down. That just might work. The trainee would have to be legitimate, however, and he will have to have registered for the trials and do whatever it is you have to do to qualify."

"Let Charles handle that end of it. He's good with stuff

like that. Or his people are. Any other problems you want solved before I turn in for the night?"

"How about some personal chitchat?" Jack asked craftily.

"Is that your way of asking about me and Ted?"

"Now that you put it like that, yeah. What's up with the two of you?"

"Nothing is up with the two of us. Ted is out there playing the field. I can't keep track of his bimbos. I'm sorry, that was unkind. He's on female number seven according to Espinosa. Not that I'm counting. By the way, I met someone I find very interesting. He's a money manager of some kind, originally from Maryland. He came by the paper one day, and I met him. We've had dinner twice. No, we have not had sex. Don't go there, either one of you. He's a tad older than I am, and that's what I find interesting. I'm actually thinking of bringing him to Annie's Thanksgiving dinner. I cannot tell you how interesting he finds me. He says I make him laugh. He says I am down to earth and cute as a newborn speckled pup. Go ahead, say it, and I'll kick both your asses all the way to the Canadian border. I'm not cleaning up this mess, either. Please try to be quiet since I'm sleeping on the couch. You do have a spare toothbrush, don't you, Bert? I really don't want to have to use yours. I get up at five, so set the coffeepot so I don't have to wait. I hate waiting for coffee. I like it ready to pour as soon as I reach the kitchen."

Bert and Jack both clamped their lips shut.

Maggie trotted off, the swinging door leading to and from the kitchen closing with a soft swoosh.

"I think that went rather well, don't you, Jack?" Bert whispered nervously, his eyes on the swinging kitchen door.

"Make sure you check your toothbrush. No telling

where those lips and teeth have been," Jack whispered in return. "Since this is your house, you can do the cleanup. Night, Bert."

Thirty-six hours later, a horde of Asians descended on Harry Wong's dojo. A titillating ceremony ensued before Master Choy was carried from the premises on a red velvet chair that was trimmed in gold. There was a lot of bowing and scraping. The ancient one slept through the whole ceremony, to everyone's delight. Yoko's eyes sparkled with relief. Jack and Bert just grinned from ear to ear, while Harry stood mesmerized as his head bobbed up and down as he listened to his new master, who was babbling in a language only Yoko understood.

"What the hell is he saying?" Jack asked uneasily.

"You want the short or the long version?" Yoko giggled.

Miffed, Jack said, "The short one will do."

"He said, 'Let's get you ready so you can kick some ass.' Then he went to sleep."

"Now, that's my kind of master. How old is this one?"

"Eighty-six! He trained the past three winners. He says Harry will be his fourth winner. Then he will retire."

"Eighty-six, huh? He looks to be . . . ah . . . at least seventy-nine," Bert said. He looked over at Jack and hissed, "What happened to Charles's taking care of this?"

Jack's eyes rolled back in his head. "Harry said this guy was just waiting in the wings and beat out Charles's guy."

Yoko giggled. "This man could wipe up the floor with you, Jack, and Harry in less than five minutes. I can ask for a demonstration if you like. But first we have to wait for him to wake up."

Bert and Jack ran to their respective classrooms. Yoko continued to giggle as she got ready to leave for the nursery. Sometimes things just worked out right. She offered up a little prayer of thanks before skipping her way out to her car. Inside, the engine running, she started to cry.

It was five o'clock when Jack and Bert finished up with their classes for the day. Once in a while they had a light day, and today had been one of them. Both were surprised when they looked up to see Harry standing in the doorway. He looked uneasy as he struggled to find the words he wanted to say. When they wouldn't or couldn't surface, Harry just shrugged.

Jack took the initiative. "We peeked in a while ago and it looked to us like you got yourself a winner this time around. The guy was sleeping just like your first master. That's a real shame that Master Choy had to leave. We know how broken up you were over that. But you know what, Harry? That, too, shall pass."

"That's the biggest crock of shit I ever heard come out of your mouth, Jack Emery. Look, I . . . what I mean is . . . listen . . ."

"It's just one lousy word, Harry. Thanks. There, I said it for you. You wanna kiss and make up now or later?"

Harry advanced across the room, his bare feet slapping on the tile floor. Jack winced, and Bert tried to wiggle behind Jack. Harry reached for Jack's shirt and had him in a bear hug before Jack could blink. He kissed him so hard on both cheeks, Jack thought his back molars were going to come loose. Harry released him and did the same thing to Bert. Then he backed up a step and bowed low. He turned without another word and slapped his way back to the door. "You . . . you rascals. I love you guys!" And then he was gone.

"Holy shit!" Jack said in a strangled voice. "I guess he didn't notice that his new master was sleeping."

"That's one for the old memory books. Jesus, Jack, Harry *kissed* us. And, he bowed to us."

"Yeah." Jack grinned. "Yeah, he did."

Back at Pinewood, Charles and Myra's home in Virginia, Charles smiled at the success of his little mission, which was no more than a blip on his computer screen. He did a double take when he read Jack's incoming text. He swore then, something he rarely, if ever, did. For all intents and purposes, Harry Wong was destined to work with sleepers. With nothing more pressing on his agenda, he made his way out of the catacombs to the main floor of the old farmhouse, where Myra and Annie were having coffee in the kitchen. Both women clapped their hands in approval when Charles reported the success, then the downfall of the mini-mission. "Harry is going to have to make it on his own, I'm afraid to say. There's nothing more I can do."

"Sometimes, dear, the best-laid plans simply don't work. It's a culture you cannot be expected to understand. You did your best. Come, join us for coffee, Charles. Annie and I are planning her Thanksgiving menu. Is there anything in particular you would like? This year, dear, you will just be a guest and not have to worry about getting everything hot to the table at one time."

"Plum pudding is a must. I can make it if you like. One has to make it just right, or it turns out to be just another pudding. I have my mum's recipe."

"That would be wonderful, as I've never made plum pudding before," Annie said.

"She's never made a turkey, either," Myra jabbed, to Annie's dismay.

"Well, I never knew how to pole dance, either, but I

managed to master that little feat," Annie snapped. "How hard can making a turkey be if you follow the directions?"

"I'm sure you'll do just fine. If you find yourself in need of my services, feel free to call on me. I seem to have a little too much leisure time these days. I think I'll leave you ladies to your menu planning and take the dogs for a run. If you need me for anything, just beep me." He leaned over and kissed Myra on the cheek before he whistled for the dogs, who came on the run.

"Are you going to get a dog or maybe a cat, Annie, when you move into your new farmhouse?"

"I don't know, Myra. I'm going to be doing some traveling, and it isn't fair to the animal. I'd love to have a whole houseful like you do, but that means I have to put down serious roots. I don't know if I'm ready for that just yet."

"Sooner or later, Annie, you're going to have to stop running. We can't undo the past. We both know that. We're in the here and now, and if you keep running, it will always be like this. I so want to see you happy. We're in our twilight years. We deserve happiness."

Annie bookmarked the page she had been looking at in one of Myra's cookbooks. "Are you happy, Myra?"

Myra tapped the side of her coffee cup with her nails. "We've had this talk before, Annie. I've come to terms with the hand fate has dealt me. I'm content. If my daughter had lived, and I had grandchildren, I would be deliriously happy. But that can never be, and I have accepted it. I married Charles because I love him, and I should have done it years ago. There isn't much left for me to aspire to is the way I see it at the moment. We have the girls in our lives, their significant others or their husbands, whatever the case may be. We've had fame, and you and I have our fortunes, which both of us share where it needs to be shared. And I now have those wonderful dogs, who make me laugh and love me unconditionally. So, let's just say I am as happy as my circumstances will allow."

Annie smiled. "I wish sometimes I was more like you, my friend."

"Don't ever wish that, Annie. Just wish to be who you were meant to be. You have so many things in your life to be grateful for. You are so loved, it boggles the mind. You do so much good that no one knows about. Like Joseph Espinosa's family. You gave up your childhood home to that family so they could have a better life. Look what you did with the newspaper. You adopted the girls, who love you more than life itself. Take the time to enjoy it all, Annie, before it's too late."

Annie played with the pages of the cookbook in front of her. She looked Myra square in the eye and said, "That sounds rather ominous, Myra."

"I know, and I meant it to sound that way. Now, are you planning on canned cranberry sauce or made from scratch? I saw a recipe for one that has orange in it. Sounded good to me."

"Then that's the one we'll serve."

"There, we made a decision. We should work on your guest list."

"Let's just invite everyone we know and do it as a buffet. We can set up separate tables since I don't have a table big enough to fit everyone."

"And another decision has been made." Myra laughed as she stared across the table at her friend, who also began to laugh. But, Myra saw, the laughter didn't reach Annie's eyes.

Chapter 3

Following his normal daily routine, Charles started to read the morning news on the computer. It was three days before Thanksgiving. He winced at the world headlines. Just once in a while he wished the headlines would be something *good,* or at the very least, cheerful. He continued to scan what he wanted to read and saw the blip that President Connor was heading to Camp David for Thanksgiving. Master Sergeant Augustus Sullivan, retired wounded military veteran, would be joining her, along with veterinarian Donald Gamble and Sullivan's male nurse and therapist. He read on and saw that Sullivan was the previous owner of the president's dog, a military K9. He smiled at what he was reading. This, at least, was some much-needed pleasant news for a change. Charles felt his smile widen.

He continued to read for the next fifteen minutes. He had not finished when his reading was interrupted by the buzzing of his sat phone. He pressed TALK and heard Lizzie Fox identify herself and quickly announce that she was at the White House, and the president was standing next to her. Instinctively, at the mention of President Connor's name, Charles stood at attention. He listened closely and found himself nodding, then realized Lizzie couldn't see him agreeing with her. "I understand, Lizzie. I'll tell Myra and the others that you'll arrive in time for dinner." He replaced the sat phone and remained standing for a few minutes, continuing to stare at the phone. He wasn't sure if he was elated or depressed at what he'd just heard. More to the point, what would the girls think when Lizzie arrived to share her news?

Lizzie's arrival meant two things—he had a dinner to prepare, and he had to call all the Sisters, since Lizzie's unexpected visit concerned each and every one of them.

These days, since their pardons and the capture of Hank Jellicoe, rounding up the girls wasn't as easy as it used to be. Kathryn was trucking again; Yoko was extra busy getting ready for the Christmas season at her nursery; Nikki's law practice was setting all-time records, causing her sometimes to work until ten or eleven at night, which meant that Alexis, her new office manager, was also working late. Isabelle was up to her eyeballs, as was Annie, with the last-minute punch list on her new farmhouse. Maggie's social life had kicked up several notches, and she was rarely available after six. Which pretty much left Myra, who was at the ready for the most part. The truth was, Myra was so bored, she was actually puttering in the kitchen with a stack of cookbooks. The dogs were eating very heartily these days. For the most part. Preparing dinner was definitely his job.

Another question facing him at the moment was the boys. Should he include them in the unexpected meeting or not? He knew for a fact that Jack and Bert were working almost twenty-four/seven, and Harry's training was just as time-consuming. Ted and Espinosa had for some reason fallen into the background as Ted grappled with his newfound social freedom and all the opportunities that had suddenly presented themselves to him. Espinosa appeared to be odd man out and was spending hours and hours of quality time with his family at Annie's old plantation home, which, in Charles's opinion, was a good thing. At the end of the day, family was where it was at.

Lizzie, if he remembered correctly, had only said call the girls. She hadn't said call everyone or call the guys, too. So that had to mean this little gathering had something to do with the meeting the Sisters had had with the president at Kathryn's surprise birthday party in Las Vegas.

For some reason, with so much time going by, whatever that had been about, he'd assumed it had fizzled before it got off the ground.

That left the boys. Or the guys, as the Sisters referred to them.

Two days ago, he'd spoken to Lizzie, and she hadn't said a word about traveling to Washington. She'd also told him that she, Cosmo, and Little Jack wouldn't be joining them this year for Thanksgiving, because the casino industry was holding a huge dinner the night before Thanksgiving and honoring Cosmo as Lawyer of the Year. The day after Thanksgiving, Cosmo was also being cited as Man of the Year by the state of Nevada, with a huge gala that would also kick off the Christmas season in Vegas.

Which all boiled down to one thing: Lizzie's meeting was important and girls only. He hoped he wasn't wrong, or the boys were going to get their Jockeys in a knot. He sighed. Sometimes, men were more angst-ridden than women.

The sun was just commencing its march to the horizon when Charles entered the kitchen to see Myra in her robe, drinking a cup of tea. He felt himself frown. Myra did like to get up early, but not *this* early.

"Bad dream, or you just couldn't sleep, old girl?"

"Both, I think. I hate it when I can't remember the dream, especially if it was a good one. I let the dogs out already, but now they are waiting for breakfast. I know you have them on certain menus, so I didn't want to disrupt your ... meal plan. I feel jittery, Charles, like there is something lurking out there we should know about."

Charles leaned over to kiss Myra's cheek. "As usual, my dear, you are spot-on with your intuition. When I was reading the paper online, the phone rang, and it was Lizzie. Despite everything that's scheduled out in Vegas, she's at the White House. Or she was when I spoke to her. Yes, before you can ask, it is early to be visiting the White House. She will be coming for dinner this evening and would like to speak with the girls. As yet, I haven't called anyone. She said 'girls,' Myra, not 'girls and guys' or 'girls and the boys.' I think, and this is just my opinion, that we are going to be finding out this evening what the president's agenda is in regard to that unorthodox meeting we all had at Kathryn's surprise birthday party. I more or less thought that, whatever *that* was, was dead in the water."

Myra perked up as she watched Charles prepare a pot of coffee. "Really?"

Charles stopped what he was doing to stare at Myra. "You're excited, aren't you?"

Myra smiled. "Things have been rather dull around here lately. I expected the pace to kick up a bit since we'll be in the Christmas season in a few days. Did Lizzie give you any inkling what this was all about?"

"Not a single clue. I assume that the president was standing right next to her. By the way, Lizzie and her little family will not be joining us over Thanksgiving." He went on to explain about Cosmo's awards and the presentation galas that were coming up. "She did promise Christmas, though."

"Oh, I was so counting on seeing Little Jack, even though he isn't so little anymore. I bought him some racing cars, bright red ones. I do so love to hear the little one's laughter. I miss that so much. So very much," Myra whispered.

Charles winced. If he didn't divert Myra, the rest of her day was going to be ruined. Quick like a fox, he said, "Call Nellie and Elias and invite them for breakfast. Like *now,* Myra, before Nellie goes out for her morning ride. I'm a little worried about Elias. He's so forgetful lately. We were supposed to play chess yesterday, and he was a no-show. He didn't even call," Charles fibbed, with his fingers crossed in front of him.

Diverted, Myra frowned as she got up and walked over to the old-fashioned wall-mounted telephone set. "That's funny you should say that, Charles. Nellie and I were just talking about that same thing the other day, when we went riding. It will be nice to have company for breakfast for a change. I love to see people eat and appreciate your efforts, dear."

Charles smiled. "And you are buttering me up . . . why?"

"Because I love you, no other reason," Myra said as she dialed Nellie's number. She nodded for Charles's benefit, then spoke for a few more minutes before she hung up. She turned to Charles and said, "Elias will come in the golf cart, and Nellie will ride her horse. Elias says it's in case Nellie breaks down. You have noticed how Elias follows Nellie in the golf cart, haven't you, Charles?"

"A time or two, but Nellie was imbibing at the time, if you recall."

Diverted even further from her original thoughts, Myra laughed. "I do recall. So what are you preparing?"

"A ham-and-cheese omelet with green onions for Elias. Banana pancakes for Nellie. Two eggs over easy for you, with Canadian bacon, and toast and coffee for myself. I am watching my waistline so I can eat hearty at Annie's Thanksgiving dinner."

"I'm not so sure I would or can be as confident as you, Charles, in regard to Annie's culinary expertise."

"Then I will gorge on my own plum pudding. I think I'll make a triple batch just to be on the safe side. Rather like Elias and his golf cart hedging his bets with Nellie and her horse."

Myra laughed again, and Charles heaved a deep breath. It was going to be a good day. The evening . . . Now, that was a different can of worms altogether.

Lizzie Fox left the White House as quickly as her feet would carry her. As she literally raced down the halls, she wasn't the least bit surprised to see staff members already at their desks, people she'd nodded to in the past, possibly had waved at or even spoken a few words to during her short tenure as the president's counsel at 1600 Pennsylvania Avenue.

Once she was a safe distance from that famous address, she pulled into a fast-food joint and ordered an English muffin and some hot coffee. She wolfed it down in the parking lot and wished she had another.

When she pulled into traffic again, she drove by her old offices, offered up a jaunty salute, but kept on going. Her destination was her old house, which she had decided not to rent out, after all. She liked the idea that she could come back to it anytime she felt like it and sleep in her old bed. She had even left some of her clothes and toiletries behind. The only thing she really needed was some coffee, but then she remembered that the last time she'd visited the house, she'd put the coffee in the freezer. Well, that meant she was good to go.

With hours looming ahead of her until it was time to go out to the farm, and with nothing better to do than think about her visit with the president, she could do a little dusting, a little mopping, and open the windows to air the place out. Then, maybe after she did that, she would build a fire and sit down and think about the meeting. It was a game plan. Of sorts.

In the end, she did nothing like that at all. She drove to Harry Wong's dojo, greeted Bert and Jack, who were between classes, allowed herself to be bear-hugged, peeped in at Harry, who waved offhandedly and continued with his training. Seeing that she was in the way, Lizzie blew kisses and headed out the door. Her next stop was the *Post* and a visit with Maggie, who was so happy and giddy, all Lizzie could do was stare at her friend.

Maggie started to babble at once, bringing Lizzie up to date on her new relationship. "Don't go getting the wrong idea, Lizzie, because we have not had sex yet. And you know what? That's okay, too. We're taking it slow and easy. He digs me, Lizzie. Do you believe that?" Not waiting for or expecting a reply, Maggie rushed on. "I'm thinking of taking him to Annie's for Thanksgiving dinner. I plan on asking him tonight. We text and e-mail all day. Well, I do it more than he does. After all, he is a big money manager and has a duty to his clients, and he has to be careful." At Lizzie's look of alarm, Maggie almost screamed, "What? What? Why are you looking at me like that?"

"Maggie, does your new beau know about the vigilantes and your friendship with them?"

"I . . . well, I didn't see the point . . . so to answer . . . no, I did not mention it. Maybe that's why I have been holding . . . off."

"What do you think he would do or say if you confided in him?" Lizzie asked quietly.

Maggie looked so stricken that Lizzie almost felt sorry for her. Almost.

Maggie sat down in her swivel chair and stared at Lizzie. "I don't know, Lizzie. Well, that's not quite true. I think he'd give me my walking papers. He said he was staying in town over Thanksgiving. I didn't . . . What I mean is, I didn't say what I was doing. I can still go to the farm on my own. That means he will have to eat somewhere alone, and that's going to bother me. It *will* bother me, Lizzie. I can't just not show up. I owe all of this," she said, waving her arms about, "to Annie. And I want to see her new house and be with the girls. It's been a while. Damn, why can't things just work out?"

Lizzie tilted her head to the side, her expression one of I don't have a clue. "That's a hard one."

Maggie suddenly bolted upright. "Lizzie, why are you here? You said last week you couldn't make Thanksgiving dinner, because Cosmo was getting all those awards, and yet here you are. What's up? And it's so early in the morning."

"I just came from the White House. I stopped by the dojo, but the guys were busy, and it felt like I was in the way. I'm on my way to my old house to check it out, you know, dust, mop up, air it out. There's a meeting at Myra's tonight. Dinner of course. Then I take the red-eye home. You're going, aren't you?"

Maggie struggled with her reporter's instincts and her

infatuation for her new beau. "Of course I'll be there. I'll just . . . you know . . . blow him off. Maybe if I'm lucky, he'll think of me as a mysterious femme fatale. Not likely, huh?" she answered herself when Lizzie grinned.

"I did not say that, Maggie. I'm just amused at your dilemma."

"Are the guys going?"

"Nope, just us girls and Charles, of course. Well, I've taken up enough of your time. I see you have a text coming in, so I'll be on my way. No, no, take care of business. I can see my way to the elevator. Give Ted and Espinosa my regards, okay?"

Maggie eyed her cell phone on the desk. She decided to ignore the incoming text and walked Lizzie to the elevator. "I'll give the guys your regards. To tell you the truth, I have no idea where either one of them is right now. Things are going to hell around here, Lizzie."

Lizzie did her best not to laugh. "I wonder why that is," she said, giving Maggie a quick hug before she stepped into the elevator.

"Yeah, I wonder why that is," Maggie mumbled to herself as she made her way back to the office, where she eyed the phone and, without checking the text, slid it into one of her desk drawers. She continued to mumble and mutter to herself as she made her way to the kitchen to fortify herself. *First comes nourishment, then comes work, then comes love. Remember that, Maggie Spritzer, the next time you go off the rails.*

Chapter 4

To Myra and Annie's delight, the Sisters all arrived within twenty minutes of each other. Seeing the girls, no matter the circumstances, was the highlight of the day. Lizzie's appearance was the cherry on top, Annie said.

They all sat around the dining-room table to be out of Charles's way in the kitchen. Pictures of Little Jack were passed around while doting mom, Lizzie, regaled them with blow-by-blow descriptions of why a certain picture was taken and where it was taken. She proudly announced that he was growing like a sprout and was now wearing a size six, which stunned everyone at the table.

"Cosmo said he's following in his footsteps, and Jack now has his own regular rocking chair, just the way Cosmo had when he was a little boy." And on and on it went, the Sisters listening with rapt attention, until Charles announced that dinner was ready.

As always, the rule that no business was to be discussed during dinner was observed, which meant Lizzie repeated all of Jack's activities for Charles's benefit.

"You should hear his God blesses when he says his

prayers at night. Every day the list gets longer as he discovers new things. He's blessing the grasshoppers, the birds, all the bugs and ants, the moon, the stars, and the clouds, plus every single toy he owns. I do want you to know, though, all of you are at the top of his list. Big Jack goes first, then all of you. It's so sweet, I want to cry sometimes. Cosmo fell asleep the other night before Jack finished with his prayers. I had to tuck him in and wake up Cosmo." They all laughed at the image Lizzie presented to them.

An hour later, Charles's delectable crown roast was just a memory. There wasn't enough left for any of the Sisters to take home, which Charles said was a good thing. He did love it when the platters were empty.

"I just love comfort food," Maggie said. "Did any of you notice how the temperature is dropping?" At their nods, she rattled on. "Our weatherman is predicting snow flurries for Thanksgiving. No accumulation, though. And, Charles, I will take a double helping of your mango banana sorbet." She continued to prattle on and on without saying anything noteworthy until Kathryn, back from her road trip, told her to zip it up.

Their nerves on edge, the Sisters rushed through dessert and coffee, all of them scurrying back and forth to the kitchen to help, as Alexis said, "to get this show on the road."

The Sisters' gaze kept going to the sideboard, to the box Lizzie had carried into the dining room. That box, they thought as one, was the clue to what this emergency dinner was all about.

The moment Charles snuffed out the lavender-scented candles and turned up the dining-room chandelier, the Sisters leaned forward.

It was time to get down to *it*. Whatever *it* was.

Lizzie, too, leaned forward. "I was at the White House

this morning before the sun came up. Actually, I was summoned. It wasn't a social visit, although the president and I did some personal catching up."

The Sisters waited.

"The president asked me to tell you that after her surprise visit while you were all in Vegas, the timing wasn't quite right to do what she originally wanted to do at that time. She said to extend her apologies. It appears that the timing for what she had in mind is now more to her liking. This is my question to you all. Have any of you changed your minds about helping her out?"

The Sisters looked at one another, then at Charles, as they shook their heads.

"That's a good thing. She was a little worried and, for obvious reasons, did not want to communicate those worries."

The ever-blunt Kathryn said, "So she wants to collect on the pardons, right? Forget that she promised them in the first place. This hand washes that hand? That's how Washington works. You know what? I'm not so sure I'm interested this time around. However, I'm open to being convinced."

"Kathryn, I would never try to convince you or the others of anything. I'm just your lawyer, the intermediary here to present . . . for want of a better word, an offering."

"And that would be . . . what?" Annie asked, her eyes shiny bright.

"It seems the president has formed a new agency. An agency that has no address and is not listed anywhere. The president left it up to me to negotiate the remuneration you would all expect. I probably shouldn't tell you this, but the sky is the limit on this one. She spoke briefly about a mystery slush fund somewhere that remuneration would come from. Another mystery fund will be set up for me to oversee and pay out. The president does have the backing of the FBI, the CIA, the DOJ, and a few other alphabet twisters."

"To do what?" Yoko asked.

Lizzie smiled. "I have no clue. My guess would be that whatever she wants done, she and those alphabet twisters don't want anyone to know about. In other words, those other agencies have to show accountability to the government and the public, whereas you will not. All she wants is to get the job done. Whatever that job may be. No questions asked, no accountability. That means you're *home free* if you take this on."

"Accountability and immunity are two different things? In writing?" Charles asked quietly.

"All you could ever want," Lizzie said just as quietly. "But nothing in writing. One cannot put something in writing if it doesn't exist. I didn't just fall off the watermelon truck, Charles. I have it covered."

Charles inclined his head slightly to show he would accept Lizzie's response.

"Proof?" Nikki, the other lawyer in the room, said.

"Absolutely one hundred percent full proof." Lizzie smiled as she looked over at the sideboard, to the box she'd brought with her. The Sisters followed Lizzie's gaze to the dark blue box sitting there like a Christmas treasure just waiting to be opened. With the overhead lighting turned on high, they could all clearly see the presidential seal on top of the box. As one, they all raised their eyebrows questioningly.

"I know you all want to know what's in the box, but my instructions were very explicit. I am not to reveal the contents of the box unless you agree to join the president's new agency."

The Sisters looked disgruntled, especially Kathryn, who

grappled with a smart-ass retort. When she couldn't come up with a suitable one, she simply scowled menacingly.

Annie took the bit and ran with it. "Let me make sure we all understand what you just said, Lizzie. The president, the same president who gate-crashed Kathryn's surprise birthday party to ask for our help, which we all agreed to give, after which we sat around for months waiting to see what she wanted us to do, that president? Now, because the timing is right *for her,* never mind *us,* she sent you here with a box that you aren't allowed to show us unless we agree to go to . . . dare I use the term, *work,* unless we all agree to work for an agency that doesn't exist and does not have an address? In addition to that, there is a mystery slush fund that will pay us whatever we want to charge. And you, Lizzie, will monitor those monies out of another mystery fund. It appears we would have no say in the . . . job . . . the venture . . . whatever you want to call it. Oh, I almost forgot, we would . . . if we take on this little . . . whatever it is . . . report directly to the president, who has approval from every agency that has initials in this cockamamy city. Did I get all that right?" Annie asked, looking around at the Sisters, whose heads were bobbing up and down.

"That's a pretty accurate summary, Annie," Lizzie drawled.

"Well then, count me in and show me what's in that damn box," Annie said gleefully. She smacked her hands together to drive home her acceptance of the situation.

Lizzie looked around at the others until she came to Myra, who was smiling from ear to ear. It was clear the others were not going to raise their hands until they saw what their fearless leader was going to do. Myra raised her arm as high as it would go.

Charles sighed and leaned back in his chair.

Lizzie reached behind her, picked up the blue box with the presidential seal, and set it squarely in the middle of the table.

"Are you absolutely sure you want to commit to this, girls? Show me your hands again."

Seven hands shot high in the air.

The Sisters leaned in toward the table and watched as Lizzie popped open the top and sat back in her chair.

"Bloody hell!" The words exploded from Charles's mouth like bullets.

"It's the gold shields!" Nikki said in awe. She quickly counted them. "There are fourteen," she said.

"One is new. It seems Jack Emery took one of the originals off an agent and gave it to Ted Robinson when the agent got overly forceful and ruptured Ted's spleen. The president said Mr. Robinson could keep it as a memento and should be issued a new one."

Annie was beside herself as she tried to figure out how to wear the shiny shield that would give her immunity all over the world. "What do you think, girls? Hang it from a chain, get a special belt and let it dangle? It's too big for a bracelet. I don't think a lapel pin will do it. It's too big," she babbled as she blew on it, then tried to shine it even more on the sleeve of the sweater she was wearing.

"They are not for show, Annie. But you are to carry them with you. It's carte blanche for all of you. All of you meaning Jack, Bert, Harry, Ted, and Espinosa. Maggie makes the number thirteen. The president didn't want any of you to feel unlucky with that number, so there is one extra shield for Judge Easter, for a total of fourteen shields."

The silence in the dining room was so total, Charles shook his head as though his ears were stuffed up. He watched as the Sisters chose their solid gold shields and stared at them, mesmerized at what they meant.

"They're very heavy," Annie said.

"And shiny," Myra said.

"The guys are going to love these," Nikki said.

"Ted can make matching bookends with his someday if he mounts them on plaques," Maggie said as she stared at her own gold shield.

"Harry does not like jewelry. He will say he does not need this. I will convince him otherwise. Two to a family is very nice. His and hers," Yoko said.

"I wish I had had this a long time ago," Kathryn said, so quietly the others had to strain to hear what she was saying.

"But then you wouldn't be sitting here with all of us," Nikki said. "I like it. I mean, I really like it."

Isabelle stared down at the badge she was holding. "I feel like Kathryn does. I wish I had had this back . . . But now is just as good a time as any to be awarded this. I, for one, am proud to accept it."

"As will Nellie," Charles added. Not for the world would he ever admit that he was jealous to the bone that he had not been awarded one of the prestigious shields. He hoped the girls couldn't see how his eyes were burning.

Lizzie got up and walked around the table. She bent down to kiss Charles on the cheek. "I bet right this moment you are thinking that you don't count, Sir Charles," she said, drawing one last shield from her pocket. She held it out to him like it was the Holy Grail.

Charles blinked.

"The president said to tell you that she is very aware of your . . . ah . . . involvement and wants you to have this as a special show of her appreciation. She is also very aware of your special relationships across the pond, as well as your knighthood. So, will you accept this shield, Sir Charles?"

"I will." Charles's smile rivaled the sun, the moon, and the stars.

"We should have a toast!" Annie said. "Charles, do we have any champagne?"

"Of course. I'll get it."

"Ginger ale for me. I'm driving." The others agreed with Kathryn.

"Ginger ale it is, ladies."

"I think this calls for my grandmother's special crystal," Myra said, getting up to head for the china closet where she kept her heirloom crystal.

Isabelle said, "I have a question, Lizzie. What happened to the previous owners of these shields?"

The girls stopped chattering, their faces startled at Isabelle's question.

"Previous administration. President Connor's predecessor retired them when he left office. I was told by the president that her predecessor handed them over to Director Yantzy at the FBI for safekeeping. At her request, he turned them back over to her right after she returned from her visit to Las Vegas."

The Sisters nodded, satisfied with Lizzie's explanation. The chatter resumed as Myra and Annie set out the glasses and waited for Charles to bring in the champagne and some ice and ginger ale.

Lizzie watched Maggie out of the corner of her eye as she let her fingers caress the shield she was holding. She thought her dear friend looked . . . defeated.

Maggie looked up at Lizzie and correctly interpreted what she was seeing in Lizzie's eyes. "No harm, no foul. Good thing I didn't take it to the next level. Relax, Lizzie. My guy is just a . . . memory."

"I'm sorry, Maggie."

"Don't be. I'm okay with it."

"You sure?"

Maggie looked her in the eye and said, "I'm sure, Lizzie.

I would never in any way compromise all of you. We're family." She turned away so Lizzie and the others couldn't see the tears in her eyes.

Ice tinkled in the exquisite crystal. Charles poured the ginger ale. "It bubbles, almost like the real thing," he said happily.

The Sisters raised their glasses and, as usual, waited for Myra to make the toast.

Myra looked around the table from one to the other, a smile on her face. "Let's toast the unknown until such time as we want to make the unknown known."

"Very well put, old girl," Charles said.

"Now what?" Alexis asked.

"Now we wait until our names are called. It's rather reminiscent of being back in grade school. I think I like the feeling." Annie chortled. "It will give us all time to let our imaginations go to work."

The good-byes were long and full of hugs and kisses.

Still holding their special gold shields, Charles, Myra, and Annie sat down at the kitchen table. They were silent because no one could think of anything to say.

"I think we all just made one hell of a commitment," Annie finally said.

"We're up to it," Myra said cheerfully. "I think it is beyond amazing that the White House thinks so very highly of us. How cool is that?" She twinkled.

"Myra, you absolutely rock sometimes. Now, Charles, since we aren't driving anywhere, get out the hard stuff, and don't stint when you pour."

"Your every wish is my command, ladies." He gave his shield an imaginary swipe and laughed out loud.

Chapter 5

It was a blustery, colder-than-normal November day, bone-chillingly cold, with a thick dampness in the air that made you wish you were wearing two sweaters under your coat. The dark gray clouds scudded across the sky as the wicked wind beat at the naked tree branches that lined the perimeter of the parking lot at Nikki Quinn's law firm. Maggie shivered even though she was dressed warmly inside the little car she was sitting in.

The parking lot that belonged to Nikki's firm was almost full, but Maggie Spritzer was able to maneuver the little Beetle she'd borrowed from her secretary into a spot with ease. She sat behind the wheel, the engine still running, the heater going full blast as she contemplated the reason she was there. Yes, she had legitimate business there; she'd made the appointment two weeks ago. But she knew she was there for another reason, too. She needed some girl talk. Time permitting, maybe Nikki and Alexis, the brand-new office manager, could find the time for a quick bite just to get out of the office.

Then again, maybe not. Who in their right mind, besides herself, would want to go out in this weather? Maggie continued to sit and watch the whipping branches. It was almost hypnotic. She had one bad moment as she wondered if the wind was strong enough to blow over the little Beetle. She had to move.

Maggie opened the door and had to use all her strength to hold on so the wind wouldn't blow the door off its hinges. She finally got the door closed and locked. She hunkered down into her jacket and tried to make a run for it, the ferocious wind battling her every step of the way, but she finally made it to the entrance and the beautiful carved teak double doors.

"You look like an alien!" Alexis laughed as she pointed to Maggie's curly hair, which looked like a messy bunch of corkscrews standing on end.

"It's wicked out there," Maggie gasped. "Even so, I was going to ask you if you and Nikki could get away for a bite to eat after my meeting. Or are you too busy?"

"I'm game, but check with Nikki. Go on back. She's waiting for you. You want coffee?"

"Sure."

Maggie marched back to Nikki's office, the last one on the right off the long hallway. Nikki got up, and the two women hugged. "Kind of windy out there, huh?"

"Sure is. I borrowed my secretary's Beetle to drive over. I hope it doesn't blow away, it's so little."

Nikki laughed and motioned for Maggie to sit opposite her. "What's up that you need my services? You want to do lunch when we're finished? It's usually slow at this time of year, what with Thanksgiving just a few days away. Legal woes seem to take a backseat around holiday time. Actually from now till the first of the year, we all get to catch our breath. This is also when we take vacations. Courts are slow, too."

"Absolutely, let's do lunch. I asked Alexis on my way in, and she said she could get away, but it really depended on you. Okay, this is why I'm here." Maggie slid a manila folder across the desk. "I made the decision to buy a house. The owner of the one I'm leasing—well, the *Post* is leasing it, and I pay the *Post*—he's willing to sell. He, the owner, married a Frenchwoman, and she doesn't like it here in the States and doesn't want to be bothered with a rental property. I lucked out, Nikki. Last summer, he put in a new AC unit, and a month ago, when the furnace went out, he replaced it. This past summer the stove just stopped working, and he told me to buy a new one, which I did. I got a Wolf, you know, those high-end ones with the red knobs.

"So, the house is in pretty good shape, a little pricey, but Georgetown prices really never go down. I did haggle and got him down somewhat. He just wants to unload it. Oh, and the roof is only five years old. I think I did good, and the best part, Nikki, is that we will be neighbors in the true sense of the word. You know, actual home owners."

"That's great, Maggie." Nikki scanned the papers and smiled. "It's all here. You did half my work for me. Do you want to close before or after the holidays?"

"I think I'd like to be a home owner before Christmas. That way, when I put up a Christmas tree, I'll feel like I'm really putting it up in my own house, not someone else's. I might even string some lights outside just to make it official."

Nikki laughed as she rang for her secretary and handed her Maggie's file. "See if you can set up the closing for December fifteenth. I'm leaving for lunch now, and if you need me, call me on my cell. On your way out, tell Alexis to meet us at the door. We're going to lunch. Sit at the front desk till we get back, okay?"

The secretary nodded in agreement.

"Where would you like to go, Nikki? My treat. I want to celebrate. God, I don't believe I am buying a house!"

Nikki laughed. "It is a bit overwhelming at first, but you settle in real quick. You got a really good interest rate, which is super. Will save you a lot of money in the long run. You're already living there, so that's a big plus. I look at it as win-win."

"I guess. I still feel intimidated for some reason. Now I have to buy my own furniture. The owner said I should donate all his stuff to Goodwill, which I will do, or I could keep it—but I don't want it. The fact that the house came furnished was the reason I moved there in the first place. Plus I love Georgetown."

Nikki reached for her coat, a long white cashmere with a belt. Maggie thought she looked like a movie star at that moment. She watched as Nikki pulled her wallet out of her purse and stuck it in her pocket.

"Let's rumble, girlfriend. I'm sensing you have stuff you want to talk about. I'll drive."

"I made a reservation at Snuffy's," Alexis said as she followed Nikki and Maggie out of the office. "They're sure to have some really good soup on a day like this. Soup, salad, and sandwich is my kind of lunch. Oh, and they have really good desserts," she added for Maggie's benefit. "I also asked for your favorite booth in the back, Nikki. We're good to go. That's if this wind lets us get there."

Fifteen minutes later, the threesome blew into Snuffy's like a tornado. Alexis couldn't stop laughing at Maggie's hair. "You look like a raspberry bush. Here, tie my scarf around your head, or people are going to laugh at you."

Maggie grimaced as she did her best to flatten her hair

down with the scarf. Nikki gave it a few artful tugs, and Alexis pronounced Maggie ready to go.

It was a cozy little restaurant teeming with patrons who loved to eat and visit in the Georgetown area, especially on a day like today.

The chalkboard hanging behind the salad station said the special for the day was hot roast beef sandwiches on sourdough bread, and Southwestern vegetable soup. Homemade strawberry-mango pie was the dessert of the day.

"That's a no-brainer," Alexis said. "I'm going to order it and get an order to go for this evening. Right now, though, I want a cup of hot coffee." No sooner were the words out of her mouth when a pot was set in the middle of the table, along with three cups. Coffee was free, compliments of the owners.

"This place is a gold mine," Maggie said as she poured out coffee.

"Depends. The owners are here at four in the morning to get everything ready for six, when they open. They close around ten, spend another hour cleaning up, and get home by eleven. They're probably too tired to do more than go to bed and get up and do the same thing the next day. But it's their life, and they seem to love it," Nikki said.

"Aren't we all in the same boat?" Maggie asked. "I'm at the paper by six, sometimes five thirty. I can't tell you how often I sleep there. We make choices in life is the only explanation I can come up with. Hey, if it works, then work it is my motto."

"Okay, let's *talk,* girls," Nikki said. "How did Espinosa take the gold shield when you gave it to him?" she asked Alexis.

"Actually, it was pretty funny. He was afraid to touch it. He said he hid it in five different places before he found one that he feels comfortable with." Alexis's gaze shifted to Maggie when she said, "Joseph said Ted was so overwhelmed, he had tears in his eyes. He doesn't know what he did with his."

Maggie didn't bat an eye at the mention of her ex, Ted's name. "What did Jack say?" Maggie asked.

"He was beside himself. At first he had this really awful look on his face when he remembered how those guys with the shields tormented him, then that big brawl when he beat the living daylights out of that agent and took his shield and gave it to Ted. At first he didn't want to take it. We talked about it for a while, and he finally accepted it. I haven't spoken to Kathryn or Bert, so I don't know what Bert's reaction was. I don't see anyone giving it back."

The waitress arrived to take their order. The moment she was gone, Maggie leaned over the table and said, "Yeah, well, I'm thinking of giving mine back."

"You are! Why?" Nikki asked in stunned surprise.

"You can't do that, Maggie. You're one of us now," Alexis said.

"I know, I know, but my . . . my life has changed. I don't mean in regard to all of you. I mean my personal life. That's what I wanted to talk to you about."

"Well, we're all ears, honey. Spit it out," Alexis said as she poured more coffee.

"You all know my history with Ted. And with Abner. Somehow, I managed to screw up both of those. I take that to mean neither of them was meant for me. I love them both in different ways. And, yes, it bothers me that it all ended like it did, but I have to think about me. I'm forty years old. I should have my personal life on an even keel, and I thought I did until . . . well, I had to rethink it all when Lizzie gave me that damn gold shield. She had this look in her eye, and I knew exactly what it meant. It meant my new beau is off-limits. I can't sustain a relationship on lies, and I would have to lie to him. He was a congressman for ten years, and very astute in the bargain. Now he's an investment counselor, which means he raises money and invests it."

"I think we all know some stupid congressmen, ex and otherwise. I don't personally know any investment counselors, at least not on a first-name basis. I do have a broker and a portfolio," Nikki said. "It's never good to start a relationship based on a lie. Having said that, it's my personal opinion that one's . . . partner, significant other, doesn't need to know *everything* about oneself. I also think each of us has to hold something in reserve and never commit one hundred percent. If things go awry along the way, we each need that little bit of reserve to carry us through."

"Men like a little mystery where women are concerned," Alexis said. "But in a way that's a double-edged sword, because they then try to find out what that little mystery is. Tough spot, Maggie. How do you feel about this new guy?"

"You know, I really like him. I met him at the *Post* one day. He was meeting with one of my reporters. No, not Ted. I gather he's sort of the new wunderkind. At least that was the impression I got out of it. I was walking across the newsroom floor, and he just up and introduced himself. We had a pleasant chat, and that was it. No sparks or anything like that. Just one of those meetings that happen every so often. One of the reporters, I found out later, was doing an article on his overnight success. He's very personable. A week or so later, he called me up and invited me out to dinner. I went. The conversation was mainly about how disillusioned he was with Washington during his five terms as a congressman. He wanted to know everything there was to know about how the paper runs. Then he popped in again on his lunch hour one day and asked for a tour. I obliged. He's real easy to talk to, nice guy.

"Full head of hair, and he's forty-eight, eight years older than I am. He's originally from Maryland. He's a lawyer and CPA. He was married, but his wife died ten years ago from breast cancer. No children. He just up and left Washington after the funeral. Then he moved to New York, went to work on Wall Street. He worked there a while, then decided to strike out on his own and moved back here to the District. He still sees his in-laws and seems to love them like his own family. And did I mention he has a really wicked sense of humor and a killer smile? No sex. We are miles away from going there. Right now, it's simply a comfortable friendship. Will it go forward? I have nary a clue, but yes, I would like for that to happen."

"That's it? You've only seen him three times? Charles drummed into our heads from day one that there is no such thing as a coincidence. You do know that, right?" Nikki said.

"No, no. We've had a few quick lunches, two other dinners. We text usually once a day, or he calls. I *never* call him. Well, I do and I don't know about coincidences. If you recall, I did not sit in on your . . . ah . . . your meetings with Charles. Usually, I meet him wherever it is we're going to eat. I was actually thinking of bringing him to Annie's for Thanksgiving, but now I don't think that's a good idea. Lizzie cut me a look that clearly said, 'Don't go there.'

"I like him more and more with each meeting. He's going to be alone for Thanksgiving, and that bothers me. He told me he used to spend holidays with his in-laws, but this year they're going on a cruise. I know he's waiting for me to . . . I don't know what he's waiting for me to do," Maggie finished lamely.

Nikki and Alexis both went silent as the waitress appeared with their food.

"Why are you looking at me like that?"

The moment the waitress left, Nikki said, "Have you given any thought to possibly . . . and I say *possibly* . . . this man sought you out knowing you know Annie and Myra? Meaning, of course, they have money and might want to invest with him? I'm not saying that's the case, but you should think about it."

"That's the first thing I thought of," Maggie said as she sprinkled salt and pepper on her food. "But then again, considering who we are, I think it's natural to think along those lines, don't you, Nikki?"

"I do." Fork poised in midair, Nikki looked across the table. "Maggie?"

Maggie felt her shoulders slump. She placed the fork on her plate, looked across the table at Nikki and Alexis, her eyes miserable. "Are you saying my meeting up with Jason Parker wasn't a chance meeting at all, and that he's *using* me?"

Nikki looked down at her plate. Alexis averted her gaze.

"Well, that damn well sucks," Maggie said as she picked up her fork and proceeded to shovel food into her mouth. "Not only does it suck, but it sucks big-time."

Nikki was determined to have the last word. "There is no such thing as a coincidence."

Chapter 6

Maggie's secretary appeared out of the blue just as the strawberry-mango pie arrived. She was as wind-blown as everyone else who was coming into the restaurant. Her face was rosy red, and there was such excitement in her eyes, the girls waited to start their pie.

"Maggie, your phone is off," she chastised.

"I know. I forgot to charge the battery. How did you know where to find me?" Maggie said peevishly.

"I called Miss Quinn's office, and they told me. I wouldn't have come all the way over here if it wasn't important. This had to be done in person," Sally, the secretary, whispered.

Maggie jabbed her fork into the pie. "I'm never going to know unless you tell me, so tell me."

"The White House called for you!"

Three jaws dropped.

"Why?"

"I don't know, Maggie. The president said she wanted to talk to you. I had to tell her I didn't know where you were. Do you have any idea how stupid I felt saying that?

Anyway, she wants you to call her back, like as soon as possible."

"Are you sure it wasn't some kind of prank call? Ted would get off doing something like that just to tick me off."

"Maggie, it really was the White House, and, yes, it was definitely the president. I see and hear her on television all the time, so I recognized her voice. Well, aren't you going to call her?"

Maggie looked at Nikki and Alexis. "My phone is out of juice. I'll call when I get back to the paper."

"She said ASAP, Maggie."

"Yeah, well, I'm eating lunch. She probably wants us to write some stuff about the White House. It can wait."

"If that were the case, as you well know, she would have called the newsroom or had her press secretary make the call. This was the *president herself.*"

"She has a point," Nikki said. "Here, use my phone."

Maggie's eyes almost popped out of her head. "You can't be serious. You want me to call the president of the United States in the middle of a restaurant with at least fifty people within earshot! I don't think so."

"Maggie, I don't think she's calling you to rattle off the nuclear codes. Just call her, and I'll bet you anything you want, she will be the one doing the talking, not you. Or, you can go to the ladies' room and talk. But we want to hear! Just call!" Alexis hissed.

Sally slid a small Post-it note across the table with the number Maggie was to call.

Maggie shrugged, looked around furtively, and punched in the numbers. "This is Maggie Spritzer from the *Post*. I am returning—"

The voice on the other end of the phone cut her off and said, "Hold for the president, Miss Spritzer."

Maggie rolled her eyes for the benefit of the girls, then jerked her head slightly to tell Sally that she should leave, which she did reluctantly.

And then she heard the voice of the president. "Miss Spritzer, this is Martine Connor. Is it all right to call you Maggie?"

Stunned, Maggie said, "Uh-huh. I mean, yes, Madam President. Everyone calls me Maggie." She rolled her eyes again at her brilliant repartee. "What . . . what can the *Post* do you for, Madam President?"

Maggie heard a tinkling laugh. "Oh, dear, I should have made it clear at the beginning. I'm not calling concerning the *Post*. This is a personal call."

Maggie almost fell off her chair. "Me personally! Wow! I mean, oh my gosh, what can I do for you, Madam President?"

The tinkling laugh again. "I'm calling to invite you to Thanksgiving dinner at Camp David. I realize this is short notice, but that seems to be the way I do things lately. At the last minute so I don't go crazy with details. If there's someone you would like to bring with you, by all means, do so. Just stay on the line so my secretary can fill you in on the details. If you're going to dinner with family, I understand."

"Thanksgiving dinner at Camp David! Wow! I mean, oh, my gosh, of course I would love to come. What should I wear?" Maggie blurted.

The tinkling laugh sounded. "Whatever you feel comfortable in. It's informal. I usually wear slacks and a sweater. Camp David can be drafty. I look forward to seeing you, then. Stay on the line now."

"Uh. Okay. Thanks for the invitation." Maggie whispered for the benefit of the girls, "I have to stay on the line for details. Do you believe this? I'm going to Camp David for Thanksgiving. I'm going to take Jason with me. She said I could. Sort of my swan song with him. Shhh."

"Yes, ma'am, I can hear you. I think that's a great idea. Just shoot me an e-mail, and I'll take it from there." Maggie rattled off her personal e-mail address, then broke the connection.

Maggie looked first at Nikki, then Alexis. "Is this a coincidence or not?"

"I don't know what it is," Nikki said, a frown building between her brows.

"I'm not getting this," Alexis said.

"I'm not either," Maggie hissed. "Why me of all people?"

"Why not you? Our president never does anything without a reason, according to Lizzie. I guess you'll have to wait till you get to Camp David to find out. The bigger question here is, how are you going to tell Annie you're blowing her off for the president of the United States?"

"I don't even want to think about that right now." Maggie reached for the check and drew some bills out of her wallet. "Don't look at me like that. I said this was my treat. Me, personally. I can't put this lunch on my expense account. I have ethics, you know."

"Cranky, aren't we, all of a sudden?" Alexis laughed. "And the best part is, not one of the customers in here knows you were conversing with the president of these here United States." She laughed again at the expression on Maggie's face.

"How upset do you think Annie will be?" Maggie mumbled as she followed Nikki and Alexis out of the restaurant.

"I think she's going to go up in smoke. This is her first dinner at her new house. And she's cooking it herself. I really think she's going to be pissed to the teeth," Nikki said with a straight face.

"You might even find yourself on the unemployment line. Annie, as you know, can be feisty. Sometimes she takes no prisoners. This might be one of those times," Alexis said, her tongue planted firmly in her cheek.

"So if it was you she called, what would you have done?"

Nikki and Alexis burst out laughing.

"The same thing you did, ninny. We're just yanking your chain, Maggie. Thanksgiving dinner at Camp David! It doesn't get any better than that. You'll be on the news, in all the papers. You are going to be famous. People will ask for your autograph. Before you know it, you're going to need a press secretary to handle all your fan mail," Alexis said.

"You sure you want to take Mr. Coincidental, also known as Jason Parker, with you?" Nikki asked.

"Who else am I going to take? I'm not going to know anyone there. I'm going to need someone to hang with. I don't see me and Martine buddying up and having girl talk. So, yeah, I'm sure I'm taking him. Then I'll blow him off when we get back."

As the wind buffeted and pushed them forward, Nikki managed to get the car door open, the three of them literally falling forward. "Which brings us to, what are you going to wear? Is it just the one day or for the weekend?"

Maggie banged her head back against the headrest. "You had to bring that up, didn't you? I don't have a clue. I guess that kind person who is sending me the e-mail might cover all of that. Why didn't I just say no?"

Nikki turned to face Maggie in the backseat. "Because first and foremost you are a reporter, and your reporter instincts kicked in. You want to know the why and the what of the invitation. Go for it, Maggie. Stop worrying about Annie. She will understand. Speaking strictly for myself, I'm as curious as you are."

Alexis chirped up. "You might want to take that gold shield with you. You know, just in case. Whip that baby out, and the world is your oyster. Didn't Lizzie say the president doesn't know or didn't want to know who we were going to give the shields to?"

"Something like that," Nikki said, turning the key in the ignition. "By the way, thanks for lunch, Maggie. And thanks for the entertainment."

Alexis giggled and agreed. Maggie just groaned.

Maggie quickly opened her e-mail the moment she reached her office. She read it once, then twice, then three times, until she had it committed to memory. The Secret Service would be picking her and Jason Parker up at her home in Georgetown and ferrying them to the White House, from where they and six other guests would be flown to Camp David on the president's helicopter, Marine One. Should her choice of bring-along guest change, she should call the number provided immediately. The e-mail went on to explain that while whatever presidential plane had the president aboard was denominated Air Force One, the helicopter with the president in it was Marine One since the Marine Corps was responsible for flying and maintaining it. Dress was informal. Departure for the return would be Sunday at 0800 hours. The last thing the e-mail asked was if either she or her guest had any food allergies. "Respond as soon as possible," was the way the message ended. There wasn't even a signature at the end.

Maggie leaned back in her swivel chair, her eyes still on the printed e-mail. Why wasn't she elated at being invited to Camp David? She closed her eyes as she pictured Nikki's and Alexis's expressions when they were talking about Jason Parker. Neither woman knew him, and yet they seemed to know *about* him. Then there was Lizzie and that strange expression in her eyes. She remembered how creepy she had felt when they talked about coincidence. Maybe she shouldn't take Jason to Camp David with her. Since she hadn't asked him, it wouldn't be a problem to cancel Maggie and guest. Then whom would she take? Her secretary? Such a dilemma.

Now she was irritated. With the situation and with herself. So irritated she barked, "Come in," when she heard a knock on her door. She looked away from her computer screen to see Jason Parker standing in the doorway. She continued to bark, "What are you doing here?" The bark didn't lessen when he advanced a step without being invited forward. Maggie clicked SAVE, and her screen went blank.

"Bad day?" Parker asked cheerfully.

"Don't you ever work? You keep showing up here out of the blue. Did we have a meeting I forgot about?" The bark was by then a snarl. She tilted her head and saw Ted Robinson motioning to her and waving a fistful of papers at her from the doorway. The snarl became even snarlier, if there was such a word, when she said, "What do *you* want?"

Ted continued to wave the papers back and forth from the doorway. Maggie held up her hand, a signal for him to wait, that she'd get to him in a minute.

Maggie focused on Jason Parker. "I do not conduct social business here at the paper. Please stop popping in here unannounced. From here on in if you want to get in touch with me, do it via e-mail or a phone call. Now, sit there while I take care of some business."

Properly chastised, Parker sat down across from Maggie's desk. He looked like an errant schoolboy caught red-handed doing something he wasn't supposed to be doing. Maggie's eyes bored into him as she made her way to the door, then closed it behind her to talk to Ted.

Maggie squared her shoulders, took a deep breath, looked squarely at Ted, and said, "What do you have for me?"

Instead of answering her, Ted said, "I think I know that guy. Isn't he that financial guru everyone in town is lined up to invest with? Don't tell me we're going to be doing another story on him. I'll pass on it if we are.

"Jesus, Maggie, don't tell me you're going to invest with him. Ooops, none of my business. Forget I mentioned it. By the way, congratulations on buying that house. It's good to put down roots. Georgetown is the place to do it."

Maggie eyed her former fiancé to see if he was pulling her leg. She decided he was sincere and thanked him. "It's a bit overwhelming at the moment, but it's like everything else. I'll get used to making mortgage payments and worrying about my pipes and wood rot. Yes, that's Jason Parker, and I don't know why he's here, and no, I am not investing with him, not that it's any of your business who I invest with." It was true, she didn't know why Jason Parker was there.

"Here!" Ted said, shoving a packet of papers at her. "The financials you wanted on that contractor you were so convinced is on the take. He's clean, so you might have to shift your focus in another direction," he said, referring to a story Maggie had assigned to him. "Looks like nothing is going on in the next few days, so I'm going to cut out and spend some quality time with Mickey and Minnie. Guess I'll see you at Annie's on Thanksgiving. You okay, Maggie? You look kind of funny."

Was she okay? No, not really. "Listen, Ted, I want you

to do a . . . *deep* background check on Jason Parker. From the day he came out of the womb. Let's keep this just . . . just between us for the time being. Oh, one other thing. I won't be going to Annie's for Thanksgiving. I was . . . I am . . . invited to Camp David for the weekend. The president herself called me while I was at lunch with Nikki and Alexis. I was . . . I was stunned, Ted." She realized at that instant how easy it was to fall back into the old familiar groove with him. A comfort zone, so to speak.

Ted's eyebrows shot upward. He grinned. "Looks like you hit the big time. Watch out for those politicians, or they'll eat you up and spit you out. Or are you thinking there is something devious about this invitation?"

"Listen, Ted, hang around for a few more minutes, until I get . . . till I see what Parker wants. I'll meet you in the kitchen. Make some coffee. Call the bakery and have them send over some cream puffs or eclairs or something sweet. By the way, where is Espinosa?"

"Men's room. Okay, coffee and sweets coming up," Ted said cheerfully. Too cheerfully to Maggie's liking.

Back in her office, Maggie's snarly mood returned. She looked at Jason Parker, sitting in the chair across from her desk, really looked at him, trying to imagine what Nikki, Alexis, and even Ted would think about him if they got up close and in his face. He was tall, fit. Just the right amount of gray in the sandy hair at his temples. Interesting face. A Kirk Douglas cleft in his strong chin. Killer teeth some dentist somewhere was proud of. Winsome smile, masculine laugh. Nails blunt cut, buffed but not polished. Strong hands. Dressed well, spit shine to his shoes. Nothing ostentatious. Drove a Lexus. That was what she saw. Three-bedroom apartment in the Watergate. That was her guess. Nikki and Alexis—now, that was different. They didn't know Jason Parker was a good kisser, didn't know that he was attentive, that he held her chair for her, opened the car door for her. They would think his smile was practiced. Maybe even calculating.

To her dismay, Ted had already formed an opinion, without even knowing she was seeing and kissing Jason Parker. *Crap!*

"Looks like I came by at a bad time," Parker said, getting to his feet. "I'll call before I stop by again. At least this little visit allowed me to warm up. I walked all the way from the office. This is where you're supposed to feel sorry for me. Ah, I see that isn't working." A second later he was on his feet. "Dinner this evening?"

"I can't. Listen, Jason, I . . . How would you like to go to Camp David for Thanksgiving dinner?"

Parker's eyes almost bugged out of his head! Maggie knew the man was rarely if ever surprised at anything, but at that moment he was stunned as well as speechless.

"*The* Camp David?"

"That's the one. Here," she said, pressing a key on her computer to print out another copy of the e-mail she'd just read. She watched as he read the terse instructions.

"Well, this would certainly look good on a résumé if I was ever going to send one out. I'd be delighted to accompany you, Maggie, and thank you for inviting me."

"Yeah," Maggie drawled. "Look, I really have to get to work. I guess I'll see you in a few days."

"Breakfast tomorrow?"

"No, I have an early engagement. I'll see you Thursday morning at seven thirty."

Parker was dismissed, and he knew it. He was out the door and almost to the elevator before Maggie got her wits about her. Her insides churning, she made her way down the hall to the kitchen. Ted was paying the bakery clerk for an oversize box of pastries. The coffee smelled wonderful. She watched as Ted poured out two cups, then reached up for the paper plates. Maggie felt a catch in her throat. She'd always loved these little meetings in the kitchen.

"So, what did that guy want?"

Maggie cleared her throat. Sometimes, a white lie was okay. "To tell me he was going to Camp David for Thanksgiving and thought it would make a good article for the Life section. He does like to beat the bushes for self-promotion."

"To which you said . . . ?"

" 'I might see you there since I'm also invited,' and no, I didn't think it was noteworthy enough to put in our Life section. I think he was disappointed."

Ted eyed the box of cream puffs as he decided if he should opt for a third or not. "And you think this means what? Is there something you aren't telling me? I'm sort of not liking what I'm thinking right now, Maggie."

"And what are you thinking, Ted?" Maggie snapped.

"Is this personal? Are you involved with this guy?"

That question didn't come under the heading of a white lie. Involved to Ted meant sex. She could truthfully answer that question, but she was splitting hairs and knew it. "No, I am not *involved.*"

She justified her answer to herself by saying that she had breakfast and dinner with a lot of people. And if you wanted to split hairs even further, she kissed some of those people. Maybe not on the lips, but on the cheek or one of those air kisses. So she was guilty of lip kissing, tongue kissing, but that didn't mean she was *involved.*

"Do I look like I'm involved? The answer is no."

Ted reached for an eclair with chocolate frosting. "So why are we doing this investigation into his background? What else do you have besides your reporter's gut instinct? Is he on some watch list somewhere?"

Is he? He was definitely on Nikki and Alexis's watch list. "Sort of . . . kind of . . . then again, maybe not. I just don't know, okay? Can you just do what I tell you and not pick it to death, Ted?"

"Sure, Maggie. Are you sure nothing is wrong? Look, just because we aren't a couple anymore doesn't mean I don't care about you. I do. I would try to move the earth for you if you needed me to do it. I'm just saying you can count on me."

Hot tears pricked Maggie's eyes. "I know that, Ted, and I would do the same for you."

Espinosa took that moment to enter the kitchen. He took one look at the intense expressions on his boss's and his colleague's face and turned around to leave.

"Come on in, Espinosa. Have a cream puff. Ted made fresh coffee. I just gave Ted an assignment, and I want you on it, too. You two kick it around a while. I have to get back to work."

When the kitchen door closed behind Maggie, the two reporters looked at one another. "Maggie has been personally invited to Camp David by the president for Thanksgiving," Ted said, his voice so flat, Espinosa reared up in his chair.

"She's blowing off Annie and the girls?" There was such outrage in Espinosa's voice, Ted actually laughed out loud.

"Guess so."

"That's not good. It isn't good, is it, Ted?"

"It is the president. It is Camp David. The president herself called Maggie. What would you do, Espinosa?"

"I'd go to Annie's. Switching up is like saying I got a better offer. Not nice, Ted, not nice at all. What would you do?"

"Well, the reporter in me would want to go to Camp David to find out why and what the president wanted from me. It's a given that she wants something. The personal side of me agrees with you. I'd go to Annie's. Obviously, Maggie made her choice based on what? I don't have a clue. That financial guru is going, too. I know that means something. Even more so now that Maggie wants us to check him out from the day he slipped out of his mother's womb."

"That far back, huh?" Espinosa grinned. "That has to mean she's onto something, and I'm sure Annie will forgive her."

Ted allowed his voice to drop to a hushed whisper. "Listen, I didn't tell this to Maggie . . . why, I don't know. I guess because she was off and running, and I wanted to hear her out. Anyway, about six months ago, I invested five thousand dollars with that guy's firm. In six months I made fifteen hundred. He guarantees to double your money."

Espinosa narrowed his eyes. "I didn't know you were the investment type. I thought you kept your money in the bank like me. Especially in this lousy economy."

"Yeah, well, I do but at one percent interest, I thought I'd take a flyer. It paid off, too, even in this economy. I heard these two Channel Five anchors talking at the Memorial Day parade, and they were both heavy investors. I figured if anyone had the skinny on the firm, they would, so I took a shot at it. My gut is telling me to cash it in now. What do you think, Espinosa?"

"I think you should listen to your gut is what I think. If Maggie is on his tail, then something smells somewhere. I saw him getting into the elevator. He reminded me of someone my mother would call a 'dandy.' He has a lot of teeth. I think they're capped."

"And that means what?" Ted said sourly.

"Too many teeth, looks like a dandy means he can't be trusted. Take your money and run."

"So where did you park your money from Global Securities?"

"In the bank, in CDs at two percent interest. I can sleep nights, Ted. That's more money than I can save in a lifetime working here at the paper, so I want to make sure it's safe even if it doesn't earn much. I thought you did the same thing."

"I did, with the exception of the five grand. Okay, okay, I'm going to cash out as soon as I get my next statement."

Espinosa crumpled up the bakery box and jammed it into the trash container. He poured the last of the coffee into his cup, then threw away the grounds and rinsed the pot as Ted watched him.

"Why are you looking at me like that?"

"You're so tidy. I admire that," Ted said.

"My mother taught me to be tidy, so the person who comes behind me doesn't call me a slob. My mother is a saint and is never wrong, in case you don't know that."

"I do know that. She raised you, and you are a fine specimen, Joseph Espinosa. I was just jerking your chain. Maggie always leaves the kitchen a mess."

"So, we're back to Maggie, are we?"

"No, we are not back to Maggie. I have accepted that Maggie and I are over and done with, but I'll go to the wall if I think someone is out to hurt her in any way. I know you feel the same way, don't you, Joe?"

Espinosa knew Ted was beyond serious, because the only time he ever called him Joe was when he was deeply troubled and needed his help in some way.

"I do, Ted. I really do."

Chapter 7

Countess Anna de Silva, also known as Annie to loved ones and friends, looked around her spanking new state-of-the-art kitchen. It wasn't exactly an alien world to her, but she definitely was not at home there, or in any other kitchen, for that matter.

Isabelle had outdone herself in the kitchen area. Annie had asked for cozy and warm, and that she did appreciate. The monster fireplace with old Virginia brick, in which one could roast an ox, for some reason was not at odds with the streamlined appliances, which gave off Annie's reflection when she stood next to them. Healthy green plants dangled from ancient beams complete with the original wooden pegs that were used instead of nails back in the day. Isabelle had saved the beams when the original building was demolished. Bright apple red crockery was everywhere and matched the fancy red knobs on her new Wolf stove.

Annie had specifically asked for a Wolf because of the red knobs and Maggie's telling her how much she loved the Wolf stove she had in her own kitchen. As Annie looked around, she realized that Isabelle had given her exactly what she'd asked for, a combination of the old world she'd grown up with and the new world she was living in.

So much for a beautiful kitchen. Now, if she only knew the first thing about how to cook, it would be perfect.

Annie hooked her feet over the rungs of the stool she was sitting on at her center island and took in the mind-boggling array of cookbooks staring up at her. It was almost midnight, and she should be asleep in her old flannel nightgown in her new bed with her brand-new silky soft Frette sheets.

Tomorrow . . . well, maybe not tomorrow, but the day after tomorrow, she was going to hightail it over to Myra's and bring home some of the barn cats and begin trying to domesticate them.

A half hour later, with two cups of tea heavily laced with brandy, Annie had reached the conclusion that country living sucked. So did cooking—not that she had tried to do any yet.

More important, her personal life sucked, too. She definitely needed a cat. Or a bird. One that talked, preferably a foulmouthed parrot that had once belonged to a pirate. She would have to ask Charles if he knew someplace she could get one. Then she wondered what her guests would think if she served them scrambled eggs.

She was pacing back and forth in front of the fireplace when her cell phone chirped to life on the kitchen counter. Annie looked at the clock on the Wolf stove. A call after midnight had to mean trouble of some kind. *Well, trouble is better than looking at these damn cookbooks,* she thought as she walked over to the phone, flipped up the cover, and barked, "This better be good, because it's after midnight, and I'm trying to make a Thanksgiving dinner here."

Annie listened to the voice identify himself and sat

down, the phone clutched to her ear as she reached for the last of her tea, which was more brandy than tea, and swallowed. "Fergus Duffy! Do you have any idea what time it is?"

"I do, dear lady. But if I recall correctly, you told me you never sleep. That's why I have been driving around for the past two hours trying to find your house. I am hopelessly lost. I was coming for a visit."

This was deep. Wayyyy too deep for Annie. "You were? You are? Don't you have a map? People from other countries should buy maps. They used to be free at gas stations. Now you have to buy them. So, where are you exactly?"

Annie listened, then rattled off directions. "You are five minutes away. I'll leave the porch light on, and unless you're blind, you can't miss it. I know it's cold out, Fergus. My house is warm. What the hell are you doing here, anyway?"

Annie blinked when she was told that explanations were better given in person. She powered down and looked at her teacup. *The hell with the tea.* She slugged directly from the brandy bottle until her eyes watered. Just as a car's headlights lit up her parking area, she realized she was wearing her flannel nightgown. She groaned and took another slug from the bottle. She told herself that if she wasn't drunk, she was so close to it that there was no point in splitting hairs.

Then Fergus Duffy was standing in her kitchen, all six feet four inches and 260 pounds of him. "What took you so long?" Annie mumbled.

"I was driving, not flying, Annie." Fergus looked around, then marched over to the fireplace to warm his hands. "This is nice. I like it. It's you, Annie. My whole cottage back in Scotland could fit in this kitchen." He shucked off his jacket and walked over to the island and sat down opposite her. "Do you always read cookbooks at this hour of the night?"

"You came all the way out here to ask me a silly question like that? The answer is no. Why are you here?"

Fergus eyed the brandy bottle and Annie's glassy eyes. "I'm retired now and doing some traveling. I had a meeting with your president earlier today, along with . . . several colleagues. I just sat in as a courtesy until my replacement can get here Monday. I was going to call you earlier, but I just didn't . . . What I mean is, I was already ready for bed, and I just knew I had to see you. That's the only explanation you're going to get from me, so take it or leave it."

Annie sniffed. "Well, since you put it like that, it doesn't look like I have much of a choice. As you can see, I'm not really dressed for company. And I've also been imbibing a little. I'm also in a state of flux right now."

"I see that."

"Would you like to come for dinner tomorrow? Well, today, actually. It's Thanksgiving. I have to warn you, though, I might be serving scrambled eggs."

"Is that a definite invitation, or are you just rambling here, Annie? I'm asking for a specific reason."

Annie squinted to see Fergus better. "Well, you're already here, and it *is* Thanksgiving Day already, so yes, it is a definite invitation. Why, are you expecting a better offer to materialize at this late date?"

"Actually, I've already gotten an invitation, but I think I like yours better. I accept."

"I thought you said you don't know anyone here. Who invited you for dinner?" Annie asked, suspicion ringing in her voice.

"President Connor. She invited me and my colleagues to Camp David. I'm to be at the White House in a few hours.

I have a number to call if I can't make it. I think I'll call that number right now." Annie was speechless as she watched Fergus punch in the numbers that would put him in touch with the White House. With nothing better to do, she picked up the brandy bottle again and took another healthy swig. She knew her eyes were crossed, but couldn't bring herself to care.

Fergus dusted his hands together dramatically, then he opened the monster stainless-steel refrigerator. Eyeing the array of food and the thirty-pound turkey sitting on a tray, he turned to look at the scattered cookbooks on the island, then at Annie. "You can't cook, can you? And just so you know, you only have a dozen eggs in that thing you call an icebox. A dozen eggs will not feed many people."

"What was your first clue?" Annie sniffed. "Have you always been such a know-it-all?"

Fergus pointed to the cookbooks, then the refrigerator. "That bird has to go into the oven around six in the morning if you plan on serving dinner late in the afternoon. And then there is all that other food you have to prepare."

"I think I'm up to the challenge." Annie sniffed again. "I suppose you're going to tell me you could whip this all up with your eyes closed."

"Actually, I can. I did many dinners like this when my wife became ill. Do you want my help?"

This was definitely not the time to be coy. "Yes!"

Fergus looked down at his watch. "We have five hours before the clock turns to six, at which time we will absolutely have to start to work. *Five whole hours?* I suggest we adjourn to your second floor and do what both of us have been dreaming about."

"I guess you think I'm easy," Annie called over her shoulders as she galloped toward the staircase in the back that led to the second floor.

"The thought never entered my mind," Fergus shouted as he whipped off his shirt and tie.

"Liar!" Annie giggled.

Five hours later, the couple, all smiles and, as Annie put it later, all kitchey-koo, descended the staircase, where Fergus immediately replenished the fire while Annie swept the cookbooks off the counter.

"I'll pick those up later," she said, grinning from ear to ear. "If you want breakfast, I have some donuts and juice. And, of course, coffee. I make very good coffee."

Fergus grinned. "I'll take it. Tell me something, Annie. Is what transpired upstairs something we aren't going to talk about, or should we beat it to death and go on from there? I just want to say that, for a woman your age, you certainly are . . . *agile*. I had no idea you had a tattoo on your rear end. I like that."

Annie stopped measuring out coffee into the wire basket. "You do? I can pole dance. Did you know that?"

"I . . . ah . . . suspected as much when I saw that pole in your dressing room. Perhaps you would give a recital for me."

"Just say the word. Oh, God, did I just say that?"

Fergus laughed. "You didn't answer my question."

"I . . . actually . . . I guess . . ."

"Yes?" Fergus drawled.

"It was the best sex I've ever had. There, is that what you wanted to hear?"

"It'll do. I think I can say the same thing. Shall we do it again after all your guests leave?"

"Make this dinner come out perfectly, and I'll give you a recital you won't soon forget."

Outside, as the sun came up, light snow was falling. Annie took a minute to stare out the window as she peeled sweet potatoes. She realized in that one nanosecond that she was happier than she'd been in years. "Just let me hold on to it for a while," she whispered under her breath.

Fergus watched Annie out of the corner of his eye. *What an extraordinary lady Anna de Silva is.* He couldn't remember the last time he'd been this upbeat, this happy, and he'd just turned down an invitation issued personally by the president of the United States. What in the world had he done to deserve this instead?

By ten thirty, all the prep work was done. What loomed ahead was a magnificent Thanksgiving dinner made by two pairs of loving hands. The kitchen was tidy; all the dishes, pots, and pans were washed and put away, the cookbooks returned to their special drawer.

Annie made fresh coffee for both of them. "This is so nice," Annie said. "I love the fire, these two rocking chairs, dinner roasting, my family coming today, and it's snowing outside. And then there is . . . *you, Fergus.* I can't help but wonder what brought you back into my life right now. Can you tell me why you went to the White House?"

"Well, I'm retired now and not bound by the same rules I once was. But I know better than to talk about things I shouldn't. What is it you want to know?"

"I think you know me and the others well enough to know that whatever is said to any of us goes no further. I probably shouldn't do this, either, but I want to show you something. Wait right here." Three minutes later, Annie returned with a gold shield in her hand. "By any chance, do you know what this is?"

"I do. We have the equivalent of it abroad. I can't say that I am surprised at what you're holding. But do you know there is another shield that tops yours and mine, because there is? I can't be sure about this, but I think only three have ever been issued."

"Who were they issued to?" Annie asked.

"I don't know. Over the years, we've all speculated, but no names were ever mentioned. I guess I can tell you what the meeting was all about, and, no, I will not insult you by asking you not to tell anyone. I know the rules.

"Your government, like all governments, has, for want of a better way of phrasing it, tons of money no one knows about. Secret slush funds. Sometimes those amounts total in the billions. Confiscated monies is what we've always been told. Ugly-gotten money to do good. Think of Robin Hood. That sort of thing. There seems to be some kind of problem—that's all I'm at liberty to tell you—concerning those slush funds."

Annie's mind raced as she tried putting two and two together with what Nikki and Alexis had told her just yesterday about Maggie and her new beau. Meaning Maggie's suddenly being invited and actually going to Camp David with that beau, no less. It all had to mean something. *But, what?*

"Maggie Spritzer, the editor in chief of the *Post,* was also invited to Camp David. She's taking a guest, some financial guru or someone involved in making and investing money." Annie tossed this out to see if Fergus had a reaction. He didn't. "She thinks something is going on. Otherwise, she wouldn't have been invited. Her reporter's instincts, I guess. We're going to miss her at dinner today."

Fergus finished his coffee and very deliberately carried the cup over to the sink. He turned and said, "All we have to do is set the dining-room table, and we're done. That gives us around three hours till we have to be back down here. Are you up to giving that recital?"

Oooh, this is such fun. "Fergus, are you partial to red or black skimpies?" Annie asked, beelining for the back staircase.

"I guess I'll put off getting that cat after the holiday,"

she mumbled to herself as she whizzed through the bedroom to her dressing room, where *the pole* awaited her.

Fergus thought he was going to black out when he
heard the runway music start. Who knew Thanksgiving
could be so exciting?

"Yoo-hoo, Fergus!" Annie trilled. "You can open the
door now!"

"Oh, my God!" was all Fergus Duffy could manage as
he watched Annie take a running start and mount the pole
as the music rose to a thrilling crescendo.

Chapter 8

Maggie felt like she was, as her old grandmother used to say, at sixes and sevens as the marine assigned to her small party drove them in a security vehicle to the main lodge at Camp David.

Once, years and years ago, both she and Ted, part of the White House press corps, had been here. She was stunned to see how beautiful it was now, even though the trees were sleeping for the winter. She'd been here in the late spring, when the entire compound was awash in color, the flowers so profuse, the shrubbery so dense, it had boggled her mind at the time at how beautiful and serene the camp was. If she were the president, she would spend every free minute she had right there at Camp David.

She risked a glance at Jason Parker, who was rattling away to the marine driver, asking question after question. She was annoyed because she could have answered every single one of them. She was also annoyed at the way Jason was dressed. He could have attended an opening night somewhere in his fine cashmere suit and pricey shoes, not to mention all the jewelry he wore. She hoped he'd brought some outdoor gear, because Camp David was all about the outdoors.

Maggie half listened as the marine recited chapter and verse about Hi-Catoctin, also known as Camp David. It had originally been built as a camp for federal government agents and their families by the WPA back in 1935. Then, in 1942, it had been converted to a presidential retreat by Franklin D. Roosevelt and renamed USS Shangri-La. Camp David received its present name from Dwight D. Eisenhower, in honor of his grandson, David. A visit to such a famous place should have been researched by Parker.

They were proceeding down the Camp David entrance road to the Gate House, where she knew that identification would have to be shown regardless of the marine driving them and the fact that they had arrived aboard Marine One. Once through the gate, the marine would take them to the guest parking area, where a shuttle would take them to their assigned cabins. Each cabin, named after a tree, could sleep six to eight people. She wondered which one she would be assigned to. She did her best to remember the names and was surprised when she was able to tick them off on her fingers: Red Oak Cabin, Walnut Cabin, Holly Cabin, Hawthorn Cabin, Sycamore Cabin, Hemlock Cabin, Linden Cabin, and Maple Cabin. The cabins that were totally off-limits, if she recalled correctly, were Camp David's presidential lodge, known as Aspen Lodge, Witch Hazel Cabin, Birch Cabin, Rosebud Cabin, and Dogwood Cabin. She stifled a laugh when she recalled how upset Jason was when his camera had been confiscated, along with a list of other things that were no-no's at Camp David. He had been less than pleased when he was told a commemorative photo would be taken. The words *no such thing as coincidence* kept running through her mind. She asked herself, and not for the first time, how she had managed to get herself into what she was now going through.

In just a few short days, she had taken a real dislike to her companion, when, prior to her lunch with Nikki and Alexis, she had been seriously considering going on to the next level. Now she didn't even want to be in the same room with Jason Parker. Not even in the same city.

Would Jason Parker in his fine duds take the Raven Rock Mountain Complex Site R Tour included in the Camp David secret tunnel tour? Probably not. She complimented herself on bringing along her stout mountain boots, fleece-lined sweats, and the down jacket she was wearing. She knew, just knew, that Jason Parker had counted on making his own little travelogue for distribution to his clients. *Such uncharitable thinking,* she thought happily.

She continued to listen to the conversation as she stared out the car window at the lightly falling snow. The marine was saying that Camp David was alleged to be one of the most secure facilities in the world, as reported by a Department of Defense journal in 1998. The facility, he went on to explain, was guarded by one of the United States Marine Corps' most elite units, MSC-CD (Marine Security Company, Camp David.)

Each marine was handpicked from the infantry field and subjected to a battery of psychological and physical tests before the successful candidates underwent specialized security training at the Marine Corps Security Forces School in Chesapeake, Virginia. A tour of duty for the marines was twelve months, and each of them was awarded the Presidential Service Badge.

Maggie risked another glance at her companion, who was looking even more irritated at everything he was hearing. When the marine got to the part that Jason would have an escort twenty-four/seven and would never be permitted to go off on his own, Maggie thought he was going to explode. What Jason did say was, "So, in other words, we're prisoners while we're here?"

The marine slammed on his brakes so quickly, Maggie was thankful she was wearing her seat belt. "Would you like me to take you back to where I picked you up, *sir?*"

"That means shut the hell up, Jason. Don't make me regret bringing you with me," Maggie hissed.

Jason slumped back in his seat and pouted. He didn't say another word until the marine brought the SUV to a stop in front of Holly Cabin. Maggie was pleased. Staying in Holly Cabin was just right for the beginning of the Christmas season.

God in heaven, what did I ever see in that man? Maggie wondered as she hopped out of the SUV and stood waiting to see if she was to carry in her own luggage or if it would be carried for her. She found out in short order, so she hefted her bag out as Jason Parker mumbled and muttered under his breath. It looked to Maggie like he had a ton of rocks in his "gen-u-ine" antelope-leather suitcase. "And to think some poor antelope had to give up its life so you could buy this case to bring here. You should have remembered to take the price tag off the side," Maggie sniped as she shouldered her Nike canvas hockey bag over her shoulder. "Just for the record, you're an embarrassment. Please do not hang around with me."

Parker threw his hands in the air. "Why are you women always so bitchy?" Not expecting an answer, he picked up his bag and trailed behind Maggie, who was loping ahead to enter the door another marine was holding open for her. A third marine checked off her name and escorted her to her room, which was plain, neat, and a tad spartan; but that was okay. She hated clutter. She knew in her gut that

Jason Parker was expecting the equivalent of the Lincoln Bedroom. Ha!

"An itinerary is on the dresser, ma'am. You will have an escort at all times. Is there anything else I can do for you, ma'am?"

"No. Thank you very much. So, if I want to go outside, do I just . . . you know, go out and someone will join me?"

"Yes, ma'am, that's how it works. It is snowing harder now, so you want to be very careful and wear good boots or shoes."

Maggie quickly unpacked and put her clothes away. Then she sat down on the edge of the bed to read through the papers that had been left for her. When she was sure she had the rules down pat, she changed her clothes and opted for a brisk walk instead of a run. She eyed the book about the history of Camp David sitting on a little table. When she got back, she would peruse it and have a cup of hot chocolate. As she switched outfits and laced up her boots, she wondered how things were going at Pinewood. She felt sad that she wasn't there, but she had called before she left to come to the Camp. Annie had sounded . . . so upbeat and was actually giggling as she talked. She'd said all the right things and told her there would be other Thanksgiving dinners and not to sweat this one. "After all, dear, an invitation to Camp David is a once-in-a-lifetime thing, so enjoy it, and we'll drink a toast to you at dinner." Maggie's eyes had misted over when she hung up.

Well, that was then; this was now. She zipped up her jacket, jammed a wool watch cap down over her curly hair, and ventured forth.

Outside, a marine fell into step behind her. She turned. "I'm just going to walk around and look at things. Is that okay?"

"Yes, ma'am."

And that was what she did for a full hour, the snow beating at her back and stinging her face, but she didn't care. When she was done and back in Holly Cabin, her reward would be the book sitting on the table just waiting to be read and a cup of hot chocolate. She hoped the chef put the tiny marshmallows in his hot chocolate.

That was her intent, but it all changed the moment she passed by Red Oak Cabin to see a man in a motorized wheelchair, another man who might have been a male nurse or an attendant, and the biggest dog she'd ever seen in her life. She rushed forward. "Do you need some help?"

The huge dog yipped once as she moved to get between Maggie and the man in the wheelchair. Maggie immediately backed away when she heard the wheelchair-bound man say, "Easy, girl. She's a friend. Otherwise, she wouldn't be here. Gus Sullivan," he said, holding out his hand.

Maggie stepped forward, looked down at the outstretched hand, then raised her gaze to look directly into the bluest eyes she'd ever seen in her entire life. Her heart took an extra beat, then another, and Maggie Spritzer, hard-bitten ex-reporter, slave-driving editor in chief, fell totally and hopelessly in love.

The man stared at her intently, then he, too, smiled. "Will you marry me? I'm free the last week in February."

Maggie laughed. "Funny thing, I'm free that weekend, also. The answer is yes. Maggie Spritzer, I'm the editor in chief at the *Post*. This is just a wild guess on my part, but is this gorgeous dog by any chance Cleo?"

Cleo yipped and offered her paw, which Maggie shook solemnly. Then she took charge the way she always did. "I think if you take him by one arm, and I take him by the other, we can get him up on the porch," she said to the attendant. The marine can't help us. They have to have hands free at all times."

"I can stand. I can actually walk a little, but I can't do steps," Gus said.

"So you get a ride. City hall or the white gown, tux, and the walk down the aisle?" she quipped as she reached out to shove her shoulder under his arm. "I gotta warn you ahead of time, I have a whole bunch of friends."

Gus Sullivan threw back his head and laughed. "I've always heard that women handle all the details, so whatever works for you will work for me." A moment later he was back in the wheelchair and inviting her into Red Oak Cabin. Cleo nudged Maggie along.

Inside Red Oak Cabin, a fire was blazing in the fieldstone fireplace. A plate of sandwiches and what looked like a pot of hot chocolate were waiting on the coffee table. Cleo walked over, circled the table twice, sniffed everything, and barked sharply.

"That bark means it's okay to eat this stuff. Cleo used to be my dog when we were deployed, but she's retired now. I gave her to President Connor when I went back to Iraq. She lets me come to see her when I'm home, which is for good now. The docs tell me I'll be walking when the spring flowers bloom. I can't wait."

"Maybe we should postpone the wedding till you can walk down the aisle," Maggie said as she poured out the hot chocolate, and lo and behold, out came minimarshmallows.

"Okay. See how easy I am to get along with?"

When was the last time she'd had this much fun? Never, that was when. Maggie removed her watch cap, and her mane of corkscrew red curls sprang to life.

"I like a woman with a lot of hair, especially curly red hair. You hate it, don't you?" Gus laughed.

"How did you know that?"

"Because I had an aunt who had the same kind of hair,

and she always hated it." He was laughing again, not at her but with her.

Maggie sat down on the floor so that she was at eye level with Gus. "Now that we've settled our marriage plans, the reporter, I should say the ex-reporter, in me wants to know about Iraq, Cleo, your past life, and your future. As your prospective bride, I need to know these things."

"You want the short version or the long version?"

"The forever one," Maggie said as Cleo nudged her to rub her belly.

They talked until midafternoon, when Gus's nurse called a halt by saying it was time for therapy and then he had to get ready for dinner at Aspen Cabin.

Maggie knew she was being dismissed, and that was okay. She couldn't remember having a more enjoyable time. She was on her feet in one fluid motion. She leaned over brazenly and kissed Gus Sullivan full on the lips, a long, lingering kiss that couldn't have been taken in any way other than what she meant it to be. "See you at dinner," she called over her shoulder as she tripped her way to the door. At the last second, as she was about to close the door, she called back, "When we return to the District, how about I do an article on you and Cleo and some of your buddies for our Life section? Maybe we can get the president to give us some quotes on Cleo. What do you say?"

"You got it, Maggie Spritzer."

And she did. Oh, life was lookin' so good. She could hardly wait to tell the girls that she was finally deliriously, hopelessly in love, and it had taken only the time for her heart to beat twice.

Chapter 9

"I think, Fergus, it's time to get dressed for our guests. I told everyone to come anytime after noon, and it is noon now. It might behoove us to put some clothes on. What do you think, sweetie?"

No one had ever called Fergus Duffy "sweetie." Fergus threw his head back and let loose with a bear of a laugh. And to think he'd dreaded this visit to the United States. "Well, you do hang out with a prudish bunch, so yes, let's get dressed."

Ninety minutes later, including a small interlude for a little tomfoolery, as Annie put it, the couple was sitting across from each other in the kitchen, sipping coffee.

"Fergus, do I look as sappy as you do?" Annie asked fretfully.

"Absolutely. Do you want to practice looking . . . oh, I don't know, maybe stupid?"

"My girls would see through that in a New York minute. I know, let's talk about something else. Tell me what you think of our president. I'm trying to figure out why she invited Maggie Spritzer to Camp David. The invitation came out of the blue three days before Thanksgiving. That alone tells me something is going on. The question is, What? and whatever 'What?' is, does it have to do with Maggie Spritzer? Why Maggie, of all people? Yes, she is a wonderful person. Yes, she is the editor in chief of the *Post*. Then there is that whole vigilante thing, where she and the paper befriended them . . . us. I can't get a handle on it for some reason. This is really bothering me, Fergus, so help me out here."

"Your president appears to me to be, as you Yanks like to say, 'on the ball.' She has her fingers on everything, not just the nuclear button. Maybe it isn't Miss Spritzer but the companion she took with her. Didn't you say the girls told you about her new paramour? Maybe that's where we should be looking instead of at Maggie."

Annie cupped her chin in her hands and stared at Fergus, all thoughts of what had transpired during the previous hours now just a memory. "But that's chancy. Maggie could just as well have invited Ted or anyone else and not the man who caused Nikki's and Alexis's antennae to start waving.

"From what I can gather, the man is not involved in politics. He's some kind of financial wizard, or so he would like you to believe. And yet, the girls feel like he sought out Maggie for a reason. Woman's intuition on that score."

"I, for one, would never argue with a woman's intuition. Especially a vigilante's intuition. For whatever this is worth, and it is just my opinion, Annie, the girls warned Maggie, and she is at heart still a reporter, so her instincts have kicked in, which is just another way of saying she will be on high alert."

"In your gut, do you think Maggie's invitation to Camp David has anything to do with *you* and your colleagues' visit to the White House yesterday?"

"Annie, I honestly don't know. Our meeting was more of a fact-finding kind of meeting. The reason for our invitation to Camp David had more to do with timing than anything else. The president had to cut our meeting short when she was summoned by her chief of staff. We had traveled here from Europe and were planning on leaving today, as a matter of fact, but the president extended the invitation so that we could meet tomorrow, finish up at Camp David, and be on our way back home tomorrow.

"As I told you earlier, I was just a stand-in for my replacement, who was scheduled to arrive Monday. Things just got bollixed up for some reason. Now, I don't know if my replacement is coming or whether he will do a webcam solo tomorrow. I'm technically out of the loop here."

"Let me ask you this," Annie said as she leered at Fergus, and there was no mistaking her intent, which was, "Tell me what I want to know, or you are outta here." Fergus correctly interpreted the look. "In your opinion, was your meeting primarily about how the European countries handle, monitor, and deal with their governmental *slush funds?* Those billion-dollar babies the public is not privy to? Or was that just a side issue?"

Fergus had a momentary vision of himself driving away from Annie's house, his visit a distant memory, as his nostrils fought the tantalizing aromas he'd helped create. He decided it was in his best interest to step up to the plate. "We did spend what I thought was an inordinate amount of time discussing the matter. My colleagues agreed with my assessment, and when we were having coffee while the president went off to do whatever she had to do, we did agree that your . . . organizational funds were at the heart of our meeting."

Annie digested the information and decided Fergus was telling her the truth as he saw it and as much of that as he was allowed to talk about. "Okay. That's pretty much what I thought." She smiled.

Fergus sighed so loud, he knew the sound could be heard all the way to the interstate. Fergus got up to check the turkey. "Have you decided on how you are going to explain my being here to your friends?" he asked casually.

"I thought I would go with the truth. You can't go wrong when you tell the truth. I . . . ah . . . might leave out a few details, but yes, I think I will just go with the truth. The girls will either figure it out or they won't. But either way, it really isn't my problem, now, is it? In case you haven't figured it out, I don't answer to anyone but myself. I might listen to other opinions, but in the end, mine is the only one that counts. What about you?"

"I don't have to answer to anyone, not even my colleagues. What is it you Americans are so fond of saying? Oh, yes, I'm free as the breeze. Footloose and fancy free. What that means to you, Annie, is this. I can stay on here as long as you want me to stay. It might be cold here, but it is ten times worse back in Scotland, and I do not have central heating. I can't fish in the winter, and I don't like hunting. There is one thing, however, and we need to get it straight right now. I pay my own way. I can't live off you. My pension is not all that big, and I have to measure out my wants and needs. I do have a nest egg, but that is for emergencies. Is that going to be a problem, Annie?"

Annie thought about what Fergus said. She understood it and admired the man for his ethics. "This is how I see it right now, Fergus. You're my guest. Guests don't pay their host for living accommodations—at least my guests don't. When and if I visit you in Scotland, I wouldn't expect you to charge me for staying with you."

"Annie, there is a world of difference between *your* accommodations and *my* accommodations. I do see your point, though. Then there is the question of airfare between our two countries."

"I have a private jet, Fergus."

Fergus groaned. "I know that. That is the problem. I will not . . . I cannot . . ."

Annie stood up to her full height, which was impressive. "You *will*! Money is not our issue. This is about you and me. We can make it work, but you have to cooperate with me. Otherwise, you can leave right now."

Fergus's vision of driving down the road in the snow swam before his eyes again. "Can we put this on the shelf to be discussed again?"

"We can," Annie said happily.

Fergus was saved from any further rebuttal when they heard the sound of a horn that announced an arrival. Annie ran to the window. "It's Kathryn and Bert! Oh, look, it's snowing harder. This is all so wonderful! Maybe we'll be snowbound for the weekend! I do love snow, don't you, Fergus?"

Fergus hated snow, but he wouldn't admit to any negatives at that point in time. "I do, dear lady. I dearly love snow."

"It's not the same when you run through the snow with a ton of clothing on as opposed to running through the rain bare-ass naked."

Fergus decided to let that little comment go right past him.

Hugs and kisses and a manly handshake between Bert and Fergus, and the greeting was over. Annie finished off the greeting by saying Fergus was taking Maggie's seat at dinner, and wasn't it wonderful how he gave up dinner at Camp David to come celebrate Thanksgiving with them?

When she started to say something about trading Fergus for Maggie, Kathryn walked over and whispered in Annie's ear, "You need to quit while you're ahead. So, was it as good as you thought it would be?"

Annie flushed a bright pink. "Actually, it was better. Are you telling me I need to tone it down for when the others get here?"

"You said it, not me, but yeah. Way to go, 'Mom'!"

"Do you girls mind if we go into the family room to watch a pregame?"

The minute Fergus and Bert were out of earshot, Kathryn hissed, "Tell me everything, and don't leave one thing out."

"Oh, my God, I don't know where to start. I gave my first pole recital!"

Kathryn was so jaded she didn't think anything could surprise her, but her eyes popped wide as saucers. "You didn't!"

"I did, and it was perfect. I did such a good job, I didn't think I would be able to revive Fergus. And at my age!" Annie cackled.

"Is this going to go somewhere, Annie?"

"Well, if it doesn't, it won't be for lack of trying on my part. He has this thing about my money. It could become an issue."

"Only if you let it, Annie. What I'm trying to say here is, don't be too quick to want it all *your* way. He's a man. He has pride. Let's face it, your lifestyle is one that most people can only dream about. Be open, okay?"

"That lifestyle hasn't gotten me a companion, now, has it? I am open. For now it is what it is, and I will not rock the boat. I wish you could have seen me on that pole. I was like greased lightning, and I didn't make a single mistake. Fergus did say he likes my agility. And he did mention that my enthusiasm was contagious."

"TMI, Annie."

"One can never have too much information, Kathryn. It is, after all, the information age."

Just then, another horn sounded. Kathryn craned her neck. "It's Jack and Nikki. While you greet them and fill Nikki in, do you want me to crack the champagne and set out the nibbles for the guys?"

"Yes, of course. I was so caught up in my . . . Well, I was caught up." Annie started to giggle and couldn't stop.

Kathryn doubled over, slapping at her sides. "I can't wait to hear what Myra and Nellie have to say."

That comment took the wind out of Annie's sails. She looked so crestfallen, Kathryn set the nibble tray on the table and hugged her. "They will be so jealous, Annie. Trust me. Plus, I know they'll be as happy for you as I am."

The door flew open, and Nikki and Jack walked in. "It's snowing harder," Nikki said as she wrapped her arms around Annie. She held out a bottle of champagne.

Jack waited his turn, then said, "Nothing smells as good as a Thanksgiving dinner. I sure hope you outdid yourself this year, Annie."

"I really did, dear, and you have no idea how *tired* I am right now."

Kathryn winked at Nikki, then raised her eyebrows. She whispered, "That lady has one hell of a story to tell you girls," before she scampered off with her nibble tray.

Myra, Charles, Nellie, and Elias were the next guests to arrive, followed by Yoko and Harry. Barely five minutes passed before Espinosa, Alexis, and Ted arrived. The only guests not yet accounted for were Isabelle and Pearl Barnes.

The men clustered in the family room while the women settled themselves around the kitchen table, where women had congregated for hundreds of years. Or as Annie put it, "The kitchen table is the very essence of family life, and that's what we're all about."

"We picked up an extra guest to take Maggie's seat," Annie said. "You will never guess who appeared on my doorstep after midnight. Fergus Duffy! I was sitting right over there at the island, scanning all those cookbooks, and there he was! And . . . get this, he was also invited to Camp David, but when I invited him for dinner, he blew off the president of the United States."

"You must have been very persuasive, Annie," Myra said.

"Myra, you have no idea how persuasive I was. I even gave my first recital on the pole, and I want you to know I aced it!"

"Oh, myyyy Godddd!" Myra said, her jaw dropping. The others simply looked stunned as Annie went into her spiel, adding and making up as she went along to make her encounter even more interesting.

"And now you expect us to sit at the dinner table, across from that man, and not . . . explode into laughter?" Nellie said.

Myra rose to the occasion and said, "Congratulations, Annie. I guess you really are a cougar."

"Oh, Myra, no. You're only a cougar when the guy is younger than you. But, I will say this. I roared like a lion, I stalked him like a panther, and then I pounced like the sleek fox I am. I showed him no mercy. Not that he asked for any, mind you. That's why I'm tired today, girls."

Yoko clapped her hands. "That was a wonderful story, 'Mom.' How much of it was true?"

"Every last word," Annie said gleefully. "Fergus is extending his visit. By the way, after dinner I have something to tell you all about his meeting at the White House and the invitation to Camp David. I really had to perform to get him to squeal. Aren't you proud of me?"

"Annie, there are no words to describe what I feel right this minute," Myra said primly.

"Stuff it, Myra. You are such a poop sometimes. You're just jealous that I am having fun, and you aren't. Stop with fingering the damn pearls. They aren't going anywhere. Oh, I hear a car. That must be Isabelle and Pearl. Isabelle had to pick Pearl up at a secret rendezvous. That's why they're late."

There were more hugs, more kisses, and Annie told her story yet again to Pearl's and Isabelle's delight.

While the girls worked in sync to get the food to the dining-room table, Annie, Myra, Pearl, and Nellie sat at the table.

"Do you want to come upstairs and see the outfit I wore on the pole?" At Myra's look of horror, Annie rushed on. "And Fergus thinks that tat I have on my ass is a turn-on. Imagine what he would think, say, or do if he ever saw yours, Myra?"

Myra's pearls broke.

Annie raised her eyes and said, "Thank you, God!"

Chapter 10

Thanksgiving at what Annie called her new digs was everything she wanted it to be. The food was wonderful; the table setting beautiful; her family's participation beyond her wildest dreams. And then there was Fergus. Tears gathered in her eyes when she said the blessing before Charles carved the turkey. And then it was delightful comments about the food, laughter, and happiness until the last bite was eaten. Annie beamed and glowed that her first dinner in her new house had gone off according to plan. She'd taken it one step further and given full credit to Fergus, who preened like a peacock. Good-natured jokes and gibes rolled off Annie's back with her saying, "The only important thing is that dinner was perfect, there are leftovers for everyone, and we're all together.

"We're starting a new tradition," Annie trilled. "The men clean up, and we ladies get to sit here with our second cups of coffee, at which point the men will retire to the family room for brandy and cigars and we ladies will adjourn to the kitchen for some serious girl talk. There will be no dissenters." And there were none.

Thirty minutes later, the women were seated around the huge plank kitchen table Isabelle had found in some ancient barn in one of her antique hunting sprees. She'd had it sanded and repaired, and it now glistened with a high shine. A red bowl of holly berries with a few sprigs of evergreen graced the center of the table on a beautiful red felt place mat.

Myra poured brandy into exquisite snifters and handed them out. The women clinked their glasses and smiled.

"Your first Thanksgiving, Annie, and it was wonderful. I am so glad you did this and that we're all together. What are we doing for Christmas this year? Not that I'm rushing time, you understand," Myra added hastily.

"That's a no-brainer, Myra," Isabelle said. "Christmas wouldn't be Christmas unless it was at your house. If you need help with the decorations, I'm your girl. None of my ongoing projects, and there aren't that many, require my full attention until after the first of the year, and you know how I do love to decorate. Plus, I don't think there is any scent that I love more than balsam."

"Absolutely! Just let me know when you want to begin," Myra replied.

Yoko held up her hand. "Isabelle, if you have some free time, I could use some help at the nursery. Starting tomorrow, I will be swamped. My first load of evergreens comes in, and I have to start making wreaths. We have a new garden building, and it has heat in it, so if you want to help, I would really appreciate it."

Within five seconds, Yoko had all the help she needed, and the girls, with the exception of Pearl Barnes, who was putting on her coat in preparation for leaving, were going on to other topics. "I'd love to stay, but I have a family of four children I have to relocate before this day is over. Thank you all for including me today. I enjoyed every minute and every bite, and the kids I am transporting will love this dinner, too." Pearl was, of course, referring to the underground railroad, where she operated outside the law to take children and their abused mothers to safe havens.

The good-byes were misty-eyed and poignant as Isabelle, who was playing chauffeur, slipped into her coat to drop Pearl off at a secret meeting place.

"It's snowing harder," Myra said as she walked back to the table. "I am going to worry about all of you when you leave to return to the District." Her hand went to her neck, but there were no pearls to grasp. The Sisters laughed at the look of dismay on her face.

"We're staying," Nikki said. "Annie doesn't want all those bedrooms to go to waste. She wants to officially christen this wonderful house with all her family, and I say that's just great. The guys are okay with it. Charles even volunteered to get up early and make breakfast as long as we shovel the snow."

"Oh, dear, didn't I tell you I have snowblowers? And I also have snowmobiles. Isabelle said I absolutely needed those so I could visit with Myra and Nellie. That young woman did not forget a thing. I am just so happy, I am giddy," Annie trilled.

"We can see that, Annie," Myra sniped.

"I'm going to ignore that comment, Myra, because you are just upset that you broke those damn pearls of yours."

Myra grimaced. "Now, let's get down to business before the men come trooping in here."

"That's not going to happen, Myra," Kathryn said. "Their eyes are glued to the game. You couldn't pry them away even if you tried. So, what are we discussing?"

"This!" Annie said, waving a piece of paper she'd taken out of the kitchen drawer. "Fergus wrote this up for me this morning. It's a list of all the guests who are at Camp

David. Along with Maggie. Notice the explanation next to each name. All big-time moneymen. Secret moneymen. You know, for all those government funds the public doesn't know about. Somehow, someway, we are going to be involved in this, so let's get a head start right now. Having said that, I think we should keep it on the down-low for the time being."

"Annie, what in the world are you talking about?" Myra demanded.

"The reason Fergus came here in the first place, along with all those other gentlemen who hired us to capture Henry 'call me Hank' Jellicoe. That's one group. The other group of guests at Camp David is the money people I just mentioned. And then there is Maggie. And that person she took with her, who also just happens to be a moneyman."

"And this means what, Annie? I think you need to be more precise. What are you driving at?" Alexis asked.

Annie sighed. "Am I the only one who thinks it's strange that Maggie went to Camp David? If I recall, Alexis, it was you and Nikki who first thought it was strange and had misgivings."

"But that was about Jason Parker, not Camp David. It was just a . . . I don't want to say coincidence that she took him with her, because she could have taken anyone as her guest. Just because he's some kind of financial wizard, and that's a term I understand he gave himself, doesn't mean anything to me."

"I own the *Post*," Annie said.

"But, dear, no one knows that. Back when you bought it, you assured us all that ownership was buried so deep that no one would ever find out. Are you saying someone knows you are the owner?" Myra asked fretfully.

"Not just someone, Myra, the president. And someone in her administration. I don't see her digging through the maze we set up. It's my opinion, and I'm sticking with it. I do have intuition, and my paper is *all-powerful*, as we all know. Everyone in Washington knows Maggie has carte blanche," Annie sniffed.

"It makes sense," Kathryn said thoughtfully.

"It does now, doesn't it?" Nikki added, just as thoughtfully.

Jack appeared in the doorway. He held up both hands, indicating he didn't mean to interrupt. "Got beer, Annie?"

She nodded.

The girls flocked to the kitchen windows and door to watch the falling snow while Jack loaded up a tray with beer. Jack watched them out of the corner of his eye, knowing full well they were up to something. He felt a flicker of alarm, but it was gone almost as soon as it appeared. The girls would handle whatever it was they were trying to keep secret. He shouldered his way through the swinging door, holding the tray high in waiter mode.

The girls scurried back to the table. "Where were we?" Myra demanded.

"I was saying Maggie has carte blanche, and the paper is one to be reckoned with. Martine Connor knows that. We just have to figure out what she wants Maggie to do. Is she going to give her hints? Is she hoping Maggie will figure it out on her own and absolve her from whatever it is she's trying to keep secret, or are we . . . you know, barking up the wrong tree, and it's all a *big* nothing?"

"It is *not* a big nothing, Annie, so get that idea out of your head right now. We're all on the same page, and if we all agree, then it has to mean it is a *big* something. We're women. We're smart. We should be able to figure this out. What's not computing for us is that guy Maggie was hanging out with. Maybe if we take him out of the mix, it will make more sense to us. So, pffft," Nikki said, snapping her fingers. "Jason Parker is out of the mix. Now what do we have?"

"Obviously, we need more brandy," Annie answered, uncorking a fresh bottle from her newly built wine rack that lined one whole wall in her kitchen. "This is just so lovely," she said, pointing to the intricate wine rack. "You pluck out a bottle and there's another one right behind it. Just lovely. Alexis, dear, add some more wood to the fire, please. We need to be cozy and warm while we ponder the present circumstances."

Yoko leaned forward. "Those financial people you say are at Camp David . . . they're all public figures with titles, right?"

Annie and Myra nodded.

"If they're public figures, and the public knows what they're doing, they can't be the ones in charge of secret funds. For one thing, there are too many of them. It has to be *one* person who oversees secret funds. And that one person is probably only accountable to *one* person. Otherwise, there wouldn't be any secret—what did you call them?—slush funds?"

"Yoko is absolutely right," Myra said. "How on earth are we going to find out who that person is?"

Nellie decided it was time to voice her opinion. "Maybe that's why the president invited Maggie to Camp David. Maybe she's going to drop a hint, hoping Maggie picks up on it. If you girls are on the right track, it leads me to believe that the other money people there might know about the mystery fund but not know who the person is who maintains it. Did that person do something illegal? Did he or she abscond with the funds? Since the funds aren't supposed to exist, you can run with any scenario you like.

"One other thing. Why do you think Fergus and his colleagues are there? I mean, he's here, but he was supposed to go there, and he didn't. To shed light on how they manage their mystery funds would be my guess. Or if those men and their countries ever had a problem similar to the one the president is experiencing. This is giving me a headache."

"Drink some more brandy. It cures just about anything," Annie said solicitously. "Maybe Maggie can contact her . . . that person who does all those illegal things when she returns. If he had the expertise to hack into the Witness Protection Program without anyone finding out, this should be . . . what's that expression? Oh, yes, a walk in the park."

Nikki, knowing the full story on Abner Tookus and Maggie's love-hate relationship, shook her head. "That's not going to happen."

"Then how about Bert and Jack going to the director of the FBI? They saved his butt not too long ago, and Yantzy owes them. Yantzy should know who that person is if he heads up the FBI. For that matter, Bert might even know," Kathryn said. She looked at Nellie and said, "Do you think Elias might know? He was Bert's predecessor."

Nellie shrugged. "I can ask, but I doubt it. I don't think anyone except the president would know something like that. Maybe one other person on her staff or someone who *used* to be on her staff. Someone she trusts one hundred percent."

As one, the girls said, "Lizzie!"

"But," Myra said, holding up her hand, "doesn't that come under the heading of attorney-client privilege or president-attorney privilege or something like that? Maybe national security?"

Myra's words and tone of voice were so fretful, Annie took a swipe at her. "Earth to Myra. And if that *is* the case, do you think *that* will stop us from getting the information from Lizzie? Lizzie is *one of us,* or did you forget that?"

Sensing a revolt coming her way, Myra backpedaled. "All right, all right, I foolishly misspoke. Please forgive me, one and all."

"That's all right, dear," Annie said, patting Myra's shoulder. "We all have these little lapses from time to time. Tomorrow morning, we call Lizzie and ask her what, if anything, she knows in regard to secret funds. Agreed?"

Every hand in the room shot high in the air, including Myra's.

"See how easy that was," Annie said airily. "More brandy, Myra?"

Myra nodded.

"On the off chance that Lizzie *doesn't* know, we need a second source. This is what I suggest. Since I personally stabilized and made Maggie's contact person rich beyond his dreams, not to mention that he owns oceanfront property thanks to my generosity, I think it might behoove us all, and I do mean us all, to visit the gentleman and show him the way we do things. Agreed?"

Once again, every hand in the room shot up.

Annie upended the brandy bottle and proceeded to pour. Miffed at what she thought was a stingy amount coming out of the bottle, the irrepressible Nellie bounded off her chair and headed directly to the wine rack. "When I say pour, I mean *pour!*"

Annie poured and poured some more.

And that was how Fergus Duffy and the others found the ladies a long time later, soused, as he put it, to the ears and feeling no pain as they laughed and giggled and congratulated each other on what they were going to do in the morning.

Feeling no pain himself, Jack Emery looked at his lovely

wife, who was trying to wink at him, and said, "Boys, don't even go there! This is one of those things that simply never happened." He turned on his heel to back out of the kitchen, bumped into Ted Robinson, who went ass over backward, knocking Elias into Fergus, who was already unsteady on his feet, and who then rolled over, tripping Bert, who tried to leap out of the way but collided with Harry, who went airborne. Espinosa was the only man left standing.

"Well, this certainly is going to be a memory I can take back to Scotland with me," Fergus bellowed.

In the kitchen, the brandy bottles lined up like soldiers, Myra tried counting them but gave up. "I have to say, Countess de Silva, you do know how to throw a Thanksgiving dinner." At which point she slid off her chair and went to sleep.

The others peered down at her and sighed as they joined her.

Annie was the last to cradle her head in her arms. To no one in particular, she muttered, "This was one hell of a Thanksgiving."

Chapter 11

Maggie crawled out of bed before she even looked at the little travel clock she had brought with her. Five forty-five! For some reason, she'd thought she would sleep in since she was at such a famous place and on a minivacation of sorts; but years of rising before the sun came over the horizon was such a habit, here she was, wide awake with absolutely nothing to do and nowhere really to go. She wished she was back in her newly purchased home in Georgetown.

With nothing better to do, she showered and washed her hair. She even put on makeup. To impress Gus Sullivan and his dog. Somehow, she managed to tame her wild hair with a handful of gel and some hair spray before she tied it all back with a green ribbon to match her designer T.J. Maxx discount sweats. At the last second, she spritzed some perfume that claimed if she wore it, men would drop at her feet. She wasn't hopeful, since she'd been wearing it for years, and a man had yet to drop at her feet. Ted didn't count, since he was the one who gave her the perfume in the first place, and he was immune to the scent.

In the kitchen of her cabin, she made coffee. While it dripped into the pot, she tried to see outside in the semi-darkness. She could see snow flurries swirling about from the glow of the outside lampposts, but the accumulation didn't appear to be more than four inches or so, if that. She knew that McLean, where Myra and Annie lived in Virginia, had gotten eight inches of snow. She'd stayed up late enough to get the weather report.

Maggie peered at the coffeepot. It still wasn't ready, so she went back to her room for her notebook and pen. By the time she got back, the coffee was ready to be poured. She settled herself and started to make notes. She was there for a reason. Now, if she could just figure out what that reason was, she would be one happy camper.

She leaned back on the cozy leather window seat and closed her eyes. *Think!* And she did think, but her thoughts were on Gus Sullivan and their meeting and how fast her heart beat at that meeting and how dry her throat was. She'd just fallen in love with a man in a wheelchair, and that wasn't a bad thing. In fact it said a whole lot for her that she could fall in love with a handicapped person. A temporarily handicapped person, who perhaps would regain the use of his legs. And if he didn't, she'd still love him, anyway. *Maggie Spritzer, I am so proud of you.*

Maggie tried once again to focus on the task at hand. She made four columns of names before getting up to replenish her coffee. The men from the different security agencies abroad went in one column. The different U.S. officials went into the second column, and the third column was made up of people like herself; Jason Parker; Gus Sullivan; the retired teacher of the year, five years running, from Bangor, Maine; a college boy from Virginia Tech who'd saved two little girls from being abducted, taken them to the police station, and walked away, saying anyone would have done the same thing. The fourth column was for the press. Whom she had yet to see. No red flags there.

No red flags my foot. They're there. I just can't spot them.

She struggled to remember what she knew about the U.S. officials who were there. Didn't they have families? Why would they give up a family Thanksgiving at home to come here to Camp David? Was it a *command* invitation? And if it was a *command* invitation, why? Why Thanksgiving weekend? No one would notice? The media wouldn't care? Unlikely. The media did care.

Maybe since she was the EIC of the *Post,* she could cozy up to one or more of them to get their take on things. Professional courtesy, that kind of thing. Then again, maybe not since she was a guest. She wondered what kind of spin the media would put on the Camp David guest list.

Maggie doodled in her notebook as she tried to come to terms with the four columns of names. As far as she could tell, all she had was the names of a bunch of people who decided that eating Thanksgiving dinner at Camp David was better than staying home. The security people from abroad were understandable. What wasn't understandable was the U.S. officials.

Maggie underlined the words *command performance.* She looked down into her empty coffee cup as she debated whether or not to drink another cup. If she did, she'd be twitching and twanging all over the place and having to pee every ten minutes. She doodled some more before she got up to clean the coffeepot for the next guest.

By the time she had finished with her uncharacteristic cleanup, it was full light. The world outside glistened and sparkled. Before she could change her mind, she took her notebook back to her room, put on her heavy jacket, and walked outside. She was just in time to see a golf cart stop at Gus Sullivan's cabin. She plowed through the snow lickety-split and came to a bracing stop just as Gus hit the last step. "Mind if I tag along?" she asked breathlessly.

Gus's face lit up like a Christmas tree. "I'd like the company, but you'll have to walk since they need to put my chair in the back. Isn't it beautiful?" he asked, waving his arm about. "When I was in Iraq, I used to dream about mornings like this."

The marine driving the golf cart drove slowly so that Maggie could keep up with them. She was winded from the cold air when they reached the dining hall in Laurel Cabin, but at the same time she felt exhilarated.

The dining room for guests was virtually empty, yet it smelled wonderful. Breakfast was her favorite meal of the day. After lunch and dinner. She wondered if her obsession with food would make a difference to Gus Sullivan.

With two more cups of coffee under her belt along with a gigantic breakfast, Maggie felt on top of the world. "The day after Thanksgiving at Camp David!" Now that was a profound statement if she had ever uttered one. "What's on your agenda, Gus?"

"Therapy. It's ongoing and never-ending. I was hoping for some kind of tour. One of the marines told me this afternoon was picture-taking time with the president. So there's that. Tonight is dinner with the president. Other than that, I plan on reading some of the books on Camp David that are in my cabin. What are your plans?"

"About the same as yours. I'm going to walk a bit, see what I can see myself. I like being alone with my thoughts in strange places. I also want to hook up with some of the press and see what their take is on this weekend. Then like you said, we get our pictures taken with the president. A personal one-on-one, then a group shot of all us outsiders.

I think I'll run them in the paper when I get back. Human interest, that kind of thing."

They talked about the paper, what it was like to be the editor in chief of such a famous newspaper, the paper that had almost single-handedly exposed the Watergate shenanigans. Her heart kicked up a beat when Gus said, "What was it like when you were covering the vigilantes? My whole unit couldn't wait to read about them. It was like one of those serial movies you watched when you were a kid. That's another way of saying, we all rooted for them, especially the women. When we heard that the president pardoned them, we had a party. Actually, the officers threw it, but no one is supposed to know that."

Maggie chose her words carefully. "It was interesting. I can't tell you how many times my e-mail server crashed, along with our switchboard, with supporters calling in to voice their opinions."

"You're friends with them, then?"

Another quick heartbeat. Maggie found herself studying the man she had just fallen in love with. She didn't see anything to alarm her. "In a manner of speaking. My people have gotten some exclusives with them. The *Post*'s readership doubled when they were active."

Gus seemed to accept Maggie's explanation. "Since I got back, my only pastime other than therapy has been to read. I read your newspaper line by line, word for word, page by page. Then I quiz myself on what I read. I don't mean online, either. I like holding the paper in my hand, and I regret the absence of ink on my hands when I'm done, the way it used to be. The funny thing is, I was never much of a reader. I was always doing something I thought was more important. Since I've been back, I think I know how Washington works." He rolled his eyes, and Maggie laughed.

"Oh, look, here's your friend, and my nurse is signaling me that it's time to go. If you want to stop by, feel free. I'm done with morning therapy around eleven. Today is range of motion."

Before Maggie could agree or disagree, Gus was steering his chair across the dining-room floor, and Jason Parker plopped down next to her.

Maggie had to fight with herself to be civil. She did her best to smile. "Good morning, Jason."

"I don't see what's good about it. Didn't you see that snow out there? It rather hampers one's day, don't you think?"

Maggie stretched her neck to peer down at Jason's feet and the expensive Bally shoes he was wearing. She pointed to her own stout boots. "I think I told you this wasn't a fashion party. Your attire is about as out of place here as tits on a bull."

Jason winced. "I lost my notebook. By any chance did you see it?"

"No. What does it look like?"

"One of those little ones that were in the cabin. The complimentary ones. I made some notes in it."

"Nope, didn't see it."

Maggie thought Jason looked upset. She wondered what kind of notes a moneyman such as he would have made. She almost asked but changed her mind.

"Since you seem to have appointed yourself the head of the fashion police, what do you think I should wear for the formal picture? I guess what I'm asking is, what are you going to wear?" Jason asked.

"What difference does it make what *I* wear?" Maggie said, deliberately not answering Jason's question.

"Well, since you brought me as your guest, I thought we should have a picture taken together."

A very unladylike sound erupted from Maggie's mouth. "Well, you thought wrong, Jason. Look, this is the way it is. I'm sorry I brought you here with me. You set me up back at the paper, and we both know it, so don't deny it. I don't know what your endgame is, but I'm not willing to be a part of it. I will admit you bedazzled me there for a little while, but it did not take long for that bedazzlement to fly out the window. So do us both a favor and stay away from me. I'm surprised you aren't out there hanging with the press."

One look at Jason's face told her he'd already tried that and either been rebuffed or unable to get access to them. She laughed as she gathered up her jacket and slipped into it.

"You are so hateful, Maggie Spritzer." Jason turned his back on her and motioned to the steward that he was ready to order.

Outside in the brisk air, Maggie took a great gulping breath. The wind was blustery, and it was hard to tell if the snow she was seeing was actually flurries or the wind blowing the snow from the trees and shrubs. She walked with her head down. When she got to Holly Cabin, she bolted up the steps and raced inside. Even though she had to go to the bathroom, she took the time to look around to see if she could spot the notebook Jason claimed to have lost. It took her ten minutes before she found the little notebook wedged between the sofa cushions in the main living area. Too pat. Too obvious. If she found it, why couldn't Jason find it? She jammed the little book into the pocket of her sweats, raced to the bathroom, then into her room, where she locked the door. She pulled out the notebook and looked down at Jason Parker's squiggles. Three pages of nothing but initials, or what she assumed were initials, then question marks. GS had to mean Gus Sullivan. MS had to mean Maggie Spritzer. She closed her eyes and let her mind roam to the other line of initials. The US contingent, all present and accounted for. Only one question mark, next to JJ, whoever JJ was. She racked her brain. No one that she knew of had the initials JJ. The European contingent, all initials present and accounted for. Ditto for the outsiders.

Jason's squiggles—his printing was tiny, a sign of an introvert. Or so she'd heard. Jason Parker, in her opinion, was not an introvert. The question now was, should she tell Jason she had found the notebook and hand it over or keep it to herself until she could figure out what he was up to? Well, that was a no-brainer. She shoved the notebook with the presidential seal on the cover into her pocket.

She was about to leave her room when the word *setup* ricocheted through her being. She whipped out her own notebook and proceeded to copy, as best she could, what she was seeing in Jason's notebook. When she was finished, she checked it again, line by line, squiggly letter by letter. When she was satisfied that she had it down right, she marched out to the huge family area. A steward was replenishing the dying fire. She sat down on the nubby wheat-colored sofa and wedged the little notebook down between the cushions, just the way she had found it. "Screw you, Jason Parker," she mumbled under her breath.

The other guests were stirring now; she could hear chatter from down the hall. The retired teacher, for some reason, had a shrill, high-pitched voice. How did that go over in a classroom? she wondered. The student from Virginia Tech barreled through the room on his way to the door. He noticed Maggie and said, "Dining is at the Laurel Lodge, right?"

Maggie nodded. She got up and headed back to her room, where she sat down in a comfortable rocker with a wonderful outside view of the snow-covered fairyland also known as Camp David. She needed to think.

Forty minutes later, with no further insight, Maggie gathered up her small backpack and her jacket. Her destination, Sycamore Cabin, to which the press corps had been assigned.

Just as she reached the door, a marine was about to enter the cabin. "Miss Spritzer, the president asked me to give this to you. I'm to wait for your verbal reply."

Maggie walked back inside and opened the envelope just as Jason Parker blew through the door. "Whatcha got there, Maggie?"

"None of your business," Maggie shot back. She looked down at the handwritten note asking if Maggie would be available for a private lunch at one o'clock. Maggie took her time folding up the note and slipping it into her small backpack. "Tell the president I would be delighted." A second later, the marine was gone, and Maggie was left standing next to Jason Parker.

Jason took what he considered Maggie's bad attitude in stride and said, "Did you find my notebook?"

"You really take the cake, you know that, Jason? Why would I look for *your* notebook? You lost it. You look for it. There are other people staying here. Ask them. You know what else? You really should dry off those expensive shoes you're wearing. You're going to find salt marks on them. How's that going to look when you get your picture taken with the president?"

Jason scurried out of the room, and Maggie left the building. Outside, she pulled up the collar of her jacket, pulled her wool cap down snugly over her ears, then pulled on a pair of bright red mittens that Myra had made for her two Christmases ago.

Maggie closed her eyes and waited for her escort to

show up to lead her to Sycamore Cabin. It seemed to her that the temperature was dropping. Damn, she hated the cold. Why couldn't the president have invited her to Camp David for the Fourth of July, when the weather was warm and balmy?

When one of the marines showed up, Maggie fought her way down the walkway that had been cleared of all the snow. She could see small crystals of ice beginning to form at the edges of the stones, which proved to her that the temperature was indeed falling. To her own great delight, she laughed out loud when she formed a mental picture of Jason Parker in his handmade Ballys, slipping and sliding and falling on his ass as he made his way to Hickory Lodge, where the pictures were to be taken. She was still laughing when she walked up to the door of Sycamore Cabin and knocked once.

Her hand was raised to knock a second time when the door was opened by Jim Matthews from CBS. "We've been waiting, Maggie. What took you so long?"

Maggie laughed. "A little of this and a little of that. I'm here now, so tell me. What's going on?"

Chapter 12

The Sisters were like a bunch of ten-year-olds when they trooped down to the kitchen to get an early breakfast before heading back to the District to honor their promise to help Yoko at the nursery.

The boys were outside blowing snow, shoveling out their vehicles, and clearing the huge courtyard so that they could make it out to the highway. Except for Charles and Fergus, who were busy at Annie's Wolf range. Annie and Myra exchanged smug expressions at how well the two men had hit it off.

As the Sisters bustled around the kitchen and dining room, Myra whispered in Annie's ear, "How long do you think Fergus will stay on?"

Annie wiggled her eyebrows. Then she winked. "Until I wear him out would be my best guess."

In spite of herself, Myra grinned. "That good, eh?"

"I have to say, Myra . . . that good."

Myra gave her old friend's arm a gentle squeeze. "I'm happy for you, Annie. I mean that sincerely."

"I know, Myra, I know. By the way, I really think we should go with the girls to help Yoko. I'm sure there's something we'll be able to do. Just because we have arthritis in our hands doesn't mean we can't fetch and carry, stack and box . . . whatever. Four extra hands could mean a big difference to Yoko and her schedule."

"Okay. I didn't have anything planned for today. I don't know about Nellie, though."

"Did I hear my name mentioned?" Nellie asked, coming up behind the women.

"You did. Myra and I are going to go with the girls to help Yoko. You're welcome to come along."

Nellie held out her hands. "I don't think so. And these new hips of mine are giving me trouble this morning. Change in weather is never good, but it is getting better, I have to say. I think Elias and I will head on home after breakfast. Annie said we could borrow two of the snowmobiles. We'll pick up our car when we return the snowmobiles. If there's anything Elias and I can do from this end, let me know." Nellie's voice dropped to a low, conspiratorial whisper. "Annie, I really like Fergus. You aren't going to screw it up, are you?"

Annie laughed. "I know you didn't mean that to come out the way it did, but the answer is yes and no."

The three women laughed just as Fergus turned to look at them. Annie wiggled her fingers in his direction, and he threw his head back and let loose with a bear of a laugh.

"Life is lookin' good, girls," Annie said, moving off toward the dining room.

The Sisters looked up, their eyes questioning.

Annie threw her arms in the air. "Nothing. Myra and I are going to go with you all to Yoko's. We're four extra hands. I'm sure we can fetch and carry and help out. Make coffee or hot chocolate. Whatever . . . We are on board with the exception of Nellie, who is going back home after breakfast. Did the boys say what they're going to do?"

Nikki and Kathryn looked at each other, then at Yoko, who nodded.

"We think they have an intervention planned. They're going to relocate Harry's second master with a dummy in another room. They said the master will never know the difference since he sleeps all day, the same way the first one did. Jack and Bert are going to take over Harry's training. Yoko gave her approval, so now it will be up to Jack and Bert to convince Harry to accept their help," Nikki said.

A bell tinkled.

"Time for breakfast," Isabelle said.

"I'll call the boys," Alexis said.

"I'll help set up the food on the sideboard," Kathryn said.

The Sisters fell to it and worked like the well-practiced machine that they were.

The rule at Annie's was the same as at Myra's: no business was discussed at mealtime. Charles's rule, a rule the Sisters adhered to.

New to their game, Fergus asked how they all thought Maggie Spritzer's visit to Camp David was going.

Myra explained Charles's rule. Fergus looked properly chastised until Annie patted his shoulder and whispered, "It's okay. You couldn't be expected to know about all our rules, even the silly ones." She glared at Charles to make her point.

The Sisters all grinned from ear to ear. Annie definitely had a thing going on, and they approved.

Breakfast progressed and, for some reason no one could explain, the Sisters and the boys split. The girls cleaned the kitchen; the boys rushed back outside to finish clearing the snow. And then it was time to leave. All questions about Maggie and any other pending business were left back in the dining room.

Ted Robinson and Espinosa brought two bright, shiny snowmobiles as close to the back door as they could. Elias and Nellie waved jauntily and sped off across the fields to their own house. Jack and Bert roared up right behind Ted and Espinosa, and Charles and Fergus hopped on two yellow snowmobiles and, with an airy wave, headed toward Pinewood.

The boys clambered into Bert's SUV, and the Sisters split up into two vehicles, Nikki's BMW and Annie's Mercedes.

Maggie looked in the mirror. She made a face at herself. She would never be a fashionista like Nikki or Alexis. And she wasn't as sporty and elegant as Kathryn or Isabelle. And there was no way she could even come close to Yoko in dress or demeanor. She was herself, Maggie Spritzer. She cocked her head from side to side. "Casual" meant casual. She decided she was casual in her black pantsuit with the leather belt that rode low on her hips. Now, if she put on the rhinestone belt, the black pantsuit would have qualified for casual evening wear. Well, it wasn't going to get any better no matter how long she stared at herself. She was even satisfied with her hair, which she had pulled back and wound into a French twist. There was nothing she could do about the stray tendrils that curled around her temples and ears. All in all, she decided she was more than presentable.

She slipped into her coat for her walk to Aspen Lodge, the president's private residence at Camp David. She was expecting an escort with a golf cart, but that had not been confirmed. Whoever was assigned to deliver her to Aspen

Lodge could just as well pick her up on the way. Besides, she wanted the fresh air to clear her head.

In the common room, the fire was blazing. A cart with fresh coffee was being wheeled in by a steward. The college student was first in line to fill his cup. Jason Parker was sitting on one of the sofas, writing something in his little notebook. When he saw Maggie, he held it up triumphantly. "I found it!"

"Good for you," Maggie snapped. What was he scribbling in that little book, and what did it all mean? Well, she didn't have time to worry about Jason Parker and his notes.

"Maggie, hold on. I heard in the dining room that Mr. Sullivan is leaving early this evening. I'm going to find out if I can hitch a ride with them. I just wanted you to know."

"I didn't know that was possible. I just assumed everyone was leaving on Sunday morning. I think I might cut my own visit short if that's the case. Thanks for telling me," she mumbled.

"It's not like you don't know everything already. I can't believe I one-upped you," Jason sniped.

"Why couldn't you just have quit while you were ahead, you schmuck?" Maggie slammed the door to drive home her point.

Gus was leaving this evening, if what Jason said was true. Why? Now if she tried to hitch a ride with him, he was going to think she was hot on his tail. Maybe she should play it cool and ride it out till Sunday. Damn, why didn't things work out the way she wanted them to? Why did something always have to go wrong at the eleventh hour? *Because it's life,* she answered herself.

When the golf cart was not waiting outside, Maggie started toward Aspen Lodge. She had taken only a few steps when she heard the golf cart before it came alongside of her. "You should have waited, Miss Spritzer. We have rules here."

"Yeah, well, I needed some fresh air. I don't mind the walk. But since you're here, I accept the ride. Where you from, Marine?"

"Edison, New Jersey, ma'am."

"I've never been to New Jersey, for some reason."

And that was the end of that conversation.

Five minutes later, Maggie found herself being welcomed to Aspen Lodge by the president of the United States. Martine Connor started off the conversation with an apology. "I'm really sorry, Maggie. Is it okay to call you Maggie? We went through this once before, I believe."

Maggie nodded.

"I had hoped to spend some serious personal time with all my guests, but some things came up that had to be dealt with. Historically, for some reason, Thanksgiving has always been business-free, with nothing going on. My luck that things changed," the president said impishly as she guided Maggie into the dining room, where a small table was set for two.

A small glass fishbowl held four white roses with assorted greenery. Maggie thought it looked simple yet elegant. Much like the president herself, who was dressed in beige slacks, loafers, and a long-sleeved burgundy turtleneck sweater. A single strand of pearls and pearl studs were her only jewelry. As for makeup, she wore a little rouge, a pale pink lipstick. There was not even a hint of perfume on her person. Her hair was pulled back casually and piled high on her head. Simple but elegant.

"I wish we had time for a real hour of girl talk, but, unfortunately, I have a meeting after lunch that is . . . very important."

Maggie relaxed. Sizing up the president, she thought she

had hit the nail on the head and that the president was going to be doing all the talking, and that she would be doing all the listening. Maggie was reminded of the news anchors who talked so fast because of time constraints. Words per minute was all-important. She waited.

"Turkey broth, turkey croquettes, and if there was a way to make a dessert with turkey, my chef would have found it. Since he didn't find one, we're having mince pie. All leftovers," the president said. "I hate to see food wasted, and it's so American to eat turkey for a week after Thanksgiving. Don't you agree, Maggie?"

Maggie nodded.

"So, did you get to meet everyone?"

Maggie nodded again because she didn't know what else to do, even though she hadn't been introduced to the *important* people.

"Isn't Gus just the most interesting person?"

Maggie nodded again.

"Cleo just loves him. I am going to be devastated when he makes his full recovery and Cleo goes back to him."

A devil perched itself on Maggie's shoulder. "Gus asked me to marry him. I said yes." Maggie giggled.

The president burst out laughing. "I know. He told me last night. He's a great guy, Maggie. He's really been into Washington politics since his return. All he does is read. He asks questions. I like that. Do you have any questions? The soup is salty, don't you think?"

What the hell? Maggie tasted the soup and agreed it was salty. When the president pushed her bowl aside, she did the same thing.

"The reporter in me wants to know why all those money people are here. The reporter in me wants to know why all those spooks from abroad are here. Personally, me wants to know if you know anything about Gus that will make sure I get him to the altar."

Well, she couldn't have been more blunt if she'd rehearsed her response. Throw out the line and see what you hook was a rule she lived by.

The president smiled. "I wish I had an answer for you. I don't. That's why I invited all these people here at the last minute. I thought you could . . . talk this up with . . . ah . . . your colleagues."

"I'm trying hard not to be stupid here, but you're going to have to tell me more. My . . . ah . . . colleagues won't . . . They'll need more. Trust me."

"Always follow the money. Isn't that a rule of something or other? When money goes missing, you start at the beginning and track it. At least that's what I've been told."

"Well, that's true. We've done enough exposés over the years to give credibility to that theory. Money trail, paper trail, it's all the same? So what's gone missing?" Maggie asked.

The president shook her head, which meant she didn't want to tell or couldn't tell.

Maggie nodded and continued to ask questions. "So you guys . . . your different agencies, you have beaucoup bucks you use . . . to pay off spies and that kind of thing? Slush funds for special agents and their expenses? High-dollar payouts to agents who go undercover to do things no one ever finds out about. I read a lot of spy novels, and that's how it works on printed pages. I think I can fill in the blanks if you just nod."

The president smiled and broke into her turkey croquette. She ladled a chile-verde sauce all over it. "It's still leftover turkey," the president said, tongue in cheek. She then nodded.

"Are there many different funds or just one?"

The president held up her fork that had four tines in it.

Maggie wanted to call a halt to this nonsense and bellow, "Tell me. Stop playing games with me." *Richard Nixon and the famous tapes.* Maggie eyed the fork and nodded. Four funds.

Maggie was shocked witless when the president said, "Money people, those investment brokers like the friend you brought with you, are such strange people. They don't operate or live on the same level as ordinary people. All they think about is money and how to invest to get the highest return or how to bilk people, like that Bernie Madoff person in New York."

Maggie blinked, then blinked again. *Oh shit.* Was the president telling her Jason Parker was a Bernie Madoff clone? Sounded like it. "I need a name, Madam President. Who controls all those invisible slush funds? One person, four people? Who has the final say, and where does the accounting end?"

In response, or should that be nonresponse, the president shook her head. She reached for her pie just as Maggie pushed up her sleeve and glanced at her watch.

Maggie figured her time would be up when the president took the last bite of her pie. She felt like she was in a puzzle house. The president didn't seem shy about talking about some things, assuming the conversation was recorded by someone somewhere, and yet she stopped short of actually giving concrete details for her to carry back to the Sisters. Why hand out those special gold shields, then pull a stunt like this one? Why not just call up one of the girls or go through Lizzie, who would then relate the request to the Sisters?

If there was one thing Maggie Spritzer hated, it was feeling stupid, and at that moment she was feeling stupid.

Really, really stupid. She was so irritated with herself, she blurted out a question she'd had no intention of asking. "How much money do foreign countries keep in those mysterious funds that don't exist?"

"Other countries?"

Maggie nodded.

"Billions sometimes."

"And just *one person* per country handles these special funds?"

The president nodded.

Maggie's mind raced. "Which one of the money people at Camp David handles the U.S. funds?" she asked.

The president shook her head.

Maggie sucked in her breath. Either the president didn't know, which was mind-boggling, or she couldn't tell her for reasons of national security. Her gut instincts told her it was the former and not the latter. All the proof she needed that the president didn't know was to see the awful look on her face. *How,* she wondered, *is that possible?*

She was the president, the leader of the free world, and here she was, admitting she didn't know. Ah, maybe something happened to that person. Maybe that person absconded with all those funds no one was supposed to know about. Maggie felt her heart start to flutter in her chest.

Maggie licked at her dry lips and nodded weakly. "Madam President, is it true that Gus Sullivan is leaving this evening? If so, can I switch up and return with him?"

The president sighed so loudly that Maggie was stunned. "Of course, Maggie. I'm sorry. I should have asked you earlier. Departure time is five forty-five. I hope you enjoyed your brief visit. I have to leave now. I really enjoyed our lunch. I hope you did, too."

"I . . . I loved it."

The president laughed, but it was a jittery-sounding laugh. "That's what Lizzie always said, but what it really meant was, 'Get me out of here as quick as possible.' I'll be in touch, Maggie."

I'll be in touch. Did the president really say that? Maggie looked toward the door, where the marine who had driven her there to Aspen Lodge was waiting to drive her back to her cabin. She stood on the side while the president explained to the marine that Maggie would be leaving on the helicopter at five forty-five. He nodded and held the door for Maggie. She turned in time to see the president waving to her; then she did something that blew Maggie's mind. President Martine Connor blew her, Maggie Spritzer, a kiss.

The marine smiled. "The president only does that to people she really likes."

Maggie felt flattered and flustered as she settled herself in the golf cart. How many people could say the president of the United States blew them a kiss? *Not many, that's how many,* Maggie thought smugly. "No kidding," was all she could think of to say.

Chapter 13

The boys and the Sisters parted company when they reached the District. The women splintered off to head toward Yoko's nursery and what Kathryn called "the evergreen" weekend, where they would trim the fragrant trees that would line the perimeter of Yoko's nursery, and fashion Christmas wreaths, grave blankets, and table centerpieces. Ted and Espinosa waved as they got out of Bert's SUV and grabbed a cab that would take them to the *Post*. Jack, Bert, and Harry headed toward the dojo.

"Amazing how the snow here is all but gone," Jack said as he climbed out of the truck. He turned to Harry and asked what was on his agenda.

Harry just shook his head like it was the stupidest question he'd ever heard. At first, Jack thought Harry wasn't going to answer, but he surprised them by saying, "I'm going to do what I've been doing for the past months, train. I lost two whole days and half of this day already by going out to the farm. That's two and a half days I can't get back."

Jack blew his top right there at the back door. "When

are you going to get it through your thick head, Harry, that you cannot train twenty-four/seven with no breaks? Catnaps and eating weeds for nourishment are not going to help you. Even with those baggy clothes you're wearing, I can see you've dropped ten pounds. That is not good. I'm not even going to mention that worthless master you hired, who sleeps twenty-four hours a day."

Harry ignored him as he unlocked the door.

"Damn, it's cold in here, Harry," Bert said. "Why did you turn the heat down so low before you closed up shop?"

Harry peered at the thermostat. "It's seventy degrees in here. Seventy degrees is not cold." He headed toward the training room. "You guys need to update next week's roster. And someone needs to call those guys at the DOJ and tell them if they miss one more session, they're outta here."

"I'll do it," Bert said as he shucked his jacket, but Harry didn't hear him. He was already gone.

"Let's go check on Harry's master. What the hell did that old guy do here for two whole days all by himself?" Jack said.

"Watched old Bruce Lee videos, is what Harry said he would do. Look! He's sitting in the same spot he was in when we left. Just waiting for Harry to get back so he can train himself." Bert guffawed.

"I think it's time you and I had a talk with the old guy. You know, shake him up a little so he contributes *something* to this training Harry is counting on. When I think of all the money Harry paid out to his organization, or whatever the hell you call it, my blood boils. I hate seeing Harry getting ripped off like this."

"Look, Jack, Harry told us to mind our own business,

and he meant it. We need to leave well enough alone and let Harry do his thing. I'm not saying I like it, but that's the way it is."

"Oh yeah! Well, check this out! This guy's dead!" Jack said, feeling the old master's neck for a pulse. "He's been into rigor and out again, and he's starting to smell. You better get Harry in here to see what he wants to do about this."

"You mean like stash him in ice and pretend he's still here *working?* I don't think that will fly. Harry is going to be so upset. I bet he cries. Two down! Harry!" Bert bellowed at the top of his lungs.

Harry appeared out of nowhere. "What?"

"Your master here . . . He's dead! That means no pulse and he isn't breathing, which translates to d-e-a-d."

"Nah, he just sits like that." But Harry looked worried as he approached his assigned master.

"Harry, I've seen a lot of dead bodies in my day, and this guy is *dead!*" Bert said. "How do you want to handle this?"

Harry threw his hands in the air. "Shit, they'll blame me. I left him here. They might send in their enforcers *to take me out.*"

"Oh, for God's sake, Harry, get real. You watch too many of those Bruce Lee movies. The guy was old. He died. People die when they get old. You didn't have anything to do with it. Worst-case scenario is, they send you another old geezer as a swap," Jack said.

"I say we ice him until Harry is done with his training. You have that big freezer in the basement. Let's just stuff him in there until it's time to . . . give him back." Bert looked at Jack and Harry to see what they thought of his suggestion.

"No! You aren't even sure he's dead," Harry said. "Are you crazy? Don't answer that. Of course you're crazy. I have to call . . . We are not . . . icing anyone."

"He's dead, Harry. Look at him. He's blue. And he's starting to smell. Okay, call whoever it is you have to call, but you should call a doctor first, right, Bert?"

"I'm going home," Bert said.

"Like hell you're going home! You found him! You have to . . . talk to . . . whoever it is that is in charge of the old guy. God, Harry, how could you have been so stupid as to get involved with these people? Now what are you going to do?"

Harry dropped to the floor and stuck his head between his knees.

"Harry, you son of a bitch, look at me," Jack ordered. "Bert and I are going to take charge. We are going to make all of this go away. Are you listening to me?"

Harry nodded.

"Okay, this is what we're going to do. Call those people and tell them to come and pick up the old guy. Bert and I will set them straight. Neither Bert nor I give two shits if you lose face with them or not.

"For starters, Harry, you are not one of them. You are American! You getting all this, you dumb shit? If not, I'm calling Yoko right now, and she's going to be pissed to the teeth that you and your problems are interfering with the evergreen party she has going on at the nursery with the Sisters. Now, make the call!" Jack said, stomping his foot on the wood floor. His eyes popped wide when the old master toppled over.

Harry winced.

"I'm waiting to hear your melodic response, Harry Wong," Jack singsonged.

"Okay, okay."

"Okay, who . . . what?" Jack snapped.

"Okay to everything. You win! You happy now? You and Bert are now my new masters. If I don't win the competition, I will kill you. You know that, right?"

"Ha-ha-ha! If Bert and I are good enough to get you to the competition, what makes you think you could take us both out?"

Harry smiled. Jack's blood ran cold as he watched Harry place his call. Bert and Jack gave up trying to understand what he was saying in what seemed like five different languages, including Russian. They did, however, grimace at Harry's grim look. Then they watched in horror as Harry went over to his desk and fished around until he found his checkbook.

"No, no, no, you are *not* paying again. Put that damn checkbook back where you got it. Right now, Harry!" Bert and Jack roared in unison.

To their surprise, Harry did as instructed. They watched as Harry walked over to his dead master, sat down, and assumed the lotus position.

With nothing else to do, Jack and Bert sat down and waited. Twenty minutes later, a dark-colored station wagon pulled into Harry's driveway. Minutes later, four Asian men walked into the dojo. Jack wasn't sure, but he thought they were the same four men who carried out Harry's first master. They watched as the men approached Harry, who was so still, Jack wasn't sure his friend wasn't as dead as the master at Harry's side.

"I'll take the two on the left. You okay with the other two, Bert?"

"I am. Harry's eyes are closed. Is that a good or bad sign?"

"Like I know! We're not going to get any help from Harry. He's in one of his trances."

"You pay now," one of the four said.

Harry remained still and silent.

The second man said, "You pay now."

"I don't think so," Jack said. "Take your master and go. Don't come back. Mr. Wong no longer requires your services."

The third man said, "You no pay, we no take master. You pay *now!*"

Harry's eyes flew open.

"Oh, shit!" Bert said.

The four men eyed Harry intently before they turned to look at the two men who were advancing behind them. The fourth man, who hadn't spoken, nodded to his companions.

"Lights! Camera! Action!" Jack roared as his feet left the floor. When they came down, the third man in the group was so dazed, he crumpled to the floor. The air moved at such a high rate of speed, the figures blurred and merged into a giant globe of human movement. Arms flailed, legs went everywhere as bodies twirled and twisted as grunts and high-pitched sounds swirled around the dojo. It was over within minutes.

Bert ran to his locker and returned with a bunch of flexicuffs from his duffel bag.

"I assume you have a plan, Mr. ex–FBI director," Jack drawled.

"Jesus, I can't believe you did this and that I helped you," Harry said, awe ringing in his voice.

"And your checkbook is intact," Bert said as he clipped the flexicuffs onto the four men. "We drag them out to that vehicle they came in and we lay the master out in the backseat. What they do after that is up to them. You okay, Harry?"

"Yeah. They'll send another master when these guys report back. That's the rule."

"No, they won't." Bert whipped out his old FBI pass and badge and told Harry to photocopy it. "I know for a fact these guys won't mess with the FBI. You're still standing there, Harry. C'mon, chop-chop. Jack and I will drag these guys out to the car. Then we'll come back to get the other two, and you bring the esteemed and very dead master. It's the least you can do, Harry."

Outside in the frigid air, Jack grunted and cursed at the weight he was dragging. "You think there will be any fallout for Harry?"

"And I would know this . . . how? I just made up that shit about the FBI for Harry's benefit. I absolutely hate it when his eyes glaze over," Bert snarled as he shoved his guy into the driver's seat, where he used another set of flexicuffs to hook his left arm to the door handle. Jack did the same thing to the man he'd pushed into the passenger seat.

"Problem, Jack. I thought these old babies came with two seats in the back. Where should we put the dead guy?"

Jack pondered the question. "Well, he should have the backseat out of respect. He is dead, you know. One guy goes on the floor. We hook his left arm to the master and his right arm to the door. Dump the fourth guy in the trunk. But you better put that on your note, or they might not look for him."

Harry looked decidedly green when he carried his dead former master to the car. He was sweating profusely. "It's snowing," he said inanely.

"No shit! And this means something?" Jack snarled.

"Well, it might mean something if you don't turn the car

heater on. It's in the low twenties, and they could freeze to death. This is just a guess on my part, but it looks to me like you guys really did a number on them. They might not wake up for an hour or so. Ergo, they could freeze to death. On the other hand, if you turn on the heater, the old guy is going to start cooking, and he smells already. Your call, boys," Harry said, turning on his heel and going back to the dojo.

"Do you believe this? He lets us do his dirty work, and off he goes."

Bert laughed. "He's going to Clorox the entire dojo. How much you wanna bet?"

"Not a cent. What do you take me for? A sucker? So, do we cook the old guy or freeze these cruds?" Jack started to laugh and found that he couldn't stop.

"Harry was right. It is snowing. So we turn on the engine and open the car windows. If the gas runs out, oh, well."

Back in the dojo, Harry Wong was indeed cleaning his dojo. The smell of Clorox was so strong, Bert and Jack rushed to the doors and windows and opened them wide.

Jack went to the minikitchen and popped two bottles of Budweiser. "I love to see Harry work, don't you, Bert?"

"I do, Jack. I truly do."

Both men walked up to Harry. They wore the most evil looks they could conjure up. "You're all *ours* now, Harry Wong!"

Chapter 14

Maggie showed up at Yoko's nursery carrying fragrant bags of food. She took one look at the tired Sisters and called a halt by saying, "I brought food, and I have news. Of a sort. I love this place, it looks so festive, and it smells just like Christmas. Go ahead, clean up, and I'll find a place and a way to set up all this food. Chinese and Italian, wine, beer, and soda, and a huge thermos of coffee. Brownies for dessert."

The Sisters scrambled to scrape the pine resin from their hands, then washed with a strong grease-cutting cleaner. When they returned to what Yoko called the "cutting room," Maggie had cleared a space against the far windows and spread a roll of colored felt she'd found in the corner of the cutting room. A picnic was a picnic no matter the time of year.

"My dear, you and this food are an absolute lifesaver," Annie said as she parceled out the food. "I'm starving. I had no idea this kind of work was so . . . taxing. Even wearing gloves, the pine sap and the branches cut through the leather. Not to mention being hard to work with as well as clumsy."

"But look what we accomplished! We made three hundred wreaths, two hundred grave blankets, and we stacked and trimmed five hundred Christmas trees. If we work tomorrow and Sunday, Yoko should be good to go for the season if we can keep our momentum," Myra said.

"I'll help now that I'm back," Maggie said as she eyed her plate of food. "It's not like I have any immediate plans, and we do need to talk here, girls."

"Charles isn't here, so we can talk and eat," Nikki said.

Between bites of food and chewing, Maggie talked and talked about her short visit to Camp David. She ended up with, "So in the blink of an eye, I fell in love. I am in love, guys! Totally, completely, heart and soul!"

The women stopped eating, their tiredness forgotten, the evergreens just a backdrop as they wiggled and squirmed to congratulate and hug their friend. Maggie flushed and blushed and beamed with happiness.

"You need to play this cool, Maggie," Nikki said. "This is uncharted territory for you. Ted was . . . Ted was . . . Well, he was what he was. If you're thinking of marriage, you need to take this slow and easy. I hate asking this, but are you sure, really sure, Maggie, that Gus feels the same way? You said it started out as a joke."

"I'm sure," Maggie said solemnly. And she knew in her heart that she was sure.

"Okayyy," Kathryn said jubilantly. "That's out of the way. Now, let's discuss what you think went on at Camp David that *we* should know about."

Maggie leaned into the circle. "For starters, Jason Parker is out of the picture. At least I think he is. It was a fluke that I invited him, so he really played no part in what went on, and I am not really sure anything went on. There is that notebook I found. Jason is so into himself, he was probably just listing the initials of the people there so he could hit them up as possible investors for when he got back.

"He'll probably send out his commemorative picture along with a brochure soliciting new clients. I racked my brain about the initials JJ and can't come up with anything. It could be something as simple as a reminder of something. I do it myself all the time. I am not seeing anything sinister in that notebook."

"Then for the moment, let's take him out of the mix. What else, Maggie?" Alexis asked.

"I guess the thing that got in my face was all those people who gave up their family Thanksgiving to go to Camp David. All those politicians. It's easy to understand someone like me, the teacher from Maine, and the college boy giving up our holidays and agreeing to go to Camp David, but those politicians have been there before and undoubtedly will go there again. So, why give up a family holiday unless it was a command invitation?

"The other thing is Fergus and his colleagues. Thanksgiving is not a European holiday, so in a sense I can understand those men coming here to the States and going to Camp David, but they've all been there before, too. That's what is not computing for me."

"Then we need to work on making it compute for you and us," Isabelle said.

"I have Ted doing a deep background check on Jason Parker. I can have him do the same for every attendee that was there. I'm sure we have tons of stuff in our archives we can pull out, but we need recent stuff. We need to know what's going on in their personal lives, personal finances, scandals, if any, friends. We need to know if any of them have stepped out of the box recently and what their *true* feelings about this president are. It's a given that every politician in this damn town has his or her own agenda," Maggie said.

"Think about this. Adam Daniels is from the CIA, Barney Gray represented the FBI, Henry Maris is a deputy over at Homeland Security, and Matthew Logan is in the DOJ. Not represented was the NSA. Now, let's ask ourselves why the National Security Agency didn't have representation there. Was the Department of Justice opposed to the NSA?" Annie asked thoughtfully. "Justice opposed to security. Doesn't make sense to me."

"Unless the NSA person declined the invitation or couldn't make it for some reason," Myra said.

"That's a possibility, but the media would have mentioned that. I met up with the media before I had lunch with the president. And they were as puzzled as I was about the guest list. They were trying to pump me while I was trying to pump them," Maggie said. "We both came up dry."

The Sisters looked at each other, their eyes reflecting the questions they had as they tried to figure out what it all meant.

Yoko closed her eyes and sighed. "Does the president think we're mind readers? If she wants our help, why doesn't she just come out and ask for it? Why all this subterfuge?"

"It's politics," Annie said, "but I agree with you, Yoko. Let's not forget those gold shields. They factor in here somehow. Maybe she thinks we should just take matters into our own hands and do whatever it is she wants. Because we're mind readers."

"Maybe her hands are tied, and she doesn't want anything bouncing back on her or the administration. Perhaps hints are all she can give us, and she has enough faith in us to trust we'll figure it out," Myra said.

"Well, that sucks," Kathryn said. "Listen, I'm tired, so I'm going home. What time do you want us back here tomorrow, Yoko?"

"Nine o'clock will be good. But whatever works for you will work for me."

The Sisters gathered up the leftover food and paper plates. Maggie folded the roll of felt and put it back where she'd found it.

"I might be a little late. I'm going to stop at the paper to get Ted up to speed and get this show on the road."

When the nursery was empty, Yoko locked up and prepared to go to bed. Harry wouldn't even notice that she didn't return to the dojo. Jack and Bert would notice, but not Harry. She felt sad, but she understood her husband's passion. She looked around at the fragrant wreaths, blankets, and the Christmas trees, and did a quick calculation as to what they would fetch. If she, with the help of the Sisters, tripled their output and sold everything, she just might clear enough money to pay the tribunal. Well, that wasn't quite right. Harry had already paid for the first master, and while Jack and Bert had run off the second group demanding payment, Yoko knew they would have to pay it somehow, someway. She felt her insides start to crumble. Harry was so stubborn.

Yoko trudged back into her office, unrolled a sleep mat, spread a blanket. She curled into the fetal position and closed her eyes, tears rolling down her cheeks.

Maggie Spritzer hated walking into the *Post* on a Saturday. It was too quiet, almost ghostly. The skeleton crew merely nodded as she passed them on the way to her office. She knew there would be no coffee or donuts in the kitchen. Unless Ted or Espinosa picked up some donuts, she would have to settle for coffee, which she would have to make herself.

She marched down the hall to the kitchen and prepared the coffeepot. She childishly crossed her fingers that Ted would bring a delectable box of Krispy Kremes. If not, she'd send him right back out.

Back in her office, Maggie booted up her computer and waited for her e-mail to pop up. Ahhhh, an e-mail from Gus Sullivan. Maggie felt light-headed as she clicked the button that would let her read the message. She wanted to cry when she saw the one-word message: HI! She was beyond disappointed at the message. Without hesitation, she typed a two-word reply: Hi, yourself! She pressed SEND, then turned off her e-mail just as she heard the elevator ping, hopefully bringing Ted and Espinosa.

Maggie beelined for the kitchen when she saw both reporters, Ted holding up a large box of Krispy Kremes. "Jelly, chocolate frosted, butter cream frosting, eclairs and cream puffs, custard filling in both. Whooeee!" Ted said as he ripped open the box while Maggie poured the coffee.

"This is sooo good. Thanks, Ted. I really needed these donuts this morning. So, tell me, did you do anything on Jason Parker? And if you didn't, it's okay, what with Thanksgiving and everything, but I need you two to get on something else, too. I want everything you can get on Adam Daniels, Barney Gray, Henry Maris, and Matthew Logan, and I want it all as soon as possible. I don't care how you get the information, who you have to bribe, or what you have to promise, just get it.

"My gut is telling me there is a common denominator here. *Find it.* It might be a thing, a situation, an event, a person. I want you to dig all the way to hell and back. Like

I said, *find it*. If possible, I want a bona fide reason why the NSA wasn't represented at Camp David over Thanksgiving. Work around the clock, get me what I want and need, and a very nice bonus will be in your next paychecks."

"What's going on, Maggie?" Ted asked.

"I wish I knew, but the fact of the matter is that I don't." She quickly gave Ted and Espinosa a rundown on her short visit to Camp David. "It's not computing, Ted. Off the top of your head, does anything strike you as . . . odd?"

"Hell, yes, the whole damn thing. For starters, I think it was something that came up not exactly at the last minute, but damn close to the last minute. Connor probably thought there would be less scrutiny at Camp David than the White House. Then you said the media were as much in the dark as you were. Ted Robinson's rule number two, 'Nothing is what it seems.' Which means Ted Robinson's rule number three is, 'Dig all the way to China for the answer.' We're on it. Where are you going to be?"

"At Yoko's nursery again. The Sisters are all going to continue helping her get her stock ready for Christmas. I stopped by last evening, just as they were finishing up. I promised to be there by nine."

"Espinosa and I can tag along and help if you don't need this ASAP."

Maggie thought about it. "No, there are eight of us, so we should be able to get a lot done. You guys do what I said. If it gets dicey out at the nursery, and we're running behind, I'll call you. Thanks for the donuts. Check in, okay?"

Ted stared at his boss, wondering what was *really* going on. He couldn't remember the last time she had been this considerate. Well, this was a new Maggie, so the best thing he could do was follow orders. The phrase *very nice bonus* was what he needed to concentrate on. Maybe if he played his cards right, shopped for bargains, he could hit the islands with that cute newbie redhead in advertising. Ted whistled all the way down the hall to where he would start pulling what he needed from the archives.

Maggie walked back to her office for her outer gear. She stared hard at her computer, then fought with herself not to open up her e-mail to see if Gus Sullivan had e-mailed her again. Nikki's cautionary words rang in her ears: *Take it slow and easy.* She grimaced as she contemplated ignoring her friend's advice. Well, the world wouldn't come to an end if she ignored the advice, and the world wouldn't come to an end if she did nothing and just headed out to the nursery.

To prove that she had willpower, Maggie left her personal cell phone on her desk and just took the special phone Charles had given to her, along with the *Post* cell, so Ted could get in touch with her. She turned off the lights, locked her door, and didn't look back. Outside in the newsroom, she called out to Ted and Espinosa as she planted her thumb on the DOWN button for the elevator.

It was a gray day, with a hint of snow. Gray days were depressing days. But only if she allowed the day to depress her. She perked up momentarily as she walked to the curb to wait for a taxi. She could make her own Christmas wreath to hang on the front door of her house, and she could even pick out her Christmas tree and take it home with her tonight. Maybe she could entice Ted and Espinosa to set it up for her. She loved the thought that her house would be permeated with the scent of balsam. Maybe she would string the lights on the tree herself. Maybe she'd even have a Christmas party, and she could invite Gus Sullivan. Her spirits kicked up even more, so much so that when she stepped out of the taxi, she was in a really good mood.

Yoko hugged Maggie. Maggie squeezed back hard.

"I know I'm early, but I wanted to make my own wreath once you show me how to do it. I might like one to hang over my fireplace, too. And, of course, I need to pick out a tree, a big one. I hope I am your first customer."

"You are my first customer. I know just the tree for your house. We need to put a tag on it and mark it SOLD. Oh, Maggie, I so hope this works."

Maggie whirled around at the anguish in Yoko's voice. She cupped her friend's tiny face in both her hands. "It *will* work, Yoko. Shame on you for thinking otherwise, but listen, you need to play some Christmas music when the nursery opens for business. You know, put people in the mood."

"That's a wonderful idea. What would I do without all of you?"

Maggie laughed. "I think we all ask ourselves that from time to time. I don't think any of us should worry about it, since we're always there for each other. Now, show me the tree that is going to grace my family room."

"Follow me."

Chapter 15

Days later, Annie looked at Fergus across the breakfast table. She knew she had a sappy expression on her face, but then, so did he. She wondered if fate would somehow throw a monkey wrench into her newfound happiness.

Don't go there, Annie, she cautioned herself. *Don't make yourself your own worst enemy. You have something good, really good, going on here. Try for once to enjoy it, and stop worrying about tomorrow and the day after tomorrow, because those days may never come.* She took her own advice and smiled.

Fergus smiled back.

"You sure you'll be all right here by yourself today?" Annie asked.

"Of course. I'll be fine. Don't worry about me. With that honey-to-do list, I'll probably still be working when you get back. Just in case you're running late, do you want me to start dinner?"

Annie almost swooned. "I would dearly love that, Fergus."

"Consider it done, then. Let me make sure I have all this straight in my head," he said, peering down at an actual list that Annie had written out. It had tickled him to no end when he read his honey-to-do list: "Set up Christmas tree. String lights on Christmas tree. Do not decorate till I get back. Hang wreath on front door. Hang wreath over fireplace in the kitchen. Attach the balsam swags to the mantel. Wash the towels. Empty the dishwasher. And, of course, prepare dinner." Then he asked, with a chuckle in his voice, "Did I get it all right?"

"You did. It sounds like a lot, doesn't it? If you think I'm taking advantage of you, tell me now. I can ask Isabelle to find someone to do it for me."

"Absolutely you are not taking advantage of me, dear lady. For more years than I care to remember, I longed to do these things over the holidays, but I always worked after my wife died so the younger men could be home with their families. I will get great pleasure doing this, and I can't tell you how I look forward to spending Christmas with you and all your friends."

Annie beamed from ear to ear. She'd hit the jackpot, no doubt about it. Fergus Duffy was one of a kind. "Okay, then. I'm going to pick up Myra. We're meeting the girls at Nikki's office. Then we're . . . Well, we have business to take care of."

Fergus's eyes twinkled. "And that business is not my business is what you're saying. Is that right?"

"That's right, Fergus. Just like your little meeting with the president wasn't my business. Imagine what we could do if we pooled our information. No, no, too late. You had your chance. Trust me, the girls and I will ferret it out, at which time you might wish you had confided in me. You think about that while I'm gone, my Scottish friend.

See ya when I see you," Annie said as she slipped into her coat and left by the kitchen door.

She was smiling from ear to ear as she climbed into her warm car, thanks to Fergus's turning on the engine and the heater earlier. There was a lot to be said for consideration. She was still smiling when she barreled through Myra's electronic gates, which opened the moment she was a hundred feet away.

Myra was waiting on the steps of the back porch. She was dressed like a lumberjack, in a red and black plaid jacket, corduroy trousers, and stout walking boots. "We already have our Christmas trees, Myra. Or are you planning on chopping down some trees for fireplace wood?" Annie giggled.

"Go ahead and laugh at me, Annie. I don't really care. It's twelve degrees outside. This is the Christmas season, when all those nasty flu and cold germs abound. I do not want to get chilled. You look . . . bundled up yourself."

"I'm layered. Lord, Myra, I don't know what to think about all of this. Do we have a mission or not? What is it the president is counting on us to do? No one has a clue. And here we are going to see Maggie's . . . ah . . . snitch. I wish I knew what our game plan was. Or if we even have a game plan, which I don't think we do. We talked it to death the past three days at the nursery, but not one of us came up with anything that makes sense."

"I know, dear, it is perplexing. Nikki seems to think that visiting Mr. Tookus will help us. We do have names. We just have to find out what they mean. Like Maggie said, there has to be a common denominator somewhere. Isn't it wonderful that Maggie has fallen in love? I've never seen her so happy."

"Yes, it is. Myra, did you think Yoko looked . . . under the weather? I know she's under a lot of stress with the

nursery and Harry's training and all that money they lost
to those awful people Harry hired to train him. I hope we
alleviated some of that stress by helping out these past
three days. This week, she has some college kids from
Georgetown helping out after class. To me Yoko just
looked . . . Remember how our mothers used to say we
looked peaked when we were coming down with something or other? Usually a good bellyache. To me, Yoko
looked peaked."

"I do remember, and yes, I agree the little dear looked
peaked, but I think it's something else entirely. I can't be
sure about this, Annie, but I think our little lotus flower is
pregnant. When I was in the storage room yesterday morning, getting those balls of wire, I heard her in the restroom,
and she was throwing up. I didn't let on I was even in the
storage room and left after she did. She was also nibbling
on saltine crackers most of the morning. One only does
that when one is pregnant. I know this for a fact, and not
only because Lizzie told me about her own case of morning sickness."

"But . . . why didn't she tell us?" Annie asked fretfully.

"I don't know, Annie. Maybe she wants to be sure.
She's probably scared to death that she might have another miscarriage, and she might think that by talking
about it, she'll jinx herself. I'm just guessing here, Annie."

"Well, it all makes sense. What can we do for her,
Myra?"

"Nothing, Annie. When she needs us, I am sure she
won't have any trouble asking for our help or our support.
She does need more help at the nursery. The college students, according to Yoko, work a few hours here or there,
between classes or after class. At best it's iffy. Plus, most of
them will be leaving to go to their homes for the holiday
break just when her business will need them the most. If

there's a way for you to find some people and pay them on the side without offending her, that might take off some of the pressure. Maybe some youth group from one of the churches. We could make a secret donation, something along those lines."

"I can do that. I'll get on it as soon as I get back home. You are a fearless leader, Myra, and the best part is you aren't tugging on those damn pearls. By the way, when do you get them back?"

"The jeweler said this coming Friday. I miss them. Stainless-steel chains don't work for me, and I don't care if they are in fashion or not. A person could choke on those horrible things, and they *clank,* Annie. Fashion or not, those chains are for young, hip people. Pearls are for people like me."

The rest of the conversation into Georgetown was about the weather and whether or not they would have a white Christmas. Annie even proposed having a pool on when any of the Sisters would first hear Bing Crosby's version of "White Christmas" on the radio.

Just as they were pulling into the parking lot at Nikki's law firm, Myra reared back and said, "Annie, I have an idea. Charles told me last week that the head of security at my candy company is retiring at the end of January. We're going to have to find someone to replace Mr. Unger. Do you think Fergus might like the job? It's not a demanding one, and he can delegate and make his own hours. The pay is good, with a year-end bonus plus really good benefits. I'm not sure how that would work legally since Fergus isn't a U.S. citizen, but I'm sure Charles would know. Or," she said slyly, "you could marry him and stop living in sin."

"You mean like you did with Charles?" Annie quipped.

"Exactly!" Myra laughed.

"It would solve a lot of problems. I'll think about it. Fergus is kind of touchy about finances."

"Feels like snow again," Myra said, stepping out of the car. "Good thing this lot was plowed, or we'd be knee-deep in the white stuff." She looked around. "Looks like all the girls are here, and we're the last to arrive."

Inside, where it was warm and toasty, the Sisters were waiting in the lobby, their coats over their arms. Conversation consisted, again, of the snow this early in the year and the traffic snarls everywhere.

"Two cars," Nikki said. "Maggie gave me directions, and just so you know, she is not at all keen on our talking to Abner. I want that clear right up front. She's okay with it, but she is feeling guilty, which is understandable. She also asked that we not . . . not come down too heavy on Abner. Just so you all know, I did not promise anything where Mr. Tookus is concerned. If you're all ready, we should leave before Abner gets his day under way. I'll take the lead. Follow me, but here is a set of directions in case we get separated. Kathryn will drive the second car." She handed Kathryn the routing instructions and wrapped herself in her long white cashmere coat.

Annie felt excitement ringing in her ears as she held the door for the others. She sniffed at the huge evergreen wreath with its gigantic red bow hanging on the door. "And the Christmas season is upon us," she muttered to no one in particular.

Forty-five minutes later, with a light tap to her horn, Nikki slowed and pulled into a scraggly parking area that was barely plowed of snow. Kathryn parked alongside of her.

"Abner Tookus lives here, in a warehouse?" Alexis said.

"Well, dear, it's my understanding that Mr. Tookus

owns the warehouse. And the warehouse next door. According to Maggie, he's become a real-estate mogul," Myra said. "She also said we shouldn't be surprised if he doesn't answer the buzzer."

"Well, that certainly doesn't sound encouraging," Annie sniffed as she jabbed at the bright red buzzer on a keypad intercom. The sound emanating outward was like the sound of a swarm of bees circling overhead.

Annie kept her finger on the buzzer until she heard a soft, cultured voice say, "I can't release the lock until you take your thumb off the buzzer."

Annie looked like she'd been stung by one of the bees in the swarm. She jerked her hand away and stepped back. The sound of the lock releasing was so loud, it was almost deafening. Isabelle stepped forward and opened the door.

The inside first floor served as a garage and storage. Two high-end cars, along with a Range Rover, were parked side by side. Inside a steel wire cage secured with a series of monster locks were wooden crates, which were stacked to the top of the cage. To the left was an elevator with a steel door so heavy that it took both Nikki and Kathryn to open it. They all stepped in, and Nikki pressed the button for the second floor. The elevator moved sluggishly until it slid gracefully into its perch. This time, Isabelle and Alexis moved the heavy iron grille.

Abner Tookus, dressed in creased khakis and a Polo sweater the color of moonbeams, stood waiting for them. He motioned toward his pristine living room, where he again motioned for the women to take a seat. He himself perched on one of the stools in the bar area. He waited.

Annie licked at her dry lips as she looked around. What she was seeing was not what she had expected. The truth was, she didn't know what she had expected. Certainly not this clean-cut, preppy young man. Well, maybe he wasn't that young and just looked boyish. The loft was decorated simply, all clean, sharp lines; comfortable furniture; pricey, colorful artwork on the walls; tongue-and-groove wood floor. But it was the fieldstone fireplace with a blazing fire that drew everyone's eye. On the raised hearth, a Yorkshire terrier watched them without making a sound. Next to the small dog was a huge cat, whose fur was whiter than the snow outside. It had eyes greener than emeralds.

Annie, for some reason, felt incredibly nervous and wasn't sure why. She made the introductions. When she was finished with the introductions, she wound down by saying, "We need your help."

"Did Maggie send you here?"

"Lord, no!" Annie blurted. "She did her best to talk us out of coming, but she did give up your address." At Abner Tookus's disbelieving expression, Annie's own features turned sour. "It's the truth. She did do her best to talk us out of coming here."

"What do you want?" Abner asked coldly.

"To hire you. Why else do you think we would be here, and why else would we be at odds with Maggie over this visit?" Myra demanded.

"I am no longer in that line of work. I retired. I work for IBM, and I was just about to leave for work." He rose and headed toward the elevator. When he didn't hear footsteps following him on the polished floor, he turned around and motioned to the elevator. He shrugged. "You can sit there all day if you want, but I'm going to work, and as I said, I can't help you."

"Why not?" Nikki demanded. "Annie made you rich, and just because you and Maggie have a hate on for each other is no reason to turn your backs on the very people who made you rich enough that you could *really* retire at your age. We need your help, and we're not budging."

The Sisters watched as Abner Tookus buttoned up a stylish navy cashmere jacket. He reached for a white scarf, which he wrapped around his neck. The last thing he did before pressing the button on the elevator was to whistle, two sharp sounds. The terrier looked up but didn't move. The cat arched its back, then settled down as two huge Dobermans pranced into the room.

"Guard!" Abner Tookus said.

"Now, wait just a minute, Mr. Tookus. We came here in good faith. I guess Maggie was right. You are so blind with love for her, you can't see straight. She said you would do this. Well, not the part about the dogs, but she said you were jealous enough that you would do *something*. I guess this means something," Myra said, her eyes on the two dogs, who were eyeing them like they hadn't eaten for a week.

"Maggie actually said that?"

Myra knew she'd stuck her foot in it, but it was too late to pull it out. "Ah, yes, she did, but we . . . we didn't believe it. Did we, girls?"

The Sisters nodded.

"That's why we're here. If we'd believed her, we would never have come to enlist your help. And also to tell you, money is no object. Maybe there's another warehouse you want to buy somewhere or, as I understand it, you are big on acquiring oceanfront property. We can make that happen for you."

Abner Tookus removed his scarf and jammed it into his pocket. He unbuttoned his jacket, but he didn't take it off as he walked back to the living room and the stool he'd been sitting on earlier. He snapped his fingers twice, and the Dobermans headed down a well-lit hallway. "For the record, I am not, nor have I ever been, in love with Maggie Spritzer. What I have been is annoyed, frustrated, and angry at the way she does things with no regard for a person's feelings. She's a bully, she's arrogant, she's selfish, and I do not care to work for anyone who works with her.

"I did not charge you for the last job I did that put my ass on the line for all of you. I could have gotten arrested and sent to jail for the rest of my life for that little caper. The only reason I did the job was because Maggie intimidated me by threatening to turn me over to the authorities. And she threatened the wrath of the vigilantes on me if I didn't do what she said." Abner laughed ruefully. "And here you are."

"Yes, Mr. Tookus, here we are. Sometimes, Maggie can be a bit overzealous. The information you garnered for us . . . Well, I'm sure you read the papers at the time and saw the result of your . . . ah . . . expertise. We . . . I . . . appreciate that you did it all gratis, which was not our intention. I respect that you were making a statement by tearing up that check, which could have bought at least a dozen more warehouses.

"But that is not helping us now. We came here as . . . as a group, so to speak, to plead our cause and to ask you to please reconsider your stance. By the way, I happen to know you do not work for IBM on a nine-to-five basis. You do work for them on a consulting basis, and your time is your own. Right off the bat here you lied to us, when, as I said, we came here in good faith to hire you," Annie said.

Abner Tookus snorted. "You came here to hire me to do something illegal."

"Well, there is that," Annie agreed.

Chapter 16

Isabelle wondered if she was the only one who could see the sadness and unhappiness in Abner Tookus's eyes. She looked around and decided, yes, she was the only one seeing it. Maybe she was seeing it because she was the closest to the stool on which Abner was sitting. Something in her made her get up and walk over to the man. She looked straight at him and said, "I'm Isabelle. I'm an architect, and I want to tell you I have never seen anything as beautiful as this loft and what you did to it. Do you mind telling me who your architect was? I'd like to shake his hand."

Abner blinked as he focused on the woman standing in front of him. "I did it myself." His voice was shy, soft, and gentle. "I worked on it for two years at night or when I wasn't . . . doing other things. I did some of the electrical work, but I had to have a licensed electrician to get me up to code. I'm not a plumber, so I farmed that out. But otherwise, I did it all."

Isabelle smiled; she didn't know why. She wanted to reach out and hug this shy, unhappy man and tell him everything was going to be all right. Instead, she said, "Well, anytime you need a job, call me. I'm in the book. I'd like a tour sometime, if it isn't too much trouble."

Abner smiled, and the room seemed to suddenly fill with light. When he smiled, he looked just like Brad Pitt, Isabelle decided. Suddenly she felt flustered and didn't know what to do.

Annie saved the day when she asked, "So, will you help us?"

"And if I don't agree to help you, are you going to peel the skin off my body or hang me from a tree over a pond of alligators?"

"No. We'll just leave," Myra said.

Abner looked straight at Isabelle, who was still smiling self-consciously. "Tell me what you want first. Then I'll decide if I want to help you or not."

"That's fair," Nikki said.

His eyes still on Isabelle, Abner said, "I'm always fair. It's always the other side that doesn't live up to the agreement."

Myra cleared her throat. She fished around inside her bag and held out a piece of paper. "There are four names on this list. Adam Daniels, who is CIA, Barney Gray, who is FBI, Henry Maris from Homeland Security, and Matthew Logan from the Department of Justice. There is no one on this list from the National Security Agency. We don't know if that's important or not. We are not even sure what their job descriptions are in the agencies these men work for. We want a complete background check on them. From the day they were born until the present. All four men spent the Thanksgiving weekend at Camp David, as did Maggie Spritzer. Just so you know, Mr. Tookus.

"We believe these men are involved in or control . . .

'slush funds,' for want of a better term, that these agencies use for . . . I guess covert operations. We want to know where those monies come from, where they are now, who controls them, and how much money is in those funds. Millions with an *M* or billions with a *B*. We want to know if there is just one huge fund or four small ones. I can't define *huge* or *small*. There might even be others, for all we know. Is this something you think you can find out for us?"

Abner's expression was unreadable as he looked down at the paper in his hand, then at the Sisters, his gaze coming to rest on Isabelle. "I'll let you know in forty-eight hours. How shall I get in touch with you?"

Faster than lightning, Isabelle had her business card in her hand and held it out. "My cell phone number is on the back."

"And your fee will be what if you take the job?" Annie asked pointedly.

Abner didn't answer right away. He stared at the women for so long, they started to squirm in their seats. "My fee always depends on the amount of risk I'm taking and the hours I work. If you have a limit, tell me now, and I'll tell you if I will consider it. Like I said, I'm always fair."

"There is no limit, Mr. Tookus," Annie said. She stood and motioned for the others that this meeting was over. No one shook hands; no one said a word as they filed toward the elevator. Except for Isabelle, who hung back.

No one was surprised to hear her say, "When would be a good time for a tour? My time is free pretty much from now till the first of the year."

"How about now?" Abner said, taking off his jacket.

"I thought you had to go to work," Isabelle said.

Abner grinned. "I do, but I make my own hours. It isn't often I get to show off my handyman expertise."

"I rode with the others. I didn't come in my own car."

"I'll drop you off wherever you want to go," Abner said.

Isabelle turned around, wiggled her eyebrows for the Sisters' benefit, and said, "Go without me. Mr. Tookus is going to give me a tour and drop me off. See ya later."

"Whoa," Kathryn said as they all piled into the elevator.

"I think it's a slam dunk," Myra said happily. "Don't you, Annie?"

"Absolutely," Annie said as the sluggish elevator descended to the first floor.

"I wonder if what just happened falls into the category of a 'Let me show you my etchings' kind of thing. If I'm not mistaken, something just happened between Isabelle and our hacker. Did you guys notice it?" Nikki grinned.

"Oh, yeah," Alexis drawled.

Upstairs, Isabelle followed Abner through the ten-thousand-square-foot loft that he had made habitable. All she could say over and over was, "This is magnificent."

The bedroom looked to Isabelle like something out of a movie. The walls were buff-colored; the floor was polished oak, the furniture simple but comfortable. A California king bed didn't dwarf the room at all. The massive headboard was hand-carved teak, a true work of art. What really surprised her was the fireplace, almost a duplicate of the one in the living room. Sitting in a stand in the corner was a giant twelve-foot Christmas tree that had yet to be decorated.

Abner noticed her surprise. "When I was a kid growing up in an orphanage, I always said I was going to have a Christmas tree in my bedroom so it would be the last thing I saw at night and the first thing I saw in the morning. Christmases in orphanages are not the things of good memories. And, I love the smell."

"You were an orphan?" Isabelle asked in surprise.

Abner nodded.

"I was, too," Isabelle said. "Anna de Silva adopted me last year. Actually, she adopted all of us except Nikki, because Myra adopted her years and years ago. I hated Christmas!" she blurted.

Abner laughed.

Isabelle thought it one of the most endearing sounds she'd ever heard. She said so.

Abner laughed again. "When you can laugh, that means life is good. But then I've laughed when life wasn't so good, too. Out of frustration, I guess. Does that mean you yourself don't laugh much?"

"Yes and no. So how did you fall into your particular line of work when you can do stuff like this?" Isabelle said, waving her arm about.

"*This* is a hobby. By the way, I own some property in Tennessee, and I'm building a cabin there. That's where I plan to retire. When that will be, I don't know. But to answer your question, I went to MIT and have master's degrees in computer science, engineering, and business. I'll officially have my doctorate in computer science next month, and you can then call me Dr. Tookus. I'm smart." It was all said modestly, almost apologetically. "My parents must have been geniuses."

Isabelle was so impressed, she was temporarily at a loss for words. When she finally found her tongue, she said, "Did you ever try to find your parents?"

"No. If they gave me up, why would they want me now to clutter up their lives? How about you?"

"I did try but came up dry. Back then, it seemed to matter. Now it doesn't. Aren't you even a little bit curious, since you're so smart and all? Wouldn't you at least like to see them, even if it was from a distance?"

"Maybe someday, but not now. Next on the tour, my prize. Drumroll . . . my bathroom. Ta da!" Abner said, waving his arms with a wide flourish.

Isabelle gaped. In her life, she'd never seen such a glorious bathroom. It was a grotto, stone walls with water trickling over green moss down into a giant tub of water that resembled a minilake.

Lighting was set deep in the ceiling and recessed in the far walls. The shower stall, with its thirty-seven jets, made her gasp, as did the carved vanity of exquisite marble. The Jacuzzi that could seat eight was flush with the floor. Blue water swirled.

"It's self-cleaning," he said proudly. He opened the linen closet, and Isabelle stared. Shelves of fluffy towels, shelves of toiletries, shelves of soaps and shampoos. More than Walgreens stocked. "Skimpy, threadbare towels at the orphanage. We used soap to wash our hair, strong soap that could take the skin off your hands if you rubbed too hard."

Isabelle sighed. "I remember," she said softly. "This is just a wild guess on my part, but I bet you have two freezers stocked to the brim and a refrigerator that is never empty and cabinets full of cookies and everything else under the sun."

Abner laughed again. "Yep."

"Tell me about this," Isabelle said, pointing to the grass she was standing on.

Abner laughed again. "My own bit of outdoors. It has four minidrains that go down to the first floor and the main drain. There's a built-in minisprinkler. My lawn is boxed in, as you can see. There was no grass at the orphanage, just concrete."

Isabelle nodded. "Say no more. It's all so beautiful. I

just never saw a bathroom with a real grass floor. But I have to ask, are you happy here?"

Abner's eyes clouded over. "For the most part. It would be nice to share all this with someone someday. If it happens, it happens. If it doesn't, then I guess it isn't meant to be. I'm so glad you like it. You're the first person I've ever shown this to. I have a guest bathroom for company. I'm not sure why I showed it to you."

"Maybe because I'm an architect, and you knew I would appreciate it, which I do."

"I guess that's it. Would you like to see my computer room?" When Isabelle nodded, Abner led her down a short hallway to what he referred to as his lair. He opened the door with another flourish, and Isabelle almost fainted. "It does have that effect on people." Abner laughed.

"It looks like something from a space station," Isabelle said in awe. "And you use all of this in your line of work?"

"Every last piece of equipment. The room is climate-controlled, just like my wine cellar, which I have yet to show you."

As Isabelle looked around, she felt annoyed with herself. "I'm not sure I could have designed this."

"I'm sure you could if your client told you exactly what he wanted. Everything you see was done to satisfy my particular wants and needs. I made it work for me. I hold classes here twice a week."

Isabelle gasped. "You mean you actually teach people how to *hack*?"

Abner grinned. "You said it. I didn't. I said I teach classes here twice a week. I didn't say what kind of classes." He looked down at his watch. "I really have to go, Isabelle. Tell me where I can drop you off."

"If it's not out of your way, you can drop me off at the Galleria. I have some shopping I need to do."

"On my way."

Back in the family area, Abner shrugged into his jacket and threw his scarf around his neck. Abner held Isabelle's coat for her. He was so close, she could smell his aftershave. A scent she liked, earthy and pungent.

"So are you going to help us or not?" she asked.

"I'm really not sure. I'll call you as soon as I make up my mind. Would you like to have dinner with me tonight?"

Isabelle didn't think twice about the invitation. "I'd love to. Tell me where you want to meet up, and I'll be there. I'll take a cab to my apartment when I finish shopping and pick up my car. By the way, when are you going to decorate your Christmas tree?"

"How about after dinner? We could do it together."

"I'd like that. I can't tell you when I did that last. I had one of those pre-lit trees last year. It didn't do much for me."

Isabelle waited by the door until Abner handed out dog treats and issued orders to the animals. She wondered if the dogs and the cat would obey them. When she asked, Abner couldn't help but laugh. A happy laugh. "Yes and no. If I'm gone too long, they get into trouble. They're my kids," he said, his voice expressing his tender feelings for them.

Abner held the gate so that Isabelle could step inside the elevator. Her heart was beating so fast, she thought she might black out. What was happening to her?

You silly girl, you know what's happening to you, so don't even go there, she warned herself.

Chapter 17

Maggie Spritzer was madder than a wet hen. Her fingers drummed on her desk as she waited for Ted Robinson to answer her call. She blasted him the moment she heard his voice. "Where are you? Your phone has been off. I gave you that assignment and told you it was ASAP five days ago." Had it really been five days? How had the time gotten away from her like this?

"My phone wasn't off. I ran out of juice and had to recharge. You need to have a little more patience, Maggie. Checking out four politicians from the moment of birth was not and is not an easy task. I'm doing the best I can, but from what I've gathered so far, there are no smoking guns, no proverbial rabbits in the magician's hat, no scandals that I can find. Those guys are just like every other politician in this town. Their wives are social climbers, mean and catty, but other than that, I'm coming up with zip."

"Then dig deeper, harder. There has to be a connection."

"Says who?" Ted asked, belligerence ringing in his tone.

"My gut, that's who. There's something there. I can feel it, smell it, taste it. Get it for me so I can own it."

Never one to argue with Maggie's gut, Ted said, "Okay, I'll do my utmost best."

Maggie broke the connection. It was four thirty, time for her to head over to Walter Reed to see Gus Sullivan. She could hardly wait, even though she would spend only an hour at the most with him. Then she would come back to the paper, finish up, and head home. She made a mental note to find someone to set up her Christmas tree.

A last thorough check of her office and the kitchen area took ten minutes. Five minutes later, she was in a cab headed to Walter Reed and the hour she would spend with Gus. She felt giddy. Today, though, it wasn't just personal. Today was business. Of a sort.

Maggie hated that it got dark so early these days, but once she was inside the massive hospital, the light was blinding. She found her way to Gus's floor and down to the common room, where he waited for her. She wished, and not for the first time, that she could visit earlier in the day, but visitation then would interfere with his therapy. He was always tired at this hour of the day, but he made a valiant effort to be as cheerful as he could under the circumstances. Just yesterday he had nodded off, so she'd left. He called an hour later to apologize.

The moment she spotted him at the far end of the room, Maggie knew he'd had a good day: he was grinning like a Cheshire cat. She wanted to kiss him till his teeth rattled, but she held herself in check. Instead, she reached for his hand, squeezed it, then pecked him on the cheek. "Listen, Gus, I need your help on something. You said you read every newspaper in the District, not to mention all the political newsletters that come off the Hill. Tell me what, if anything, you know about these four guys. Adam Daniels,

Barney Gray, Henry Maris, and Matthew Logan. I need to record your responses. I hope you don't mind," she said, putting her minirecorder in the middle of the table.

Gus's brow furrowed. He closed his eyes for a minute. "Daniels is with the CIA, Gray is in the FBI, Maris is something or other in Homeland Security, and Logan is at the Department of Justice. Money guys. Daniels and Maris are the two guys who can freeze money, freeze assets. Gray and Logan, I think, are actuaries. Of a sort."

"Do you think or know if those four guys interact either personally or through their different agencies? Aside from various interagency meetings. Did you see anything in the Hill publications? You know, stuff the public doesn't know or care about."

Gus thought about the question. "I didn't get back here until June. I wasn't in shape for six weeks or so to do much reading or anything else. By August I was reading nonstop. I don't recall seeing anything that made me think about it or go back and reread the article." He quirked an eyebrow in Maggie's direction. "Maybe if you told me specifically what you're looking for, it might trigger something in my mind."

Maggie thought about it. Did she really want to involve Gus Sullivan in her work life? If she did, she knew in her gut she would be opening up a whole big can of worms. She waited so long before responding, Gus nudged her. *What the heck.* "I am trying to figure out why those guys were at Camp David over Thanksgiving. They have families. Not to mention the Europeans. I spent a few days researching past guests at Camp David over the holidays. There hasn't been a guest list like the one you and I were on in the last twenty-five years. Does that answer your question?"

"Well now, that's a rib tickler if I ever heard one. What

are you thinking? You said earlier that you talked to the media guys while you were there. What did they think or share with you?"

"The same thing I shared with them—nothing, nada, bupkes. They were as much in the dark as I was. We kicked it around for a while, each of us trying to pick the other's brains, but it was like picking strawberries in the middle of winter. Our yield was zip. The only thing we could agree on was that, as guest lists go, it was exceedingly strange. None of the media could figure out *my* last-minute invitation. Hell, I still haven't figured it out."

"Do you think, and this is just a wild guess on my part, but could it have something to do with your *friends?*"

Maggie felt a sudden chill on her neck. "What *friends* would those be, *Gus?*"

Seeing Maggie's attitude change in a nanosecond, Gus retreated. "I think I should quit while I'm ahead. What I was referring to was your colleagues, your reporters who normally cover the White House beat. Since you are the editor in chief, you aren't reporting anymore, right?" Even Gus knew his explanation sounded lame; she could read it in his expression.

That wasn't what he'd meant at all, and Maggie knew it. She looked down at the oversize watch on her wrist. She still had plenty of time before her hour visit was up. "Would you look at the time! I have to go." She shut off the mini-recorder, jammed it into her pocket. A second later she was literally running from the common room and down the hall to the entrance. She didn't even say good-bye or wave. *Well, Maggie, if you stick your foot in someone's mouth, be prepared to get bitten.*

Maggie lucked out. Just as she reached the main door, a cab pulled up. Two men got out, and Maggie hopped in. She rattled off her home address and said, "Go!" just as

Gus's electric wheelchair collided with the two men entering the hospital. She didn't look back. So much for going back to the *Post*. She'd never felt so alone. She realized she didn't want to go home to an empty house. But where could she go on a Friday night? Everyone was a couple these days. Well, there was alone and then there was *alone*. Maybe she could take a stab at putting up her Christmas tree. How hard could it be to put a tree in a stand, turn the screws, and stand it upright?

When she stepped out of the cab in front of her house, Maggie saw her next door neighbor's high-school-age son walking a gorgeous German shepherd named Pretty Girl. "Drew, hold on a minute," she said as she paid the driver. "If you aren't doing anything, I'll give you fifty bucks to put up my Christmas tree."

"Sure, Miss Spritzer, but you don't have to pay me. Just let me take Pretty Girl in and tell my mom where I am. Where's the tree?"

"In a bucket of water on the little porch. I'll get the stand out. If you have a saw, you better bring it with you, or we'll have to use a butcher knife to trim off the lower branches."

"I'll do that. Be over in a few minutes."

"At least I won't be alone for a little while," Maggie muttered as she entered the house, turned off the alarm, and turned up the heat. She ran upstairs and changed into jeans and a sweatshirt. With nothing else to do, she went back downstairs to wait for her neighbor. To while away the time, she opened the storage closet under the stairs and rummaged till she found the Christmas ornaments and the neatly coiled lights that she had wrapped around a cardboard paper towel cylinder last year. It was a household hint she'd seen on Martha Stewart's morning show one year. And it worked. Good old Martha.

Maggie's cell phone took that moment to ring. A second later her doorbell chimed. She looked down at the number on the phone: Gus. She turned the phone to vibrate and shoved it in the bread box sitting on the kitchen counter. She ran back to the front door, where her neighbor was standing, holding a tray of food.

"Meat loaf and roasted potatoes and some carrots. Mom makes great meat loaf. Eat it now, while it's warm, she said. I can get the tree in the stand, if you tell me where it is." He handed over the tray of food, then picked up the tree like it was a toy, shook off the water, and carried it into the house.

Maggie pointed to the corner by the fireplace.

"Good choice. Go ahead and eat. I really can do this. I put our tree up over the weekend."

Sometimes, Maggie liked taking orders, like now, especially when food was involved. She kept her eyes on the bread box as she ate. She could tell the phone was vibrating by the way the bread box moved against the ceramic canisters.

Two hours later, Maggie was sitting alone in her family room, the only light coming from the TV, which was on mute, and the colored Christmas lights twinkling on the tree. It was beautiful, even though the ornaments weren't heirloom quality. She stared at it and felt sad. So sad she wanted to cry. *Big girls don't cry,* she told herself. And then she cried. When she was done sniffling and chastising herself for the tears, she hauled out her laptop, which she'd wedged between the sofa cushions, and powered up. *Drown yourself in work,* she told herself. *That way you don't have to think.*

Maggie Spritzer, you are so stupid. Just because Gus Sullivan mentioned your friends doesn't mean he was referring to your relationship with the vigilantes. Yes, it does, she argued with herself. *He was making a point. You got too close, too quick. You acted like a ninny when you ran out of there. Now what are you going to do?*

Maggie craned her neck to look into her kitchen. She could see the bright red bread box. All she had to do was get up and go into the kitchen, take her cell phone out of the bread box, and listen to Gus's messages or read his texts. That was all she had to do. It seemed like a monumental task. She shook her head to clear her thoughts.

Gus Sullivan was not Ted Robinson. She could not treat Gus the way she treated Ted and Abner. Not that she mistreated Ted and Abner, she sniffed. No, she just took advantage of them. She told herself it was apples and oranges, but she knew it wasn't true.

As much as she hated to admit it, she knew she had to work on her emotions and her attitude. Maybe if she slept on what she considered her situation, she'd have a plan in the morning. Then again, maybe she wouldn't. Tears in her eyes, she stared at the beautiful Christmas tree. Sometimes, life was such a bitch. She needed a hug. She leaned back into the softness of the sofa she was sitting on and closed her eyes. Sleep came quickly. The dream came just as quickly.

"Why are we standing in a straight line, and why are we sporting these gold shields?" Nikki Quinn asked. "No one is supposed to know we have them."

"The president gave them to us for a reason. She didn't tell us what the reason is or was. So, I suggest that we make them work for us," Annie said.

"How?" the ever-combative and verbal Kathryn barked.

Charles Martin stepped out of the straight line and turned to face the group like a bandleader. In his hand, instead of a baton, he held his gold shield. "The names on

Maggie's list, that's how. Pay the men a visit, flash your shields, and then do what you all do best."

"That's brilliant, Charles," Myra said happily as she blew him an air kiss.

Charles beamed as he stepped back into line.

"But they'll know who we are," Alexis said fretfully.

"And who are we, dear? Today we are ordinary citizens who have been entrusted with these exquisite shields by the president of the United States. I see absolutely no reason why we can't use an assumed identity or go with our own identities," Myra said. "But first and foremost, we need a plan."

"What's wrong with making an appointment with these people and keeping the appointment? And then, when we gain entry to their offices, we flash the shields and get them to talk. We should have the reports on what Ted and Abner have been able to dig up for us. There's bound to be information that will point us in the right direction and tell us who we should lean on. The only problem that I see is, do we go as a group or do we split up, and do each of us take one of those politicians?" Isabelle said.

The straight line scattered as the group milled about.

"What are you writing, Maggie?" Annie asked.

"Just that the CIA is the one who controls all that money no one is supposed to know about. It isn't Adam Daniels who controls it, either. It's someone with the initials JJ."

"How do you know that, Maggie?" Yoko asked.

"I just know. My gut instinct. We have to find someone with the initials JJ in government, then put the squeeze on him. Adam Daniels is just there to field inquiries. He has no control at all. A shill, for want of a better word."

"But you're guessing," Yoko persisted.

"Yes, but I'm never wrong when it comes to stuff like this. Maybe Abner can find out. Ted can only do so much, whereas Abner can tread where angels fear to tread."

Maggie stirred, woke confused for a moment as to where she was. She blinked at the sparkling Christmas tree and knew she'd had a meaningful dream. JJ. "Okay, I get it," she mumbled to herself as she set about locking up and turning off the tree lights before she made her way to the second floor and bed.

Chapter 18

It was just a few minutes shy of five o'clock when Maggie wrapped herself in her winter coat and trudged three doors down the street to Nikki Quinn's house. Just as she reached the stoop, the outside light came on, and Jack Emery walked through the door. He didn't appear surprised to see her heading to his house at such an early hour.

"Hi."

"Hi, yourself. Is Nikki up and dressed?"

"She is. She's still upstairs. Here, I'll open the door for you. Court is in session today because the heat was off for the last two days, and the judges don't want to lose too much time trying to play catch-up. Happens two or three times every winter. Coffee's ready. You know where everything is. Everything okay?"

"Probably, but not sure. You doing okay with Harry's training?"

Jack laughed. "We're getting there. See ya."

Maggie entered the house, stood at the foot of the stairs,

and shouted up to Nikki. "I need to talk to you. I'll be in the kitchen."

Five minutes later, Nikki was in the kitchen, pouring coffee for herself. "Kind of early for a visit, not that you aren't welcome. What's up?"

"Something. Maybe nothing. I put my tree up last night. Well, that's not true. My neighbor Drew down the street set it up for me, but I did decorate it. It's beautiful. Is your tree up yet?"

"Jack set it up over the weekend, but we haven't decorated it yet. Myra never used to put ours up till around the fifteenth of December. Now, if you don't put it up after Thanksgiving, there are no trees to be had. Traditions change over the years. Still, we get to enjoy it longer, I guess. Why am I babbling like this, Maggie?"

Maggie shrugged and related her encounter with Gus Sullivan. "I overreacted. At least I think I did. I knew he was talking about you and the others, even though he said he wasn't. I went into protective mode. But that isn't why I'm here.

"I usually do my best thinking in the shower. I don't know why that is. It just is. I should clarify that in the summer I do my best thinking in the shower, because I can stand in there for an hour. In the winter, I'm in and out of the shower in ten minutes, so I dream about my problems and usually come up with a solution to them. It's winter now."

Nikki sipped at her coffee. "Uh-huh."

"I had this dream last night." Maggie went on to relate the dream in detail. "You guys need to ask Abner Tookus to figure it out or run one of his many programs to find out who JJ is. I know it sounds kind of like trying to find a needle in a haystack. There are probably thousands of politicians, aides, staff, and the like who have the initials

JJ. But if anyone can find it, Abner can. As you know, I can't ask him. You said he took the assignment, right?"

"He did, and Isabelle is in charge. She and Abner hit it off. They even had dinner one night and lunch yesterday. This is just a wild guess on my part, but remembering how you said Abner worked at the speed of light, it's surprising he hasn't wrapped it up. We all think it's because of Isabelle. You aren't upset over that, are you?"

"Heck no. You know what? They are a perfect match. I can see them as a couple. That's really great. Abner is not . . . He's not a geek. Well, he was back in the day, with the long hair, baggy clothes, the glasses, etc. That was just a front. He thought that's the way a geek was supposed to look. I don't have the words to tell you how smart that man is. Plus, he's one of the nicest guys to walk the planet. If anyone can find JJ, it will be Abner."

"I liked him. I had a bet with Kathryn that he wouldn't take the job. Kathryn didn't want to take the bet until Isabelle stepped forward. Then it was a whole new ball game. It only took him a day and a half to get back to us. The plan is to meet out at the farm when he submits his report. I'll pass this on to Isabelle as soon as I get to the office. Now, about Gus. Do you want some advice, or are you comfortable winging it?"

"Talk to me."

"Well, your Christmas tree *is* up and decorated. Don't you want to show it off? Of course you do, so why don't you invite Gus to dinner? You said he's allowed to leave the hospital if he has somewhere to go. Give him somewhere to go. In fact, send the *Post* car for him. No point in having a perk like that car if you don't abuse it once in a while. That's another way of saying Annie will approve. So what if he brings his nurse or aide, or whatever he calls the people who surround him? Let them watch television or eat in the kitchen, and you two eat in the dining room. Be sure to use scented candles and a pretty tablecloth. That's how I hooked Jack.

"Be up front. It's pretty much all a matter of public record, anyway. The world knows the *Post* came down on the side of the vigilantes. You don't have to protect us anymore, Maggie. And you *are* one of us. Tell him right up front. Then I would show him that gold shield. It's when you try to hide stuff that problems surface. So, how many messages and texts did Gus leave?"

Maggie grinned. "Twenty-one."

Nikki laughed. "Then I would say you have that boy hooked. Don't call him, though. Send him a text. I like seeing the words as opposed to hearing them. I suspect Gus is the same. Just a gut feeling, Maggie."

"Okay. Hey, thanks for talking to me. I didn't mean to intrude this early in the day. Talk soon, okay?"

Maggie trudged home just as the dark turned to light. She stood on her little porch and looked across the street as lights started to peek out of the windows. The barren tree branches shivered in the wind just the way she was shivering. She scooted through the door, ran to the kitchen, made coffee, then headed for the stairs and her room, where she dressed for the day. Downstairs again in her kitchen, she poured herself a cup of coffee. She sat at the table and realized again how alone she was. That was when she finally realized it was Saturday, and she didn't have to go to the paper. Here she was, dressed for the day with nowhere to go. "Crap," she said succinctly.

As she sipped her coffee, Maggie pondered Nikki's advice. Nothing ventured, nothing gained, she thought as she sent a text message to Gus Sullivan, inviting him to dinner. When she was finished, she went back upstairs to change her clothes again. Back in the kitchen, she rummaged in the freezer for meat and frozen vegetables, which she dumped into a Crock-Pot. She threw in some herbs, some salt and pepper, a little canned beef broth. An hour before serving time, she'd toss in some wine and hope for the best. She had frozen dinner rolls, packaged greens for a salad, and a Boston cream pie she only had to thaw out.

With nothing else on her agenda, Maggie called for a cab and was told one would arrive in seven minutes. She dressed once again for the weather and walked out to her porch. She was sure Yoko could use her help at the nursery, and it was better to be busy than to sit around the house moping. In the cab, she sent a text to her driver to put him on alert to pick up Gus at Walter Reed if he accepted her invitation.

As Maggie climbed out of the cab at Yoko's nursery, she was shocked to see Fergus Duffy. He greeted her with a hug. "I'm just helping out. Annie said Yoko could use all the help that's available. Yoko put me in charge. Do you believe that? Having said that, I need to assign your work. How do you feel about making red velvet bows?"

Maggie shrugged. "I love red bows. There is something special about a big red bow. Anticipation, excitement, a sense of mystery, not to mention cheerful."

Fergus smiled as he showed her the box of red velvet ribbon and a gizmo to wrap the ribbon around and through. The end result was a beautiful handmade-looking bow.

Maggie screwed up her first, second, and third bows and was starting over just as Isabelle Flanders rolled over in bed and debated if she should answer the phone or not. With a nudge from Abner Tookus, she clicked on the phone and listened to Nikki's greeting, which was, "Sorry to call you so early, Isabelle, but I just spoke with Maggie, and we need you to get a message . . . well, it's more like a request, to Abner Tookus, and if he accepts, Abner is to tack it on to his bill."

She explained Maggie's dream and wound down by saying, "So, we know that two initials are like finding leaves in the wind, but Maggie said Abner has special software that should work. How soon do you think you can pass this on to Abner?"

Isabelle giggled. "How about right now?"

Nikki looked down at her watch. She wiggled her eyebrows for her own benefit. "Oh," was all she could think of to say. A grin stretched from ear to ear when she heard Isabelle giggle. In all the years she'd known Isabelle, she'd never heard her giggle. Not ever. "Well, I'll hang up now. When you have time, give me a call and let me know what . . . what Abner's decision is." She broke the connection before Isabelle could respond.

"Way to go, Isabelle," Nikki chortled to herself as she shuffled papers on her desk. She wondered if the other Sisters knew about Isabelle's new relationship. Well, Isabelle's love life was none of her business. Or was it? She hoped that Abner Tookus knew how lucky he was. If he didn't, the Sisters would make him aware of it lickety-split. "Damn," she said happily. Who knew?

While Nikki hustled over to the courthouse for an early morning hearing on a motion, Isabelle relayed Nikki's request to Abner, who groaned. Isabelle laughed as she swung her legs over the side of the bed. A long arm snaked out and drew her back under the covers. "This is where we pretend we're kids again in the orphanage, and we're waking up Christmas morning to this glorious Christmas tree whose lights I leave on twenty-four/seven. We have to imagine, for the moment, that there are hundreds of presents nestled underneath, with both our names on them.

All of them are from Santa because we were both good all year. Close your eyes, and when you open them, squeal with pleasure. Can you do that, Isabelle?" Abner whispered.

"I can," Isabelle said softly. When she opened her eyes, tears were rolling down her cheeks, but she still managed to squeal, a high-pitched keening sound that Abner echoed. She looked at Abner through her tears and saw that his eyes were just as wet as her own. She wanted to say something, but she couldn't find the words. She hoped she would forever remember this moment. Abner squeezed her hand. She squeezed his back. The moment was preserved. Forever and ever plus one more day.

The dogs barked on cue. Abner groaned again and got up. He threw on some clothes and his heavy jacket. By the time he got to the elevator, the dogs were waiting with their leashes. In spite of himself, he laughed. He couldn't ever remember a time when he felt this good, so at peace with himself and his life.

Isabelle heard the elevator thirty-five minutes later, just as she flipped the last of the pancakes. "Just keep them warm till I brush my teeth," Abner said, loping off to the bathroom.

They ate in happy silence, silly smiles on their faces.

"You'll do it, right?" Isabelle said.

"Of course. It shouldn't take long. I want to go over the final report on the other stuff, and then you can take it out to Ms. de Silva. What time is your morning meeting over?"

"Depends on the client. Some of them like to chat it up, you know, be reassured that the plans will be exact. Some of them don't understand Murphy's Law and inspections. To be safe, I'd say noon. I'll come back here. By the way, why do you keep calling Annie 'Ms. de Silva'? She likes to be called Annie."

"She never told me to call her Annie, and she is my employer and as such deserves my respect. To be totally honest, I am worried about what Maggie might have said to you all."

Isabelle looked Abner in the eye and said, "Maggie never ever said a negative word about you. In fact, we never even knew your name until a month or so ago. Maggie holds you in the highest regard. She was very hard on herself where you were and are concerned."

Abner seemed content with Isabelle's explanation. "You go ahead and take the bathroom. I'm going to feed your latest request into the computers. I can shower and shave later. I'll clean up, too."

"Don't forget to add water to the tree stand," Isabelle called over her shoulder.

"Yes, 'Mom.'" A moment later, Abner was off his stool and barreling down the hall to his workstation, where he typed furiously for several minutes, sat back, then typed some more. Two hours, tops, and he should have every JJ in the District of Columbia plus fifty miles around.

Abner pressed another button on a different computer and waited for the printer to activate. He watched, a smile of satisfaction on his face, as page after page flew out of the printer. Within minutes he knew he had more than a ream of paper. Translated, five-hundred-plus pages of background material on the four subjects he'd been hired to vet.

Now all he had to do was make sense of it all. He looked up at one of the many clocks that adorned his walls. He had plenty of time. He was, after all, a computer whiz, wasn't he?

As he was stapling and sifting through the stack of papers, Isabelle appeared in the doorway. "I watered the tree. If I'm going to be late, I'll call you, okay?" She wanted to go over to the stool where Abner was sitting and kiss him, but she held back. At that moment, he was in another world, a world that didn't include her. She forced cheerfulness into her voice and said, "Bye."

Abner looked up and over at the sound of her voice. Isabelle watched as the transition from computer world to personal world fought a battle. For a nanosecond, she thought she had lost the battle, but Abner scooted the stool he was sitting on across the floor and leaped off. A second later, she was in his arms, and he was kissing her so hard, she thought her back teeth were going to come loose. She'd never been kissed with such passion in her whole life. And she liked it. No! She loved it. She said so.

Abner laughed, a heartwarming sound that stayed with her all the way to her office.

Isabelle Flanders was in love.

Back in the loft, Abner scooted his stool back to his workstation, but for the first time in his life, he didn't want to do what he was doing. He wanted to chase after Isabelle, grab her in his arms, and run somewhere far away. Far, far away. Maybe to Hawaii and that glorious beachfront property he'd purchased last year.

Abner Tookus, soon to be Dr. Abner Tookus, was in love.

Abner looked at his housemates, at the two Dobermans, who were watching him, and the Yorkie, who was clamoring to be picked up, at the cat, who was already in his lap, and said, "Holy shit, guys, I'm in love!"

Chapter 19

Ten minutes later, Abner was back in his other world, the world he'd lived in for so many years, a world that hadn't included Isabelle Flanders and love. He was like a whirlwind as he moved from computer to printer, back to computer and on to another printer. The room hummed with sounds as he sifted and collated the papers, separating them into neat piles according to each government agency. Now all he had to do was sit down and read what he had in front of him. No small task, to be sure. He thought then about how much he was going to charge for this assignment. Satisfied that it would be enough to finish his cabin without his touching any other money, he let loose with a sigh so loud, Dolly, the big white Persian cat, leaped off his lap and hissed at him before she stalked her way out of the room.

Abner decided to go with the big gun first and pulled out the stack of CIA printouts. Adam Daniels's, the money guy. He read through the file as it related to Daniel's tenure at the CIA. A career guy with a paunch and a bad hairpiece. He studied the picture that accompanied his file from all angles. Married thirty years, two kids, a boy and a girl, who lived in New York. Three grandchildren. Lived in Old Town Alexandria, in a rather nice Federal-looking house complete with blue door. Beach house on the eastern seaboard, nothing elaborate. A five-year-old Boston Whaler that he kept in dry dock. No traffic tickets. Mr. Upstanding Citizen. Wife, Arlene, was a retired fifth-grade schoolteacher. Either Mrs. Daniels didn't like to cook or wouldn't cook, because credit-card receipts said they dined out seven nights a week. He wondered what the couple did for the other two meals of the day.

Abner continued to flip pages, scanning each intently before turning it over. He wanted to make sure he didn't miss a thing. Not good for his image. Gold's Gym. Two visits in the last five years. He'd played squash at the indoor cage at CIA headquarters with . . . Matthew Logan from the Department of Justice. Once a week Daniels went to the shooting range without fail. Excellent shot, won two awards from the NRA. He liked to shoot skeet with . . . Henry Maris from Homeland Security.

Daniels had put in twenty years at the Treasury Department before going over to the CIA. Abner sucked on his lower lip as he tried to figure out if he was missing something. Adam Daniels was just Mr. Ordinary. "Ahhhh, what have we here?" Abner turned over another page. Best friends with ex-Director Span of the CIA before the latter's forced retirement. Span was best buddies with Hank Jellicoe, now rotting away in a federal prison.

Abner tapped at his chin with a pencil. Span and Jellicoe. All those lucrative government contracts he'd approved for Jellicoe back in the day. So much money one person couldn't count it all. He plopped a paperweight on the papers, rolled across the floor to a computer against the far wall, and tapped furiously. Then he made two phone calls, waited, checked his e-mails, and tapped some more.

Ten minutes later, sheets of paper started piling up in the trays of three different printers. He tapped some more. Another printer went crazy as even more papers spewed out. Now he finally had what he needed. At least he hoped so. Director Span had okayed lucrative contracts to Hank Jellicoe for years and years, but if he remembered correctly, the amounts of money paid to Global Securities never added up when he snooped in Jellicoe's bank records. If he remembered correctly, there was way too much money unaccounted for, with no trail to follow, and there were no "clients" at the time other than the government.

He made a mental note to tell Isabelle to get those files from Maggie, because he did not keep copies of anything once he turned the job over to the person who hired him. He preferred to be as pure as the driven snow where all that was concerned. Once he invaded—he hated the term *hacked*—a subject's life, he made a point of never doing it again. So if Maggie or her boss hadn't made copies, they were all SOOL.

Abner scooted all around his work area, gathering the papers from the various printers. He scanned them, collated and stapled them, and added them to his other files. There was something there. He was sure of it because the fine hairs on the back of his neck were moving. He scribbled notes on a yellow legal pad.

A break was called for. Abner loped off to the kitchen, reached for an apple, and crunched down. Just the act of chewing sometimes triggered something in his head. He'd never been able to explain it even to himself.

As he munched and chewed, he wondered if everyone but himself kept their lives on their computers. He had his life secured thanks to Suze Orman, the financial guru whom he'd trust with his life.

Five minutes later, Abner was back in his workroom. He fiddled and diddled, whistled to himself, tapped his foot as he punched the keys; then he was looking at Adam Daniels's computer.

He'd broken the politician's password the previous day. He typed it in and proceeded to go through Daniels's files and e-mails again to see if anything had changed. He wondered what the fussy little man would think if he knew his computer had been compromised. Abner had the knowledge and the power to crash Daniels's computer if he wanted to. Actually, he could bring down the entire computer system at the CIA if he wanted to. But not yet. Maybe soon, though. He shut down and rolled back to his stack of files.

Next on his list was Barney Gray of the FBI. Gray was two years away from retirement. A widower with three children, all living in California, the land of orange blossoms and sunshine. He lived in the Watergate, saw different women occasionally, nothing out of the ordinary. Definitely not a playboy. Lived within his means, healthy, stable bank account. A consistent saver. Loaned money to his kids from time to time. Active Lutheran church member. No gym for him. Rarely charged on his Visa card. Used the ATM every other day but did not withdraw more than a hundred dollars at a time. Charged his groceries and gas on an American Express card that he paid off every month.

All his records reconciled. Played bridge twice a month but with neighbors, no government people. He liked to fish and hike and belonged to two different clubs, a fishing club and a hiking club. His three children, two boys and a girl, visited each year around the Fourth of July, when, as a family, they went camping or white-water rafting. No grandchildren to dandle on his knees.

The only interaction between Gray and the other three moneymen was either a meeting where the directors were present or by chance out somewhere. Nothing was pre-arranged. In Abner's mind, Barney Gray was clean. That meant the FBI was clean. He separated the FBI's files and scooted them over to a bare shelf. He plopped a sticky note on top that said "Clean."

Next up was Henry Maris from the Department of Homeland Security. Well, if ever there was an organization that could rival a Chinese fire drill, the DHS was it. Maris was like dog poop in a park—he was all over the place. He was in debt up to his eyeballs, three months in arrears on his mortgage, and in danger of losing his town house; spent way beyond his means; charged everything under the sun. Liked designer clothes and custom-made shoes. As of the moment, his checking account said he had $345 in it. He had overdraft protection. He had tapped his re-tirement account three times in the last seven years and hadn't paid back a penny of it. He drove a leased Mercedes-Benz and was two months behind in his lease payments. No unexplained cash deposits into his bank account.

The guy simply lived high and didn't worry about a rainy day or tomorrow. He had lots of friends but mostly drinking buddies or neighbors. He charged a lot of liquor on his MasterCard, which had a two-thousand-dollar limit. He had only seventy dollars of credit available. All he was doing was paying the interest every month. He had what Abner considered way too much porn on his com-puter. No secret e-mails, nothing in his files. He was seen having lunch last week with the new director of the DHS.

A ninety-minute lunch, with each man drinking two glasses of wine. The director picked up the tab.

Nothing here to ring any bells, Abner thought. He stacked the files neatly and added a sticky with a large question mark on top.

Abner moved on to the last name on his list, Matthew Logan, or Matt, as everyone called him. His first assessment when he ran the files was that Logan was a stand-up guy. Good education, a veteran, well liked, played well with others, no known enemies. His bank accounts and charge accounts were normal. He drove a three-year-old Lexus; his wife of thirty-three years drove a Ford Taurus. Children scattered across the nation, two grandchildren, who visited from time to time. Wife, Claudia, was a buyer for a local department store. She would retire this year. Logan himself was just two years away from retirement. Friends all over the place. Both his and his wife's friends. They did the Washington party scene in the spring and summer but stayed away in the fall and winter.

He met from time to time with the other three, but it was always business and one director or the other hosted the meetings. Nothing there of any consequence.

And yet, all four of these men had gone to Camp David for Thanksgiving. That meant Daniels's and Logan's wives stayed home by themselves. "That's weird," Abner muttered to himself.

Abner mumbled and grumbled to himself as he stapled more papers. He really had nothing to show for all his hacking. He hated it when this happened because with no results, how could he bill a client? He couldn't; it was that simple. So, back to the drawing board. And then an idea hit him.

With all his power and knowledge he could send the

four men an e-mail and arrange to intercept their replies by setting up a bogus e-mail account for all four men. *Toss out the bait and see what hooks itself on your line.* He'd done it before and always come away a winner. He smacked his hands together in glee, then flexed his fingers the way a pianist would before a recital and started to type away with a vengeance.

Abner worked steadily for over an hour, lost in his own world, oblivious to the program he was running, which should, if he was successful, spit out who belonged to the initials JJ.

Time lost all meaning for Abner, so much so that he didn't hear the phone ringing to tell him Isabelle was going to be late because a walk-in client had appeared. He came up for air at three o'clock in the afternoon because his stomach started to protest.

In his kitchen, Abner became the Abner in love. He sat down and munched on a ham-and-cheese sandwich, his expression dreamy. His world was so right side up, he made a fist and shouted it to the world.

Across town in Georgetown, Maggie Spritzer wasn't entirely sure her world was right side up. She hoped it was since Gus Sullivan had accepted her apology and her invitation to dinner. And he was coming without a nurse or a handler.

Maggie knew she was an emotional mess, a feeling she hated but one she couldn't seem to control. A hot shower to remove all the pine resin that coated her clothes, hands, and arms from working at Yoko's nursery might be a good start. Maybe even a little perfume, perfume she'd bought herself, not perfume Ted had given her. She always felt better after a shower. As her thoughts trailed off, she sniffed appreciatively at the stew cooking in the Crock-Pot.

Maggie was back in the kitchen thirty minutes later, dressed in gray flannel slacks, penny loafers, and a cherry red sweater. Her wild curly hair was tied back with a matching cherry-colored ribbon. Her skin glowed, and she thought she smelled wonderful.

She had decided earlier on the ride home that she would serve dinner on the old plank table in the kitchen, which sat in the middle of the wraparound windows. As she was walking out the door, Yoko had shyly presented her with a beautiful evergreen centerpiece with a fat red bayberry-scented candle.

The house smelled so good, the cooking scents vying with the fragrant odors from the Christmas tree in the living room and the centerpiece. She wondered if it was true that the way to a man's heart was through his stomach and his nose. She hoped so. She checked the mess in the Crock-Pot, sniffed, and then tasted the rich gravy. Perfect. She added the wine and covered the pot. Next, she set the table and held a match to the shiny red candle. The last thing she did was build a fire in the living room and turn on the tree lights. It was all perfect, so much so that she crossed her fingers the way she had when she was a little girl and wanted some good-luck fairy to make her wish come true.

Her stomach in knots, Maggie sat down in front of the fire. She propped her elbows on her knees and let her mind race. This was a whole new ball game. Her emotions had never been this twisted, this unpredictable. She couldn't ever remember not being in control. The feeling was so alien, she wanted to cry.

Work versus love. Love versus work. Not exactly. Factor in the Sisters, and it wasn't just work or love. Why did it have to be one or the other? Why couldn't she blend it all together? Millions of women did it. But, she argued with herself, those millions of other women didn't have a loyalty to the infamous vigilantes. Common sense told her to just let things play out. Whatever was meant to happen would happen.

Maggie continued to watch the flames, mesmerized as they danced and frolicked and raced up the chimney. There was something about a good fire in the winter with a Christmas tree that was so comforting, she couldn't put it into words. *And I'm a reporter,* she thought, *so I should have the words.* The best she could come up with was, it evoked childhood memories, belief in Santa coming down the chimney. She remembered asking someone, an aunt, she thought, why Santa's pants didn't catch on fire. She smiled at the memory just as the doorbell rang.

Maggie uncurled herself and took a deep breath before she walked to the door. She actually wanted to run to the door, but she held herself back. She opened it, a welcoming smile on her face. The smile turned into a wicked grin when Gus said, "I'm staying the night." He had a small canvas bag under one arm and was walking with two canes. "Because of the weather. I hope it's okay. On Sundays, my therapy doesn't start till one o'clock."

Maggie noticed for the first time that it was sleeting out. Gus's curly hair was glistening with little ice crystals. "Sure it's okay. When did it start sleeting?" she asked inanely.

"Oh, about four hours ago." Gus laughed as he made his way inside.

"I didn't notice. Well, I have a nice fire going and my tree is up, and if I do say so myself, it is spectacular. Follow me, and I'll hang up your jacket. How about a glass of wine? Wow, Gus, you're walking pretty good."

"I know. My doctors are pleased with my progress but

not as much as I am. One more operation next month, more therapy, and they tell me I'll be good to go by late spring. Everything depends on my progress, though. We've had to revise deadlines several times. Good thing I have lots of patience."

They were in the living room, and Gus turned to view the tree and the fire. "Oh, this is the perfect end to a great day. You were right. This is a spectacular tree. I love sitting in front of a fire and just daydreaming. The Christmas season really is here."

"I was doing that when you rang the doorbell. When I was a kid, I remember asking one of my aunts why Santa's pants didn't catch on fire coming down the chimney. I don't remember if she answered me or, if she did, what she said. Grown-ups hated me because I was always the kid with the questions no one wanted to answer."

"I guess you were meant to be a reporter even back then," Gus said, lowering himself to one of the chairs by the fireplace.

Maggie laughed. "Yeah. You want some wine or a beer?"

"I'm a beer kind of guy, Maggie. And I like drinking it right out of the bottle, and the brand doesn't matter. Smells good in here."

"I need to tell you right up front, Gus, I am not much of a cook. I throw stuff in a Crock-Pot, cook it for hours, and hope for the best. We're having stew. Kind of goes with the weather outside. You know, comfort food. Be back in a minute with the beer."

Gus leaned back in the chair and closed his eyes. He hoped the pain in his back and legs would abate a little so he could enjoy the evening. He looked from the fire to the beautiful tree and made that wish. Either he was dreaming, crazy, or he was out for the count, because the minute he made his wish, he felt like he could get up and dance a jig. "Thank you, God," he whispered.

Maggie was as good as her word. She was back in a minute with two bottles of beer. She handed one to Gus and then curled up at his feet by the fire.

"We should make a toast. How about to Santa coming down the chimney, pants smoking, and we douse him with our beer?" Gus said, clinking his bottle against Maggie's.

Maggie laughed so hard she almost choked. "That'll work."

"Before we get off on the wrong foot again, and I'm willing to take the blame for speaking out of turn, let's talk about your last visit to the hospital. I don't want anything hanging over our heads if you and I decide to go forward with . . . with whatever is happening between us."

Maggie bit down on her bottom lip. The rubber was about to meet the road. "Yeah, okay."

"Let me go first. Then if you want to say something, feel free to interrupt me."

Maggie nodded as she stared into the fire.

"I've been at Walter Reed since June. I met the president in person in August. That's just background. I had a lot of nurses, both male and female, and the females were always trying to take my mind off my pain, my body, and what I was undergoing. They were wonderful to me. The ladies would jab at me when they thought I was slacking and say things like they were going to sic the vigilantes on me. When I didn't know what they were talking about, they enlightened me.

"A lot of them had theories, and they weren't shy about presenting them. One feisty grandma type had this theory that the *Post* was somehow involved with the ladies. Your paper always seemed to have a jump on what they were doing, and you had the banner headline when the ladies solved something. Which led the feisty nurse to come to that conclusion. I didn't think much about it back then, but I put it all together the other day, when you went flying out of the hospital and didn't return my calls.

"I deduced, because I am a clever kind of guy, that you and the vigilantes were on a first-name basis, and you have a loyalty to them. What I want you to know, Maggie, is, I don't care. I hope you are friends with them, and I respect your loyalty to them as a group. Maybe someday you will be comfortable enough with me to let me be part of that, but if not, I'm okay with that, too. I know how to compartmentalize, just as you do. Any questions so far?"

Maggie shook her head.

"I have tons of time to do nothing but think. I even try to shift my mind to other things when they're trying to twist me into a pretzel. Sometimes, I think I have pretzel logic, but at least it's logic of some kind."

Maggie turned from the fire and stared up at Gus. Her expression told Gus he needed to do a little more explaining.

"I understand now why you wanted to know about those money guys who were at Camp David. I did my own little survey at the rehab ward by asking the guys and some of the women what, if anything, would make them give up their own Thanksgiving dinner with their families, and they all said pretty much the same thing, something earth-shattering. Even then, that didn't satisfy me, so I turned to my laptop, the Internet, and Google. I have to say I didn't come up with much. Then I remembered this four-star general who was getting daily therapy, along with the senior senator from Texas, who sits on just about every committee there is. In rehab, titles don't count, at least where I was.

"We were just a bunch of guys trying to get whole again. We'd try to bolster each other up if one of us was having a bad day. What I'm trying to say here is, I over-heard quite a few conversations that I probably shouldn't have listened to but at the time didn't mean anything. I also heard private cell-phone conversations.

"The general and the senator still come in for therapy twice a week, and most times they look me up and we chat a bit. When they found out I was invited to Camp David, they were a little . . . nonplussed . . . for want of a better word. Then, when they heard that you, the editor in chief of the *Post,* was going, they actually looked . . . I wouldn't say worried but more like concerned. Any questions?"

Maggie set her beer bottle down on the hearth and stretched her arms over her head. "But why?"

"I don't know, Maggie. I can tell you one thing, though. Both those guys hate the CIA. They aren't fond of the FBI, and they think Homeland Security sucks. As for the De-partment of Justice, they said those guys don't know their asses from their elbows."

Maggie shrugged. "A lot of people in this town don't trust any of the alphabet agencies. So where does that leave us?"

"With a problem. I'm unbiased, a freethinker, at least at the moment. I'm not a politician, thank you, God. That's just another way of saying I don't have a dog in this race. No pun intended. Cleo is not part of this. Just off the top of my head I'd say those guys are having trouble with their respective slush funds. If you think for one minute that an agency that suddenly needs money for something or other goes to the Treasury Department and they just hand it over, then you are out of your mind. But there has to be one major person, I'm thinking, who oversees it all, and I think because the CIA is the most powerful, it has to be someone there. Hey, like I said, that's just my opinion. I'm probably so off base, you could hit a slam dunk and still have room to drive an eighteen-wheeler through the hole."

"Any idea who that could be?" Maggie asked.

"Nope. Do you?"

Maggie shook her head.

"I can try and find out tomorrow. Both the senator and the general will be at rehab, even though it's Sunday. The two of them like to do the weekends so they don't eat into their office time. I sense a little self-importance there, like the Senate and the Pentagon can't run effectively unless they're in their respective offices. They might open up or let something slip. It's worth a try if you want me to go for it."

Maggie grimaced. "Show me a politician who doesn't think like that. Sure, see what, if anything, you can find out."

"Your turn, Maggie," Gus said quietly.

"You were right. I guess you could say I'm an honorary member of the vigilantes. I believe in them, and when we reported anything, it was true and accurate because we had the inside track. Have I myself broken any laws? Not really. But I have skirted the edges and danced away in the nick of time. I'd do it all over again if I had to. Thanks to all of those women, I have the job that I have, and I do have a fierce loyalty to them. Today they are ordinary citizens with full pardons. Or, as Annie likes to say, today they are on the side of the angels."

"Do you ever see them going back to their . . . original line of work?"

Maggie laughed. "Never say never." She wondered what Gus would do or say if she showed him her gold shield. She was tempted to follow Nikki's advice but squelched the thought as soon as it popped into her head. "If you're hungry, I think we can eat now."

"I've been ready since I got here. Even though the food is okay at the hospital, it's not the same as home cooking. My mouth is watering. So, we're okay, Maggie. I mean me and you."

Maggie thought about it for a few seconds. "We're okay, Gus. Oh, oh, wait. We have to make a wish. You know, on the tree, like when we were kids."

Gus just looked puzzled.

"You're supposed to make a wish the first time you see someone's tree. Okay, okay, I made that up, so let's each just make a wish. Close your eyes and wish hard."

"Okay, I made my wish."

"I did, too," Maggie said. "We can't tell each other what it is unless it comes true. You know that, right?"

Gus nodded solemnly and grinned.

Maggie just smiled.

"So, it's okay for me to stay over. I have to do the couch, though. There's no way for me to do those stairs of yours."

"It's not a problem. The couch in here opens up. You'll have the benefit of the fire and the tree at the same time." *And me, if you want me,* she thought as she left to get the sheets and blankets to make up the sleep couch into a bed after dinner and more visiting.

"Uh-huh," Gus drawled.

Chapter 20

Gus Sullivan hobbled into the room using both canes. He looked around and was surprised to see that he was the only patient, but then again, he was twenty minutes early. Even his therapist wasn't there yet. Not surprising, the weather being what it was. For all he knew, his two-hour therapy session might even be canceled. Doubtful but entirely possible.

Most days the smell of stale sweat and the powerful disinfectant the cleaners used bothered him. Today he barely noticed it, his thoughts back in Georgetown with Maggie Spritzer. He wished he had someone to confide in. Someone like Cleo, who would listen and nuzzle with him, but Cleo came only during the week.

Gus lowered himself to one of the benches, propped up his canes, and leaned back. He closed his eyes as he tried to project how much pain his therapist was going to put him through that day. And, of course, how cooperative his body would be. He thought about what he'd promised Maggie. He wondered how successful he would be. Four-star generals did not have loose lips, even though in this room they were just two guys fighting to get their bodies back into some kind of livable shape. In here were no spies, no secret recording machines. What there was, was a lot of cussing, moaning, and groaning—even tears. He had certainly shed his share and didn't care who saw the tears rolling down his cheeks. He'd seen the general swipe at his eyes, and the senator had turned white and almost blacked out a few times. Therapy was a bitch. But the alternative didn't bear thinking about.

Gus's thoughts shifted to his evening with Maggie. It was the kind of evening he'd dreamed about when he was in the desert, finding that perfect mate, making it work, and going on with your life as a couple. The evening had been so endearing, so sweet, so perfect, he thought he was dreaming. Forty-seven years old and he was just now finding true love, and that true love didn't care if he was a cripple or not.

What was it Maggie had said? "If you go back to being a hundred percent, fine. If you don't, I'll take care of you." That had blown his mind. Absolutely blown his mind. He hadn't known what to say, couldn't find the words. Maggie was the one who knew all the words. When she saw him struggling to say something, she'd put her fingers on his lips and say, "That's a promise." And he believed her, heart and soul.

Gus was so deep into his thoughts, he didn't hear it when someone came into the room. When the air stirred around him, he opened his eyes to see the general easing himself down onto the same bench he was sitting on.

"How's it going, son?"

"Today is better than it was yesterday, sir. How are you doing? I didn't see you last week."

"Had to go to Rhode Island to a funeral. Old army buddy. I got so caught up in my memories, I just didn't feel like coming here. I hate to admit it, but I needed to wallow a bit."

"I understand, sir."

The general looked around. He gave a snort of laughter and said, "Maybe you and I are going to give each other therapy. No one is here. The weather is bad, but when that happens, you have to leave early to make sure you arrive on time. You and I know that, son. It's these civilians that march to a different drummer who don't understand it. So, what's new in your life? Have you made any concrete decisions about what you're going to do when you get out of here?"

Gus grappled to find the words. Finally, he blurted out, "I'm in love. I met the woman I've waited all my life for, and she doesn't care what condition I'm in. I'm going to write a book. I always wanted to do that, so I'm going to try my hand at it. Then I'm going to breed dogs. I've been researching real estate on the Net, and I came up with a few possibilities."

"Sounds like a plan. What kind of book?" the general asked curiously.

"Espionage, spy stuff, illegal funds. I guess you could say political." Gus sucked in his breath as he waited for the general's response.

"That stuff sells. My wife loves thrillers. How do you plan on doing your research?"

"I haven't gotten that far in my thinking. Any idea who I should be talking to? I'm not up on Washington politics. The flip side of that is, why would anyone even talk to me? I'm a nobody."

Gus was surprised when he felt the general's hand on his arm. "Son, I don't ever want to hear you say you're a nobody. You are somebody. You're a soldier who almost gave his life for his country. And you're suffering and undergoing unbearable pain as a result. You get a résumé in order, and when you call around to make appointments, you toot your own horn. I can steer you in a few directions."

Gus felt his heart start to pound in his chest. *Careful, careful,* he warned himself. "Which agency should I start with, sir?"

"There is no such thing as full disclosure among agencies, so you'll have to talk to all of them, depending on what it is you're going to write about. In other words, your plot, son. I've never written a book, so I don't know if this is good advice or not."

"You should think about writing your memoirs, sir. When you retire."

"That's what my wife keeps telling me."

The worms crawling around in Gus's stomach settled down. He heard noise from out in the hall. The therapists must have arrived. Before he could change his mind, he blurted out the question Maggie had told him to ask. "Who would I need to talk to about the different money funds that are not controlled by Congress? I read, so I know that they're out there and that the general public doesn't know about them. There has to be a person or a committee or a group of some kind that controls huge amounts of money. Do those people have control of the money, or do they report to the president?" There, he'd said the words out loud. He stared at the general to see his reaction.

"Sounds like you know what you want to write about, son—money and power. You can never go wrong with that. I'm thinking you might want to talk to JJ, but I'm not sure he'd give you the time of day. The man is like a phantom, from what I've heard. He answers to no one, not even the president. Or so the story goes. This is Washington, son, and stories abound. Quirky kind of guy and, by the way, this is just scuttlebutt."

Gus felt a surge of panic when the door opened and a gaggle of people entered the room. One of the therapists clapped his hands and said, "Okay, let's get to it!"

"Sir, who is JJ?"

The general pierced Gus with a look Gus couldn't define. He held his breath as he waited for the general's response.

"Jody Jumper. He knows where all the bodies are buried, or so I've been led to believe. And you didn't hear that from me, son."

Gus thought he was going to faint. "Hear what, sir?"

"Okay, Sullivan, you're up!" his therapist said as he held out his hand to pull Gus to his feet. "You okay? You look a little . . . white."

"Forgot to eat, that's all. I'm ready."

Back in Georgetown, Nikki Quinn Emery was staring at her husband, a wide smile on her face. "I can't believe we're standing here like this on a Sunday afternoon, both of us. And that you just invited me out to brunch. I accept, Jack. And we need to do this more often. You do know the weather is pretty shitty out there, right?"

"I really don't care. I've been cooped up with Harry and Bert so long, I don't know what it's like outside. Let's just bundle up and go to the Knife and Fork. It shouldn't be so busy now, and the weather will keep a lot of people indoors. I'll hold your hand," he said and laughed.

Nikki was already slipping into a long all-weather coat the color of burgundy. She plopped a rain hat on her head, pulled on boots and gloves, then held out her hand. "I'm ready, husband of mine."

"I love the way that sounds."

What should have been a three-minute walk to the Knife and Fork turned into a twenty-two-minute walk with hard, icy rain pelting them. In the end, Jack guided Nikki to the cobblestone road and held her arm tightly. It was slush up to their ankles, but they managed. Both of them sighed when they entered the small eatery. Both of them were surprised when the hostess told them it was a ten-minute wait. They hung up their coats and took a seat along with four other couples waiting to be seated.

"Maybe this wasn't such a good idea, after all. The temperature is dropping. By the time we leave here, it's going to be pure ice out there," Jack said.

"Nonsense, and do we really care? No, we do not. Think of this as romantic," Nikki said. "We held hands the whole way here. If we have to, we can slide on our bums all the way home."

Jack laughed and mouthed the words *I love you*. Nikki mouthed the same words in return.

Fifteen minutes later, when they were finally seated, Nikki said, "Jack, did I tell you I think I have Alexis convinced to go to law school? You know I was in court all day yesterday, even though it was Saturday, because court was dark for two days with no heat. When I got back to the office, there was Alexis, manning the fort. She's a natural. I think between you and me, and a few other people I know who can pull strings, we can get her into law school if she wants to go.

"The firm will pay for it as long as she signs on to work for us when she graduates. She wants to, but she doesn't think she's got the smarts to do it. I also think she thinks she might outshine Joseph Espinosa. I don't know whom she loves more, Joe or his family. She absolutely adores Joe's mother. I don't think she would want to put that relationship to the test, and she might back away for that very reason."

"Do you want me to have a little preemptive talk with Espinosa?"

"Yeah, that would be great, but don't come on too strong. Talking to Ted might also help since the two of them are so tight."

"Consider it done," Jack said, picking up his menu and perusing it. "I love their Canadian bacon, so I think I'll go for that and two eggs over easy. And some fresh-squeezed orange juice. Wheat toast with some of that blackberry-raspberry jam they're so famous for. How about you, Nik? You as hungry as I am?"

"I'll have the same, but let's split one of their potato-onion casseroles, too."

Jack gave the order to the waitress after she filled their coffee cups.

Jack leaned back in his captain's chair and smiled across the table at his wife. "Seems like the only time we get to play catch-up is on the weekends. What's new?"

"That's so true, Jack. We really have to make more time for *us*. I thought that would happen when you and Bert took over Harry's training."

"Yeah, well, if Harry hadn't screwed things up, it would have happened. We got him going in circles now. Bert cracks the whip, I can tell you that. Harry has agreed to everything we set up. I wish we could take the credit, but down deep I know it was Yoko who set Harry straight. He's coming along well, and I think he has a really good chance of taking the title in the spring."

"Did Yoko tell him yet?" Nikki asked.

"Tell him what?"

"Well, Myra and Annie swear Yoko is pregnant, but she hasn't said anything to any of us to confirm or deny it, but by the same token, we haven't asked. Morning sickness," Nikki said, as if that would explain everything to Jack, who just looked blank.

"That's really great if it turns out to be true. Harry can't keep a secret to save his life, so I have to say no, he doesn't know. If he knew, he'd be out running the streets, shouting at the top of his lungs. No, he doesn't know," Jack said emphatically.

"Don't say anything, Jack. If it's true, Yoko will tell us when she feels the time is right. She might be afraid, considering what happened the last time. Asian people are often superstitious when it comes to things like this. Promise you won't say anything, Jack."

"I promise. That the sum total of your news?"

"No, I have more." Nikki giggled. "Fergus and Elias are working at Yoko's nursery, pro bono. They're getting along like two peas in a pod. They make Yoko sit and drink tea, and they do all the heavy lifting. You know, hefting those Christmas trees to roll into the barrel so they can net them up. Fergus told Annie business is brisk, and Yoko is very happy when they tally up the receipts at the end of the day. And in February, Fergus is going to head up the security at Myra's candy factory.

"Mr. Unger, who replaced Charles, is going to retire. Lizzie is working on getting Fergus the right paperwork so all that can happen. Annie is happier than a pig in a mud slide, I can tell you that."

"That is a lot of news. You're right. We have to spend more time together. I can't believe I didn't know any of this." Jack grinned sheepishly.

"Wait, there's more," Nikki continued, giggling again. "I saved the best for last."

"Hit me!"

"Gus Sullivan, Maggie's new amour, went to her place for dinner last night and spent the night. I know nothing more, so do not ask questions. Maggie is definitely in love. She said Gus loves her, too. And, Gus has the inside track with some general who goes to Walter Reed for therapy.

He's going to ask him some questions this afternoon. Seems the general prefers weekends for his therapy so he can be in his office during the week. Just two military types who are sweating the same bullets and hoping they can walk away whole when it's all over. She promised to call me when Gus reports back to her at the end of the session."

"Yep, that was news."

Nikki leaned across the table and hissed, "So, share. What's your news?"

"I really don't have any, Nik, unless you want to hear all about Harry's idiosyncrasies. He wears boxers. He sleeps on the floor. He eats crap. He's lost weight, but we're putting it back on him. We have him on such a tight schedule, all he does is curse us. Bert actually bought earplugs. We train for two hours, and then we make him shower and eat a small protein meal, wait thirty minutes, and go at it again. It's paying off. He's got more stamina than ever. We call it quits at seven thirty, when Yoko gets home. Like it or not, he has to go upstairs with her. He's getting ten hours' sleep a night. He's looking good. Actually, Nik, I'm so proud of the three of us, I could just bust."

"That's hardly newsworthy, Jack. That's it!"

"Well, Ted Robinson stopped by a few days ago with a very pretty young lady on his arm. I think he wanted to show her off. She's a real-estate broker in Arlington. Late thirties, early forties, nice-looking. Definitely in shape, and she was hanging on to Ted for dear life, and he was loving every minute of it. Her name is Rachel Ryan. Never been married, no baggage, as Ted calls it. We all liked her. Sweet personality, just right for Ted. And speaking of Ted, which makes me think of Maggie for some reason, what's up with her hacker? Is he on the job?"

"Oh, good Lord, how could I have forgotten to tell you

about *that?* Not only is he on the job, but he is on the job with Isabelle. They are now an item, as in a couple, as in love. Annie said she has never seen Isabelle this happy, but yes, they are working on what . . . you know . . . what he does. We should be hearing or seeing results in the next few days."

Their food arrived just as Nikki finished talking, and they dug in. They chatted about the weather, the law, and nothing important during the meal. When they were finished, Nikki said, "This was a good idea, but I am stuffed. Dinner tonight will be a salad and some soup."

"That works for me, but what about dessert?"

"Let's go home and make some peanut butter fudge and hit the sheets."

Jack leered at his wife. "As in . . ."

"You want a diagram?"

"No, ma'am, I figured it out." Jack stuffed some bills under the saltshaker, got up, held Nikki's chair for her. They both raced to the door and bundled up.

Outside, the precipitation was a mixture of sleet and snow. Laughing like two kids, they made their way home, slipping and sliding and giggling the whole time.

Gasping for breath, they climbed the few steps to the front door. While Nikki fumbled with her keys, Jack said, "I love you, Nikki Quinn Emery."

"Not as much as I love you, Jack Quentin Emery," she said, thrusting the door open. They both barreled through the door at the same time and headed for the stairs.

"I thought we were going to make peanut butter fudge?" Nikki grumbled.

"Are you nuts! No pun intended," Jack managed to blurt out.

Giggling, Nikki sprinted up the steps, Jack hot on her trail.

Chapter 21

Charles Martin stood at the back door in the kitchen, straining to see the weather outside. Sleet crashed against the windows and even found its way to the panes in the kitchen door, even though there was a protective overhang. For sure, winter was here. And early this year, in his opinion.

In the background, Charles could hear Myra laughing and the dogs barking as she did her best to wrap Christmas presents in the living room. He'd peeked in earlier, while he was readying a prime rib to put into the oven. So much food for just the two of them, but Myra said she was in the mood for prime rib, so prime rib it was. He turned and walked to the door leading into the living room. Myra was actually rolling across the floor, a skein of scarlet ribbon in her hand, which one of the pups was intent on getting. A mountain of gaily colored paper and ribbons were strewn everywhere. As fast as Myra fixed a bow, one of the dogs snatched it from her. Charles smiled as he listened to his beloved's hysterical laughter. He knew at some point she would have enough, at which point she would whistle and say, "Enough!" and the dogs would retire to the fire-place, where their beds were lined up. Of course, she would have to bribe them with chew bones, whereas all he had to do was give a command, and the dogs fell into line. The dogs knew who was boss and whom they could trick.

Charles did one last check of the kitchen for tidiness—he did sooo hate a mess—as well as looked at the banana cream pie he'd baked earlier. Satisfied that he had a good two hours before it was time to serve dinner, he headed for the war room. He decided to make his way through the dining room, out to the hall, then to the hidden opening behind the bookshelves that would lead him to the dungeons under the old farmhouse. No sense in disturbing Myra; she was having too much fun, something that was sorely lacking in her life these days.

Charles took a moment to look around what the Sisters called his "lair," the place where they said he made things happen. That was back in the day, he thought ruefully.

These days, the upstarts were showing him up. He hated to admit it, but his sources simply hadn't kept up with the times. But, he did have the manpower.

He touched a few keys to see if he had incoming e-mails to go to the printer and was disappointed that there was nothing there for him to analyze. He stared down at the round table where his chicks, as he thought of the Sisters, had sat so many times, plotting a revenge to right some wrong. He focused on Julia's chair, Annie's chair now. He said a little prayer for Julia, the way he always did when he got in one of his moods. Julia might be gone, but she would never be forgotten.

He thought about the wager he'd made with himself, a wager he hadn't even told Myra about. When this, for lack of a better word, mission, this elusive something or other the Sisters were supposed to tackle was completed, he thought they would finally pack it in and get on with their lives. He'd seen all the subtle changes: their personal lives and happiness were starting to be more important than missions and righting wrongs. They had been flattered, even excited, when Lizzie had brought the gold shields and dispersed them. But . . . they had been *more excited* at seeing the video and pictures of Little Jack.

He felt sad and yet almost relieved that the girls were finding happiness at last. And they so deserved happiness after all they'd been through. Myra was the one—Annie, too—who worried him the most.

He hated to admit it even to himself, but he was concerned about his own well-being. What would he do with his time? Cooking certainly wasn't his main goal in life. He supposed he could dabble at writing a cookbook. The minute the thought popped into his head, he rejected the idea. He turned to look at the computer that had just given off a ping, signaling an incoming e-mail. He hit READ and almost gasped aloud. It was from Pappy, telling him Pappy's father, Spiro, had passed away. Charles bowed his head and offered up a prayer for his soul. He read on:

The powers that be finally granted me and my family immunity, but it was too late for Pop. We will be going back to my homeland so my family can see where Pop and I lived for so many years. It's time for them to meet what's left of my family. I'd like to lease, if possible, Annie's mountain in Spain. Tell me if that is something she would consider. And then the mindblower. The last sentence of the e-mail made the fine hairs on Charles's neck stand on end: Do you and your people want to buy Big Pine Mountain?

Charles bit down on his lower lip. Thoughts of the years he and his chicks had spent on that mountain, perhaps the only safe place for them in the entire country, raced through his mind. He left his lair so fast that he almost tripped over his own feet. He flew up the moss-covered steps and into the living room, where the dogs, finally giving way to exhaustion, were sound asleep and Myra was seriously wrapping presents. He blurted out Pappy's news and waited to hear her reply.

"Oh, dear, how sad. Spiro was such a lovely man." Myra bowed her head, much the way Charles had, and offered up a prayer. "But how wonderful for Pappy and Samantha and the children. One always wants to return to their roots. Do you think Annie will want to buy the mountain?"

"Why don't we call her and ask?" Charles said, tongue in cheek.

Myra worried her lower lip. "Did he say how much he wants for the mountain?"

"No, he didn't, but Pappy is a fair man. And, old girl, as you know, everything in life is negotiable except death. First, we have to find out if Annie is interested. Perhaps the two of you could buy it together. You certainly have the money to do it, Myra."

"We were so happy on that mountain, weren't we, Charles? We were so insulated and safe. Not that we aren't insulated and safe here on the farm. Living on the mountain was just different. Personally, I loved it. Annie did, too. Even though the girls got antsy from time to time, they loved it, too. Knowing we owned it would make it a wonderful retreat for all of us. Hurry, Charles. Call Annie and see what she says. Do you think we should ask the price first?"

Charles rolled his eyes. "Do you really think Annie is going to quibble about the price? Either she wants it or she doesn't. If she expresses an interest, then I'll go back to Pappy."

"Where . . . where is Spiro buried?"

"On the mountain, but when Pappy's immunity came through, he made arrangements to have Spiro's body taken back to Greece. Pappy and his family are already back in Greece. I didn't sense any urgency in Pappy's e-mail."

"If Annie agrees, I have a feeling she'll jump on it. So, are you going to call Annie or not?" Myra asked, impatience ringing in her voice.

Myra's fist shot in the air when she heard Annie's squeal come through the phone. Charles grinned. He was still grinning when he hung up.

"Annie wants to know when we'll have our first re-union. Dinner will be in an hour, so you can wrap some more presents, and I'll go back to my lair and send off an e-mail."

"Lovely, just lovely," Myra said happily as she returned to the living room and the mound of presents still to be wrapped. The dogs looked at her to see if it was time to play, and she shook her head. They went back to sleep.

Below, in the war room, Charles's cell phone chirped. He listened to Maggie's excited voice. When he could get a word in edgewise, he managed to say, "Unbelievable, and the information just fell in your lap, in a manner of speaking. Thank your young man for all of us. I'll get right on it, Maggie." He listened a moment longer as Maggie groused about the miserable weather. Then they both broke the connection.

Jody Jumper! Who in the bloody hell is Jody Jumper?

Charles debated a moment before he made the decision to text Isabelle. If Myra's intel was correct, Isabelle was camped at Abner Tookus's place of business. Weren't they going to be surprised when Charles came up with the name ahead of the best-known hacker in the country. He was almost giddy when he typed off the name.

Within minutes he sent off nine different e-mails to people who would, as Kathryn was fond of saying, have the skinny on Jody Jumper. He knew replies would take a while, so he composed an e-mail to Pappy and told him Annie agreed to purchase Big Pine Mountain and what was the price and when did he want to close the deal?

The reply, when it came minutes later, stated an astronomical price that made Charles blink. The e-mail said the closing could be at Annie's convenience. Before he committed further, he called Annie again, who didn't have any problem with the price for Big Pine Mountain, but she came back with a lease amount for her own mountain in Spain that made Charles chuckle. He wasn't so sure that Pappy would chuckle, but he sent off Annie's offer and again waited.

The return e-mail was even quicker than the last one, saying Pappy agreed to Annie's ten-year lease and to notify him of the closing on Big Pine Mountain. He included the routing numbers for a wire transfer to an account in Greece. As far as Charles was concerned, it was a done deal all the way around.

Belatedly, he sent off an e-mail to Lizzie and asked her if she would handle the closing. With nothing else to do, Charles kept his eye on the e-mail and waited. How long, he wondered, would it take for someone to get back to him on Jody Jumper? He decided nothing would come to him until tomorrow, so he closed up shop and went upstairs in time to see Myra packing up all her Christmas wrapping materials. A neat, tidy row of presents, each box prettier than the next, sat under the Christmas tree. He breathed in the scent, then exhaled. There was something about a Christmas tree that he absolutely loved.

"Old girl, how would you like to have dinner here in front of the fire so we can see the tree? I know you want to talk all this to death, and I do have other news that just came through."

"Am I going to like your news?"

"I think so. I'll finish up dinner if you set up the card table and take the dogs out."

Myra strained to see through the window. She knew she'd have to bundle up, and the dogs might not even go out, but she was game. She whistled for the dogs, who stared at her. A second whistle meant business, and all of them bounded through the room to the kitchen, where they waited for her to put on her outerwear. "Okayyyy, let's go!"

The dogs beelined out the door, ran to the nearest spot under a dripping hemlock tree. They ran back inside, shaking the sleet and snow from their coats all over the kitchen floor. Melted snow on Myra's rain gear trickled onto the floor. Charles looked at the puddles with a jaundiced eye. Myra sighed as she walked into the laundry room for an old towel. Charles handed out his rewards, and the dogs ran back to their beds in front of the fire.

"You do the eleven o'clock outing, dear," Myra said as she threw the towel in the washer. "I'll set the table."

An hour later, Myra sighed happily. "It was a wonderful dinner. Actually, Charles, it was a wonderful day all the way around except for the weather, and we're snug here inside, so I guess the weather really doesn't count. Now tell me your news."

He did.

"Jody Jumper! It rings some kind of bell, but I can't put a face to the name, and I can't truthfully say I ever heard the name. But for some reason I think . . . Oh, I don't know what I think, Charles. Maybe he's the invisible man who controls the invisible money fund no one knows about. I guess Isabelle hasn't gotten back to you, eh?"

"No, not yet. I have my people working on it. All it is, is a name, Myra. The fact that a four-star general just popped it out for a fellow soldier really doesn't mean he is our elusive JJ, even though he told Mr. Sullivan he didn't hear the name from him."

"And Maggie?"

Charles shrugged.

"Knowing Maggie as I do, I am sure that she is, as we speak, on Ted Robinson's case to go through the archives to see if there is any kind of background on a Jody Jumper. With a strange name like that, you would think people would be lining up to volunteer information on the man. It might even be a woman, for all we know. I do believe there are film stars with the name Jody. They might spell it Jodie or not. I'm babbling, Charles.

"Dear, I know you want to get back downstairs, so I will clean up and feed the dogs. Run along. I can handle this. I also want to call Annie to congratulate her on buying the mountain. I wonder if she called the girls to tell them."

"Babble away, dear one. I do want to go downstairs to see if any more e-mails have come through."

"Take your time, dear. I might even wrap some more presents after I clean up. Then again, I think I might want to watch some television for a little while."

Charles kissed Myra's cheek; then he kissed her lips.

"Ahhh." Myra smiled. "I like it when you find the right spot."

Charles chuckled all the way back to his lair, arriving there just in time to hear his computer pinging away. And the evening was still young.

Chapter 22

Isabelle looked at the sea of white littering the floor in Abner's workroom, a look of pure dismay written all over her face. "What can I do to help, Abner?" she whispered. When Abner didn't respond, she backed up when her cell phone chirped. She continued to move backward as she clicked on the phone to hear Charles's voice. She moved farther back into the hallway to guard her conversation, her gaze on a befuddled Abner as he stirred and moved the papers on the floor.

"Okay, Charles, I will tell him. Is there anything else?" She listened again before she broke the connection. What did it all mean? She hesitated before she advanced into the room again.

Isabelle squatted down next to Abner. "What is all this?" she said, pointing to the mountain of discarded papers.

Abner grimaced as he stroked his chin. "This," he said, waving his arm about, "is the thirty-seven thousand four hundred fifty-six men and women who live within a fifty-mile radius of Washington and have the initials JJ. As far as I can tell, and I've been poring over this for hours, there is not one name out of the thirty-seven thousand four hundred fifty-six names that fits the criteria your people gave me. Not a single one."

"I think I can help you out here. JJ stands for Jody Jumper." She relayed Charles's message.

"There is no Jody Jumper on this list. I can do a hundred-mile perimeter and see if it pops up," Abner said as he scrambled to his feet and started to beat at the computer keys. He hit the PRINT key and waited. Nothing. He looked over at Isabelle and shrugged. "If there was a name like Jody Jumper in this database, it would have popped out by now. I ran one from the FBI and the CIA. There is no Jody Jumper."

Seeing his distress, Isabelle winced. "Maybe it's a code name or a nickname. Would that show up?"

"Not really. A name has to be an identity. This is mind-boggling. Who came up with the name?"

Isabelle sucked in her bottom lip, debating whether she should tell Abner what she knew. Finally, she said, "Maggie has a source who got the name from a four-star general."

Without missing a beat, Abner said, "Then have Maggie go back to her source and ask that source to call the general and ask him if it's a code name or a nickname. Can you do that now?"

Isabelle swallowed hard. "I can do that." She yanked out her cell phone, scrolled down, and hit the number three on her speed dial.

Maggie picked up after one ring. She listened to Isabelle and mumbled something that Isabelle took to mean she was on it.

Isabelle powered down, looked at Abner, and said, "She's on it."

*   *   *

Gus Sullivan listened to Maggie's voice mail and winced. How in the hell was he going to call a four-star general and actually get to talk to him? There was no doubt in his mind that he would give it his all, but would he be successful? Maggie was not the kind of person who took no for an answer, and he now knew Maggie didn't know the meaning of the word *defeat*. Maybe he could sweet-talk the general's therapist. He knew for a fact the therapist had the general's number in case of an emergency.

Since it was after hours, he had to call his own therapist at home, something he didn't relish doing. But if Maggie needed him to do it, he would do it. He'd never complained, never bothered his therapist after hours, so maybe he would accommodate him this once and do him the favor.

When he finally reached his own therapist and told him what he wanted, John Long whistled. "Gus, I can't do that. Listen, what I can do is call Jerry Brantley and ask him to call the general and have the general call you. I don't know if Jerry will do it, but I'll give it a try. I'll tell him the general is helping you with your book. Swear to me, Gus, that this is on the up-and-up. I don't want to mess with a four-star by invading his privacy and get written up or even lose my job."

Gus took a huge deep breath. He was committed now. He was going to have to write a damn book whether he liked it or not. "It's on the up-and-up, John. It's important, or I wouldn't have called you. I don't want to have to wait till next weekend, when he comes in for therapy."

"All right, I'll call you when I know something."

Gus struggled back to his room, flopped down, and yanked out his cell. He relayed John's information and said he would call again when he knew something more.

An hour later Gus's phone rang. It was his therapist. "I have bad news and more bad news and a smidgin of good news. You ready, Gus?"

"Yeah, give it to me."

"It's taken me this long to really track down the information to make sure it was true. When the general left us after his therapy, he slipped on some black ice, knocked himself out cold, and blew out one of his new hips. He had to have emergency surgery, and he's four floors up. You could try to visit him. I don't think the nurses will fight you. Hell, most of those women on that ward were the ones who took care of you when you had your surgeries. Sweet-talk them."

"Damn," was all Gus could think of to say. He thanked his therapist, struggled to his feet, and went out to the hall, where he eased himself down into one of the wheelchairs.

Minutes later, he was on the surgical floor and schmoozing with the nurses on duty. He stated his business and waited. "I can wait if he has visitors, or I can come back, but it's not easy. I just need to ask him a question if he's awake."

A chubby nurse with fire red hair laughed and said, "Oh, he's awake, and he's been cussing up a storm since he came out of recovery. His wife said she wasn't listening to him anymore and left. He might be glad of the company, but you know the rules, Gus. I have to ask him first."

Gus slouched in the wheelchair as the nurse walked away on her rubber soles. He hated the squishing sound they made. To him, the sound was the same as nails scratching a blackboard. The nurse stepped to the door and beckoned him forward. Gus sent the chair down the hall at a fast clip. He couldn't believe his good luck.

"He's a little groggy, but he's up to speed. He wants

some Jack Daniel's, and if you are packing some, hand it over right now."

"Sorry. I came empty-handed," Gus said as he sailed his chair through the doorway. The nurse laughed as she closed the door behind her.

Inside, the general looked smaller than he did when he was in the rehab room. Gus hated seeing all the tubes and monitors. "Hi, sir. Sorry to see you back here."

"No sorrier than I am, son. One minute I was upright, and the next minute I was kissing the ground. Didn't even see that patch of ice. Enough of me. What are you doing up here? Didn't you spend enough time here? How'd you find out I was even here? Never mind. News travels fast in a hospital, just the way it does at the Pentagon. They're going to kick my keister out now."

"I hope not," Gus said sincerely.

"They will. I should have retired last year, but I couldn't bring myself to walk away. The board will just tell me to leave, and I won't argue. Now, did you just come to visit, or do you need my help on something?"

"Both, sir. I'm sorry I don't have any Jack Daniel's. Maybe tomorrow I can get a friend to smuggle some in. I was going to start on my research, and I can't find anyone who knows anyone named Jody Jumper. I tried Googling it, but nothing came up. Is it a nickname?"

"That's been his name for as long as I can remember. He works in some dark, strange places, was the story I got. In the bowels of buildings where no one goes, and he's free to do whatever the hell he wants. That's called real power, son, when you don't answer to anyone but yourself. The story I was told was, when he crawled out for air, he would jump all over the place. Stupid, if you want my opinion, but there you have it. He's worked everywhere, State,

Treasury, and I think he did a stint at the Office of Management and Budget. I told you previously this guy knows where all the bodies are buried. He's your Alan Greenspan, Ben Bernanke, and Tim Geithner, and then some, all rolled up into one. The son of a bitch is a sneak. No one likes him. He doesn't answer to anyone, not even the president, and do not ask me where he got his power, because I don't know."

"What's his real name?"

"Owen Orzell."

Gus thought he was going to black out in relief now that he had a real name. He could hardly wait to get back to his room so he could call Maggie. He hoped she would do that cooing thing in his ear.

The general's eyes were drooping. Gus hoped he didn't fall asleep on him. "Can you give me a clue as to the best way to get in touch with him? If I'm understanding you correctly, the man is invincible as well as invisible."

"Stalk him, son, would be my advice."

"But, sir, I need a jumping-off place. A go-to person who can tell me where he hangs his hat."

"Son, I can't help you there. Maybe you could hire one of those fancy D.C. private-eye firms."

Gus started to say something, but then he realized the general had fallen asleep. He offered up a crisp salute, turned his chair around, and headed for the door. He had to struggle to get the door open, but he managed. At the nurses' station, he stopped to say good night and to thank the red-haired nurse. "The general fell asleep."

The nurse nodded. "He's on some pretty powerful pain meds. Take care, Gus. Come back and visit, and I don't mean operation-wise. The general will be glad of the company. His wife . . . she doesn't stay long. Hospitals depress her, she said. All they do is fight. At least they did when he came in for his initial surgery. Shhh, don't say anything."

"My lip is zipped," Gus said as he wheeled himself to the elevator.

Back in his room, he whipped out his cell, called Maggie, reported his news, and waited to see if she would coo in his ear. She didn't; instead, she hung up on him. He was so disappointed, he wanted to bawl. Instead, he brushed his teeth and stripped down. He was in bed with the lights out ten minutes later. Maybe he could dream that Maggie was cooing in his ear.

Isabelle relayed Maggie's information to Abner as Maggie was giving it to her over the phone. Abner's fingers flew over the keyboard. He sat back and waited. It took exactly forty-seven minutes to gather the information on the phantom known as Owen Orzell.

Abner was so gleeful, Isabelle couldn't help but laugh. "Is this our reading material for the evening?"

"It is. And it will wrap up my assignment for your . . . people. Then we can start to enjoy the Christmas season."

"I hate to burst your bubble, Abner, but my job will just begin once you turn over all your information to . . . my people. But I am sure I can squeeze in some quality time with you," she teased.

Abner pretended to pout. "Enough time to take the shuttle to New York, to Rockefeller Center to see the tree and ice-skate. I do it every year. Then I go to see the Rockettes and do some Christmas shopping. I've been doing it for years, but I thought it would be something you would enjoy."

"Absolutely I would enjoy that. I love New York, but I wouldn't want to live there," Isabelle confided.

"We'll make it work," Abner said confidently as he parceled out the papers he was plucking from the various printers. "Let's make a fire, have some wine, and go through this stuff. Then we can do other things. I'd like to turn this over to your people first thing in the morning. Be sure to thank Maggie for her due diligence."

"Why don't you thank her yourself? She's not your enemy, Abner. She loves you like the brother and the friend you are. Don't be stubborn. Friends are hard to come by these days, especially good friends, the kind you can count on through thick and thin. I'm going to feel really bad if you two don't make peace. She is my friend, Abner, and that is never going to change."

"I'll call her tomorrow."

"No, you should call her tonight."

Abner sighed and reached for his cell. He punched in Maggie's number. "Hey, Maggie. It's Abner. I just wanted to thank you for the heads-up. I was chasing my tail on that JJ business. I got everything you guys want and need. I'll turn it over in the morning. I just wanted to say thanks. You doing okay, Maggie?" He listened, then laughed. "Good luck."

"You were right, Isabelle. I'm glad I called. She was really nice, and she thanked me. She said she's in love with a guy in a wheelchair."

"She is. He's going to get out of the chair in a few months. Even if he doesn't, she'll be with him. I think it's wonderful."

"I agree. Maggie is one of a kind."

"That she is."

"But then so are you, Isabelle Flanders."

Isabelle laughed. "Tell me more. I love to be flattered."

"How about . . . ?"

Chapter 23

The ice storm that descended on Washington, D.C., and lasted four days, according to the weathermen, was the worst storm in over forty years. The nation's capital shut down; government workers were furloughed because of road conditions, heating problems, and loss of power. A generator was a luxury if one was fortunate enough to find one. Salt and sand were also luxuries that couldn't be had. Sanitation workers were working double shifts and could barely keep their eyes open when they did report to work. Even the news anchors were unshaven and wrinkled when they faced the cameras to offer grim hope that it would all soon be over.

And when it was over, it rained, which caused flooding. Then it started to snow late Sunday afternoon, when the Sisters had all made it safely out to Pinewood for dinner. The talk was mostly about the weather until after dinner, when Isabelle presented Abner's report.

The group was clustered around the table in the war room. Everyone was present except Nellie and Elias.

The boys, honorary members of the Sisterhood, were in

awe that finally, they were being permitted to sit in on and participate in a working meeting. They were stunned when Charles said their input would be appreciated.

Charles stepped down from the dais, where he usually held court. In front of each chair was a copy of Abner Tookus's report. "It's all some heavy reading, so I thought Isabelle could give us a short summary, and you can all follow with the report."

Isabelle didn't bother to stand up and address the group. She leaned back in her chair and said, "The short version is that Maggie found out, thanks to Gus Sullivan, that JJ is Owen Orzell. That's what took so long. With that information, Abner was able to develop the information you see in front of you. JJ, or Jody Jumper, is or was a less-than-endearing nickname given to Mr. Orzell by people in the Treasury Department. There's a picture of him in the file, and it is not a good one. Mr. OO, as Abner calls him, seems to have an aversion to the camera. It was the only picture he could come up with.

"Mr. OO is all over the map. Sometimes he's at Treasury, sometimes, at the State Department, and sometimes, inside the E-Ring at the Pentagon. He's one of those people who is so ordinary, you don't look at him twice. That's Abner's assessment. He was not able to find any association with the men on your list. Daniels, Gray, Maris, or Logan. There were meetings scheduled with all five men, but it was always recorded, and those meetings didn't bear any fruit that Abner could find.

"Mr. OO did have a meeting six months ago, back in June, a luncheon meeting with Jason Parker. Abner found that out strictly by chance because he does the security for the Occidental Restaurant, where all the power brokers like to go and be seen. When he was running the tapes, he just happened to see the two men. We have to decide what that means. When I left, he was working on doing a 'deep hack job,' as he put it, on Jason Parker. He promised to download it and send it on if he came up with anything that will help us.

"Abner said that there is no such thing as full disclosure among the agencies. Each agency guards its turf ferociously. Abner found four funds that are monitored and that Congress knows about. Standard, nothing wrong there, all agencies abroad have them just the way we do, but there is accountability.

"For the most part, no questions get asked when those monies get disbursed. The *big* fund that seems to be in question and guarded by Mr. OO . . . On that one there are no leads, no trails, no numbers to follow. In other words, for all intents and purposes, it simply does not exist. At least on paper or in a file somewhere. Abner and a lady who needs to remain anonymous are the ones who wrote the software for the CIA. If Abner can't find it, it isn't there. Which brings us to the question, where is it?"

Everyone started to jabber at once. The questions flew all over the room.

"How much money are we talking about?"

"Millions with an *M* or billions with a *B?*"

"Is it in a bank or a brokerage house?"

"How can someone hide that kind of money?"

"Is there just one signatory on the account?"

"In this day and age, how could any agency not have safeguards in place and allow just one person to control that kind of money with no accountability?"

Annie bristled. "If that fund is so secret, and the president wasn't aware of it, how did she find out? Why did she set up that nonexistent agency that she wants us to work for? Why did she give us the gold shields? We were to name our own price, and she didn't quibble about it, according to Lizzie. Of course we haven't been paid the money up front, like we requested."

"We haven't done a job yet, dear," Myra said.

Ted Robinson cleared his throat. "Maybe when she tried to get the money to transfer it from the other agencies, since she seems to be in the dark about the *big* fund, there wasn't enough, then somehow the four different agencies let it slip that she should tap the *big* fund as opposed to their own. Think about it. It makes sense. The CIA is the eight-hundred-pound gorilla here. That's just my opinion," he added as he looked from one face to the other.

"You know what, Ted? That makes real sense," Jack said.

The others agreed.

"Maybe we should arrange one of those Come to Jesus meetings with those guys," Bert said.

"And that would be what exactly?" Kathryn asked.

"Get Daniels, Maris, Logan, and Gray in a room someplace. Sweat them. Or do it separately. *Before* you go after Mr. OO," Bert said.

"That makes sense, too," Jack said as he looked around at the faces watching him the way they had homed in on Ted.

"It's counterproductive to go through the four agencies. Let's cut to the chase and go after Mr. OO," Nikki said. "Let's make a plan. What do we have, Isabelle, in the way of an address for Mr. OO?"

"Abner did find one. It's on page three."

The only sound in the room was the sound of pages turning.

"It's a run-down three-story brownstone on Kilbourne Place in Mt. Pleasant," Charles said. "Unless it's a decoy, and we won't know for sure until we investigate. I can have one of my people on it within minutes. What say you all?"

In unison, they all said, "Do it!"

Charles moved quickly back to his workstation and typed out a directive. He was back within minutes. "One hour to put my people in place, another hour to infiltrate the building. We should hear something in a little over two hours. Remember now, it's Sunday, so if Mr. OO is in residence, all we can do is surveillance, which means my people will be in place to follow Mr. OO in the morning, when he goes to work. If he's home, we'll know something in a little over an hour."

"Then let's spend the time studying this report," Yoko said.

"As we read it, let's throw out questions to each other," Alexis said.

"First, let's see exactly who Mr. OO is. Let's all read his profile, then run it up the flagpole," Myra said. The room went silent as all eyes turned to the briefing materials Abner had prepared.

"As long as it isn't that *other* pole," Nikki quipped.

The room went silent again as more pages turned. Soft murmurs could be heard as the group digested what was on the written pages.

Charles waited until Yoko, who was the last to finish, turned the final page. "Comments please."

"I think the guy is stealing from the fund he controls," Jack said.

"I think he leads a double life," Ted said.

"Where did he get the money to buy a three-floor brownstone, run-down or not?" Kathryn asked.

"It's in a run-down neighborhood, and it's a cover," Bert said. "I think he has some fancy digs somewhere else," he added hastily.

Esposito spoke for the first time. "Do you want me to go up there and take some pictures? If Ted is agreeable, we could talk to some of the neighbors, maybe say the *Post* is running some kind of special something or other. People love getting their pictures taken and being in the newspaper. We could even do a Google Earth thing right now if you all want to see the neighborhood."

Charles immediately clicked on the big-screen TV hanging on the wall. The room grew quiet the way it always did when Lady Justice, scales in hand, appeared on the screen. Charles pressed more buttons, then clicked and clicked. "There it is! That is Mr. OO's address." He pressed another button, and the picture became so clear, they could see vehicles and the license plate numbers on the cars.

"No pedestrians are out and about. Of course, the weather could have something to do with that. So, ladies and gentlemen, do we want Mr. Esposito and Ted to take a trip to Mt. Pleasant?"

"Tomorrow morning would be good," Maggie said. "People do not like to open their doors at night to strangers. Sometimes, they even call the police."

Charles nodded. "We should be hearing from Avery Snowden's people shortly. Go back to Mr. OO's profile."

Annie flipped pages. "Here we go. Mr. OO was born and raised in Boston. He attended Boston University. He was the valedictorian of his class. He got a master's at twenty-one and had his Ph.D. at the age of twenty-four. Smart man. Both his parents were professors at Boston University. Equally smart, so it's easy to see where the man got his brains. He's forty-nine years old. He'll turn fifty in February. Maybe he's having a midlife crisis," she said, tongue in cheek.

"He went into government service early on and has

stayed on the government's payroll. As to where he got the money to buy the brownstone, it looks like he bought it about fifteen years ago, when his parents passed away. Their estate passed to him, and it was rather robust. There isn't much activity in his brokerage account, which also came to him from his parents. It's all invested in safe, conservative holdings. Once in a while, he makes a modest investment in stocks, but never more than five hundred shares at a time. I don't see anything here that raises a red flag."

"It says here that Mr. OO had a close friend in college. Joel Jessup, who was a financial wizard much like Mr. OO. Abner scanned a picture of him from his college yearbook. Big guy. Just as brainy as Mr. OO. His peers wrote messages in the book and almost all of them refer in one way or another to gambling. One even said in the years to come, he would take over Las Vegas. Another message referred to him as Mr. Lucky. I guess that's why he and Mr. OO were such good friends. Before you can ask, neither man is gay. Both dated heavily when they were in college. Nothing serious for either man. Mr. Jessup died in a skiing accident in Austria nine years ago. Mr. OO was with him but not skiing that day. They had just traveled from Monaco because both men liked to gamble. Mr. OO was feeling poorly that day, and that's why he didn't go skiing," Yoko said.

"How did Abner get all this?" Bert asked, awe ringing in his voice.

"You don't want to know, so don't ask," Isabelle snapped. "You wanted information, you paid for it—or, at least, you will pay for it, I trust—and here it is, so stop right there."

"Okay, okay," Bert said, looking at Kathryn, who was

glaring at him as much as to say, "You're here, but you have to keep quiet." Bert's lips snapped shut.

"Is that when Mr. OO went to ground and became a recluse?" Alexis asked.

"Yes," Charles said, reading ahead.

"Maybe he wigged out at the loss of his best and only friend," Nikki said.

"More than likely," Myra said, as she fingered the pearls at her neck. "Neither of them was married, is that right?"

"No, dear, neither man was married. Mr. Jessup ran a think tank in Washington. He was very wealthy, according to his financials," Charles said.

"When he died, where did his money go?" Ted asked.

Charles smiled as he looked down at the papers he was holding. "To Mr. OO."

"Do Mr. OO's financials bear that out?" Annie asked.

Charles smiled again. "No, they do not. That has to mean Mr. OO has another bank or brokerage account somewhere else. Under another name would be my guess, or possibly a corporation offshore, which is more likely. The man is considered a financial genius, so bear that in mind."

"I guess, then, we have to pay Mr. OO a visit and get our information firsthand," Nikki said, her eyes sparking dangerously.

The Sisters hooted their approval of her suggestion.

"Uh-oh, what's this on the next-to-the-last page?" Jack said, holding up a sheet of paper. "Oh, I see, it's Abner's personal note that he thinks the CIA is in danger of either being divided up, castrated, or put out to pasture. Can that be?" he asked, a dumbfounded look on his face.

"In this day and age, anything is possible," Charles said. "The current administration has had nothing but trouble since Martine Connor took office. It's almost as if her administration is out to get her and destroy her in the process. I'm going to take that one step further and say it's because she is our first woman president. That should get you ladies all fired up," he said quietly.

"I'm already all fired up," Kathryn shot back.

"So are the rest of us," Annie said.

"She's not going to run again," Ted blurted.

"And you know this . . . how?" Maggie barked.

"Hey, it's my opinion, okay? I do cover the White House. My colleagues agree. We see and hear stuff. If you're smart enough to put it together, that's what you come up with. It's all whispers and snide comments, but it's out there. You know as well as I do, Maggie, when it's out there, *it's out there!*"

Maggie had the good grace to look sheepish. "Ted's right. Where there's smoke, there's fire. Sorry about the cliché."

"That doesn't make any sense, no offense to you, Ted and Maggie. If she is thinking about not running again, why go through all this? Why set up a nonexistent agency? Why hire us? Why give us those gold shields? We must be missing something," Annie blustered.

Myra had a death grip on her newly strung pearls. "I agree with Annie a hundred percent. This is not making sense."

"This is Washington, Myra. It's not supposed to make sense," Nikki said.

"When something doesn't make sense, it is usually a lie," Isabelle said.

They all agreed with Isabelle. Ted and Maggie both pouted.

Isabelle's phone took that moment to chirp. She looked at it and handed it to Charles, who rushed to his workstation. She turned to the others then and said, "Abner's download on Jason Parker."

They talked then in soft whispers so as not to disturb Charles. Lady Justice, who was still on the big screen, stared down at all of them.

Charles actually looked gleeful when he returned to take his position at the round table. "It seems that our friend Mr. Tookus was able to . . . ah, tap into Mr. Parker's computer and view his day planner. Remember the picture taken of Mr. Tookus and Mr. Parker having lunch at the Occidental Restaurant? According to the notation in Mr. Parker's planner, he was having lunch that day with one Joel Jessup. Now," he said, tongue in cheek, "we have to ask ourselves, how is that possible since Mr. Jessup died nine years ago, and Mr. Tookus was kind enough to provide a death certificate issued by the Austrian authorities?"

Alexis leaned across the table and gaped at Charles. "Jason had lunch either with a dead man or with a man who assumed his identity. Is that what you're saying?"

"Yes, dear. Remember now, we only have that one picture of Mr. OO, or someone we think is Mr. OO. The man having lunch with Mr. Parker might not even be Mr. Orzell. But then you have to ask yourselves why Mr. Parker would enter the name of Mr. Jessup in his day planner. His day planner was safe and secure in his computer— or at least he must have assumed that it was."

All eyes turned to Maggie, as though she might have the answer. She shrugged. "I do not have a clue. I really didn't know the man all that well. I can tell you that he is not shy about seeking publicity for his firm. Within a week of coming back from Camp David, he was sending out brochures with a picture of himself and President Connor.

He even ran a tagline that read, 'Does she or doesn't she invest with Parker Investments?' "

Harry Wong spoke for the first time since entering the war room. "I think he's a clone of Bernie Madoff. Now that I'm opening my mail on a daily basis," he said, looking pointedly at Jack, "I see those stupid brochures he sends out on a weekly basis. I didn't think for a minute that the president would invest her funds with someone like him. I still can't figure out why she allowed someone of his ilk to go to Camp David. He's a charlatan."

Ilk. Charlatan. Jack blinked, then blinked again. Good old Harry was on a roll. "And you know all this because you now open your mail. That is stupendous! You know what else, Harry? You are absolutely right. I agree with you one hundred percent."

Harry flexed his fingers in Jack's direction in a not-so-subtle threat.

"Okay, okay, I'll quit while I'm ahead." Jack turned to Charles. "Did Abner run Parker's financials?"

"He certainly did. And we now have his client list. You might be surprised, Mr. Robinson, to find out you are on Mr. Parker's client list."

"*Was.* I bailed out," Ted said defensively. "I made money, so I can't complain." Maggie glared at him as though he was a traitor. "Hey, Maggie, I wasn't doing kissy poo with the guy like you were." Maggie continued to glare at her star reporter.

"At least you had the good sense to get out," Harry said generously.

Charles looked down at the papers he had printed out. "Mr. Parker has a very impressive client list. He appears to have considerable financial savvy. His biggest client is the aforementioned Joel Jessup. Said person appears to be very much alive, because he places orders on a regular basis.

He's making money at the speed of light, and Mr. Parker is racking up some very impressive commissions."

"Did Abner do a due diligence on Parker?" Nikki asked.

"He did, and he also ran a Dun & Bradstreet check. He started his business eight years ago, slowly at first. It looks like Mr. Jessup was his first client, and he brought in more clients. Slowly. Our deceased Mr. Jessup's initial investment was ten million.

"Now, Mr. Jessup's net worth at death was four and a half million. Plus two properties, a car, and a pickup truck. The properties are worth less than five hundred thousand dollars combined, and it appears that Mr. Orzell still owns them. The car and truck were sold for a total of twenty-six thousand dollars. After all bills were paid, his estate was worth precisely $4,111,067.87.

"Given the tax regulations at the time he died, Mr. OO would have had to pay taxes on the amount he inherited above two million. And yet this deceased man, or someone presenting himself as this deceased man, invested ten million. Even an idiot can figure out that none of this is computing," Charles said.

"So that can only mean he is playing fast and loose with the CIA fund. And it's possible our Mr. Orzell has other investment accounts spread all over the place, using even more monies from that *big* fund. Mr. OO keeps the earnings and no one is the wiser. Is that what you think, Charles?" Nikki asked.

"Even though the economy is bad and the market has taken a hit, we're still talking serious income no one knows about. Wonder how his tax records are done. We need to find that out. Like really soon."

Isabelle was already texting Abner to tell him what Nikki had said.

"Done!"

Chapter 24

The group was about to retire to the main part of the house at nine o'clock when Charles received his first call from Avery Snowden. He held up his hand, a signal that everyone should wait. The Sisters sat down as the boys milled about.

Charles listened for a good five minutes before he powered down and advanced toward the group. "For starters, it's snowing heavily in the District, which makes visibility difficult, but Avery does have Zeiss night-vision binoculars. There are lights on all three floors. Using the binoculars, Avery was able to see the nameplates on the mailboxes. It appears Mr. OO lives on the second floor. The names on the first-floor mailboxes are Evan Holloway and Denise Pomroy. Owen Orzell is on the second floor, and the third floor is rented to Joel Jessup."

"Well, now, isn't that amazing?" Annie said.

"Now what?" Myra asked.

"Now we're going upstairs, and I'm going to make us some hot chocolate, which I will serve with my four-layer Black Forest cake."

"Shame on you, Charles. There go my hips." Nikki giggled.

Back in the main part of the house, the dogs welcomed them with joyous barks. Charles opened the door, and they barreled out into the snow.

"Do you want us to go to the barn and get the snow-blowers?" Jack asked.

"Morning will be soon enough. It looks like it's going to snow through the night. No sense in doing double the work," Charles said, pretending not to see the relief on the boys' faces.

The dogs were back in the house within minutes, shaking off the snow. Charles poured hot chocolate while Myra cut the cake. Annie passed the plates around the table.

Kathryn was the first one to say she was tired. She offered to help clean up, but Yoko held up her hand and asked everyone to wait a minute. When she had everyone's attention, a smile split her features. "Harry and I want you to know we're expecting. I'm almost four months along."

The room rang with excitement as the Sisters crowded around Yoko, hugging and kissing her, then hugging and kissing her again. The boys crowded around Harry, who looked so out of it that Jack slapped him on the back and said, "You son of a gun! You're going to be a father, Harry!"

A second later, Harry was flat on his back on the floor.

Yoko looked down at her husband. "Ignore him. Every time he thinks about becoming a father, he does that."

The others roared with laughter as Bert and Ted hoisted Harry to his feet. Bert slung Harry over his shoulder and ran through the house and up the stairs, with Harry's body twitching every which way, but he didn't say a word until Bert set him back on his feet.

"C'mon, Harry, you are going to be a great father. You already got your feet wet when we took care of all those babies in Bryan Bell's baby ring. Even Espinosa said you were as good as he was, and he had, what, nine, or was it eleven brothers and sisters to take care of when they were babies?

"Listen, Harry, you need to stop thinking about yourself and think about Yoko now." Bert waved his arms about and started to wax poetic. "Think of this as a stage play. You stand in the wings and watch. Yoko is the star performer. That's another way of saying, you don't count, Harry. End of story. Wait a minute. You reach star power for the 2:00 a.m. and 4:00 a.m. feedings, providing Yoko supplements the baby's milk with bottles. Most mothers do that these days. I heard that on the Discovery Channel."

Harry, his eyes as round as he could make them, looked at Bert and said, "Eat shit, Bert!" He stomped off and then stopped and turned around. "I meant to say, Eat poop. Yoko said I have to stop cussing and being so violent. That's why I didn't kill you just now."

Back downstairs, the kitchen was tidy, and the girls were getting ready to head up to the second floor. They all crowded around the door for one last look at snow that was coming down heavier than ever.

The good nights were brief; then the kitchen was silent.

"I can't believe I'm spending the night when I just live down the road," Annie grumbled.

"It's like old times, dear," Myra said. "Isn't it wonderful that Yoko finally told us what we already knew?"

"I so hope it's a little girl," Annie said. "Yoko is so tiny. Do you think the baby will be tiny like her?" Annie asked fretfully.

"I don't think Yoko's baby is going to be a bruiser like Little Jack. Normal, six pounds and a few ounces, would be my guess. It will all depend on Yoko. She did say her morning sickness has abated, and she's feeling really good. You're missing Fergus, aren't you, Annie?"

"No, of course not. Yes, Myra, I am. I don't know what's come over me where that man is concerned."

"Do you think, Annie, that you might be in love with Mr. Duffy?"

Annie flopped down on one of the kitchen chairs. "I'm thinking I might be, Myra."

"That's so wonderful. Stop being such a sourpuss. Enjoy what you have and don't go . . . you know . . . screwing it up."

Annie laughed and reached for Myra's hand and squeezed it. "I'll try not to. So, tell me, what do you think of tonight's discussion?"

"Which part? We discussed quite a few things. If you're referring to Mr. OO, I think we can handle that with very little sweat. If you're referring to the gossip about the president, then I have to tell you I don't know what to think. Why would she set us up, then abandon us? If she decides not to run for office, we are out of the loop. I suppose the whole thing could be a one-time-only job, for want of a better way to put it. We clean up Mr. OO, find the money, and then we're done. What do you think, Charles?"

"What I think is, I'm going back to work. I'm worried about Avery and his men on the stakeout in this weather. Since our quarry appears to be in residence, it is highly unlikely that he'll go anywhere till morning. If they're back on the job by five o'clock, that should work."

"Run along then, dear, and tend to your business. Annie and I are going to bed."

"Are we really going to bed, Myra?"

"Absolutely not. Let's go in the living room and look at my Christmas tree. Do you know any gossip?"

"Myra, I've been with you all day. How could I hear any gossip?"

"Because you're you, Annie, that's how." Myra smiled.

"Well, since you put it like that, I might have overheard *something*. I saw Bert showing the boys a ring he bought for Kathryn for Christmas. *An engagement ring,* Myra. Ted personally took him to Dorchester Jewelers in Summerville, South Carolina, two weeks ago. The same store where Ted bought Maggie's ring. They drove down over the weekend, and Jill and Patsy opened the store on Sunday just for them. Since I was sneaking around, I couldn't see the ring, but the boys whistled, so I guess it's something pretty special."

"But I thought Kathryn didn't . . ."

"That was back then, Myra, when we were all at sixes and sevens. Everyone has their lives back now and is thinking straight. Kathryn is a different person these days. She's shed a lot of the guilt she's been carrying around since her husband's death. The girls have talked to her. I've talked to her. She does love Bert. That's a given. She told Nikki she'd like to have a spring wedding."

Myra made a face. "Why didn't I know any of this?"

Annie made a face right back. "In order to know things, you have to ask questions. It's called being nosy, Myra. I am nosy. Therefore, I get the news, the scoop, the information I am now telling you."

"You should be ashamed of yourself, Anna de Silva. That's terrible. What's even more terrible is, you admit to it. What else do you know?"

"Nothing. I'm going to bed."

Disgruntled, Myra followed her friend up the stairs. She looked at the big four-poster and longed to have Charles with her. She sighed. Charles was Charles and was doing what he loved to do, even if it was the middle of the night. She turned the dials on the electric blanket on her side of the bed. "When you can't have the real thing, improvise," she muttered as she prepared for sleep.

*   *   *

It was 5:00 a.m. and still dark when Avery Snowden and three of his men arrived at Kilbourne Place in a rusty pickup truck with a plow hitched to the front. Metallic signs on the doors read SANITATION DEPARTMENT. A second truck was behind him with identical metallic signs but no snowplow attached. The game plan was to plow out the cars on the street so Mr. OO wouldn't be tempted to stay home. While Avery maneuvered the plow, the occupants in the other truck watched the brownstone with eagle eyes.

"The lights went on at exactly the same time on floors two and three. At five twenty. The first floor stayed dark," one of his men reported.

As Avery worked the plow, he listened to his operatives report. "That's because he probably controls the switch for the third floor. No one lives on the third floor. Don't argue with me, Simpson. Just keep your eyes on the front door, and you peel outta here the minute the dude starts up his car. I'm going to plow the road now."

By six o'clock, the street was completely plowed, but the cars were blocked with the exception of two, one registered to Owen Orzell and the second one to Joel Jessup. It was still dark out, but there was no sign of life or light on the first floor. At 6:15, the lights on the second and third floors went out.

"Look sharp, lads!" Avery ordered as a tall, thin man walked out of the door of the brownstone. He looked around, shook his head, and made his way down the snow-covered steps by holding on to the railing, then picked his way carefully to his car. He was dressed in a camel-colored shearling jacket. He wore stout rubber boots and a black watch cap pulled low over his ears. A plaid scarf was wrapped and draped around his neck. He pulled on gloves he had in his pockets.

It took Mr. OO a good fifteen minutes to scrape the snow off his windshield and the back window. All the while the car was running, with the heater going full blast. From time to time, he stopped to look around as the street came to life and residents came out to ready their cars for another day of work.

Avery moved his truck with the plow slightly forward and got in front of the gray Saturn Mr. OO was driving. The second sanitation truck had been joined by a third truck, equally battered and junky-looking. "Just in case he makes one of us," Avery said into the mike on his collar.

The moment all three trucks moved into traffic, a small black car slid into Mr. OO's parking spot. Two men bundled up for the weather got out and walked up the steps to the brownstone. It was just turning light when the door opened. The two men stood a moment to see if an alarm would sound. None did.

Inside, they split up, going from room to room. One of the men snapped pictures; the other one looked through everything, being careful not to touch anything, per Snowden's instructions.

It was a comfortable apartment, but it had only one bathroom and three bedrooms, one of which was an office. The kitchen was big enough to hold a round table and four chairs. The dining room had a complete set of furniture, as did the living room. The furniture was neither new nor old. It looked used and comfortable. A seventy-six-inch television set hung on one wall. The bookshelves were full of technical and financial books. The bedroom had a king-size bed that had not been made but otherwise was neat and tidy. The bathroom was old-fashioned, with a claw-footed tub and shower curtain. The floor was covered with black-and-white tile that was chipped in a few places. There was no vanity, but there was a medicine cabinet that was loaded with vitamins and shaving gear. The sink was a pedestal style, also chipped. It was as clean as the tub, but both had brown rust stains running from the faucets to the drains.

"Jensen, come here and look at this!"

Jensen looked to where his colleague was pointing as he snapped picture after picture. "I'm betting this set of stairs leads into the third-floor apartment. This trapdoor beats building in a set of steps. If you're trying to be sneaky, that is. Look, here's the light switch. Watch, it turns on the light at the top of these steps as well as the light in this bedroom."

"After you, Jensen," Collier said as he snapped more pictures. "What's up there?"

"It opens into a bedroom just like the one down below. Not much in here, from what I can see. Secondhand furniture, from the looks of it. No one lives here. There's dust and spiderwebs everywhere. Hold on till I check the fridge. Nope, it's not even plugged in."

"What did you expect? A ghost? Snowden said the man whose name is on the mailbox is dead."

"If you got all of your pictures, Collier, close it up and be sure to turn off the lights. Snowden said not to touch anything, just take pictures."

"Just want to take one of the inside of the refrigerator and freezer. Who knows what might or might not lurk in there? You didn't touch anything did you, Jensen?"

"Well yeah, but like you, I'm wearing latex. Hurry up, Collier. I'm hearing noises coming from downstairs. Whoever lives there is probably getting ready to go to work. We are not supposed to be seen."

"The guy likes frozen food. There are enough Hungry-Man dinners in this freezer to feed an army. Keeps his vodka in the refrigerator. He doesn't eat healthy. There's not one vegetable or piece of fruit anywhere. Everyone has bananas," Collier grumbled. "And get this," he said, opening one of the cabinet doors, "the guy must be addicted to Cocoa Puffs. There are eight boxes here." He clicked his camera, the shot preserved forever. "Okay, I'm ready. Let's split."

"Try not to make any noise going down the steps. We don't want to have to answer any questions on the way out."

The two men literally tiptoed down the stairs. Jensen was holding the door open for Collier when the door to the ground-floor apartment opened.

"You coming or going?" the tenant asked.

Before he could answer, a surly-looking woman bundled up like Nanook of the North followed her partner out the door.

"Just leaving. We came by to pick up Joel, but he said he isn't going into work today. It's a mess out there, buddy, so be careful. Oh, you're going to need a shovel. We plowed all you people in."

At the tenant's stormy expression, Jensen said, "Look, we didn't have a choice. The city says plow, we plow. Like I said, get your shovel. And you should think about shoveling and salting these steps. Someone could have a serious accident."

"Hey, buddy, I don't own this dump, so tell that to the owner. I just live here."

While Jensen was carrying on his dialogue, Collier was uploading his pictures and texting Avery Snowden on what was going on.

"Good work, lads," Avery said happily. "Meet us at O'Rileys, and I'm buying breakfast. Our bird just went into the Pentagon. Wait for us if you get there first."

Collier sent off a text that read, Will do.

Chapter 25

It was ten o'clock, breakfast was over, the kitchen cleaned, the boys were outside with the snowblowers, and the girls headed to the war room with Charles. They took their assigned seats at the center table. Charles clicked on the remote, and Lady Justice welcomed them with a burst of sound. Seconds later, the pictures of the interior of the brownstone in Mt. Pleasant appeared on the screen. Charles did a running commentary as he used his pointer to indicate what he thought might be of interest, particularly the pull-down stairs that led to the third floor and a close-up of the electric switch, which he followed with a picture of the nameplate over the mailbox outside the front door that read JOEL JESSUP in neat block letters.

"Since Mr. Snowden's people didn't have any problem picking the lock, I assume you ladies won't have a problem, either. There is no alarm system, something I personally find strange," Charles said.

"He's lived in that house for years, and nothing happened. Now, if he acts like he's done something wrong and has security out the ying yang, then, yes, that would be cause for concern," Annie said.

"He feels safe," Myra said.

"How many people do you think know his best friend passed away? Probably no one, and if they do remember a friend dying, it is doubtful they would remember the name. I think Mr. OO is very confident and also very clever," Nikki said.

"Not clever enough. We found him, and the best part is that the man doesn't have a clue that his world is going to come crashing down around him," Kathryn said.

"So what's our game plan?" Alexis asked.

"This is what I think we should do," Isabelle said. "Let's round up Jason Parker and invite him to Mr. OO's house. We, of course, will already be there waiting. We bring him in early, work him over, pick his brain so that when Mr. OO arrives, we have it all nailed down. Quick in and out, and we collect from the president and go about our lives.

"One more thing. This might not be the right time or the right place, but my heart and my gut are telling me it is. When we finish up here, I want to give back my gold shield, and I don't want to do this anymore."

The silence in the room was so deafening, it was eerie. All Charles could do was stare at his chicks in stunned surprise.

"Oh, Isabelle, I am so glad you had the courage to say it first. I have been trying to find a way to say it since I arrived. With the baby coming, I just want to be a mother. I want to spend all my time with my little family. Harry feels the same way. He is trying to find a way to tell Bert and Jack he doesn't want to go to the trials in Hong Kong. He is determined to look after me while I'm pregnant, and

I cannot deny him that. We also want to give back our gold shields," Yoko said.

Alexis jumped in and said, "I made the decision to take Nikki up on her offer and go to law school full-time. If I can, I'll work part-time. Joseph and I talked about it, and we will get married at some point but not right now. Neither one of us wants the gold shields. We want to live someplace where we have neighbors so we can put down some roots. Grady needs me to spend more time with him, too."

"Jack and I have been talking about this for months," Nikki said. "We both agreed that after Harry went to the trials, we would also pack it in. That was in the spring, but after Yoko's announcement, right now is looking even better. We had our time in the sun, we made a difference in quite a few lives, and I, for one, have no regrets. But I do want a life with my husband. We're thinking of buying a bigger house with a yard, and we are seriously thinking of adopting. We want some dogs and neighbors we can count on, and like Alexis said, we want to get our lives back. Jack is going to join the firm. We, too, want to turn in our gold shields."

"There's nothing much for me to say other than that I agree with all of you," Kathryn said. "I told Bert I would marry him when the cherry blossoms are in bloom. Bert is going to join Nikki's firm with Jack. I'm going to keep trucking for a little while, and we're also going to look into adopting and getting a companion for Murphy. I, for one, can't wait to give those gold shields back."

Annie was so stunned, she didn't know what to say. She was finally able to get her tongue to work. She knew what she said now was probably going to be the most important thing she ever said in her life. "Please, you all look like you're going to cry. You should be happy that you will be getting your lives back, and each of you deserves that plus more. It's like Nikki said. All good things have to come to an end. I'll be going back and forth to Scotland with Fergus when he has free time. I think I speak for Myra and myself when I say whatever you all want to do is okay with me. Except for one thing. I'm keeping that damn gold shield. I think I earned it. What about you, Myra? If you keep yours, we can make bookends, and you get them one month, and I get them the next month. Joint ownership."

Myra forced herself to smile, even though she felt like she'd been kicked in the gut by a mule. "Damn straight! I'm with Annie all the way. Joint ownership of the bookends it is. This will give me more time to knit afghans for hospice, like my old friend Claudeen does in Arizona."

All eyes turned to Charles. "I understand, and I congratulate all of you. I'll be more than happy to turn in my gold shield so you can send it along with the rest. I'll get back to writing my boring memoirs and planning Sunday dinners for you all. I hope that won't change. We're family."

The Sisters all started to cry. Annie the loudest. "Okay, okay, you can have the damn bookends to send along. It won't be unanimous unless we all turn them in, right, Myra?"

Myra reared up. "No," she said, tears rolling down her cheeks. "I'm keeping mine! I want something tangible in my hand to remember how it all started and how it all concluded. I'm keeping it!"

And no one argued.

"Well, now that that's settled," Charles said, with a catch in his voice, "let's all get back to the matter at hand so we can wrap up this one last mission and go out in a blaze of glory."

*   *   *

It took another two hours before the Sisters had their plan down pat. When they returned to the main part of the house, they were surprised to see the boys cooking up a storm in the kitchen, to Charles's dismay.

"Whatever you're cooking, it smells wonderful, but did you really have to use every pot and pan in the house?" Charles asked.

"Don't worry, dear. We'll clean up. Just sit down and enjoy whatever the boys prepared for us," Myra said.

What the boys prepared turned out to be homemade chicken soup from the freezer, which just needed to be thawed and heated, grilled bacon and cheese sandwiches, and Jell-O that failed to set so they had to drink it out of cups.

Ninety minutes later, when the kitchen had been restored to its normally pristine condition, the Sisters took center stage, first by saying that everyone now knew that the vigilantes would retire after the completion of the current mission. The boys' collective sigh of satisfaction was duly noted.

"Now, this is what we decided while you guys were out there playing in the snow," Nikki said, an impish grin on her face. "We ran off copies of the plan for all of you, so follow along with us. The pictures are of the interior of Mr. Orzell's house. We plan to get there around noon tomorrow afternoon and will wait for him to come home from work.

"Right now we are waiting for Mr. Snowden to get back to Charles so he can tell us about what time we can expect Orzell to get home from the office. What we want you guys to do is go to Jason Parker's residence, wherever that may be, pick him up, and bring him to Mr. Orzell's house. We'll stash him in his client's, Joel Jessup's, third-floor apartment until Orzell gets home. Nice, neat, and tidy. Everything will be contained."

"What about the tenants on the first floor?" Ted asked.

"First thing in the morning, before they leave for work, one of Snowden's men is going to tell them they're installing a new furnace and there will be no heat until the next day. They will also give them some money to go to a hotel. Just in case Orzell doesn't leave first, the way he did this morning, Snowden's men will wait it out. After we are all safe inside, they'll stretch yellow caution tape across the front and put a new lock on the foyer door."

"Who is picking up Parker?" Bert asked.

"All of you. Ted is going to say he's bringing him new clients. Espinosa is going to be taking pictures for a phony layout and say that Ted is going to be doing an article. That should work like a charm because the man loves good press. How you get him to Orzell's is something you all have to work out. We have our own details to take care of. Any questions?" Annie asked.

The boys shook their heads.

"Then we should hit the road," Jack said. "The temperature is dropping, and the roads are going to freeze up again. Thanks for everything, Myra."

Twenty minutes later the caravan of cars was gone. Myra closed the door and turned to look at Annie and Charles, her eyes misty.

"Well, that damn well sucked," Annie said.

Myra ripped at the pearls on her neck and sent them flying across the kitchen. Annie and Charles gasped in horror as a flood of tears rolled down Myra's cheeks. "Tomorrow night, we'll be . . . *retired*," she sobbed.

The two women clung to each other as they sobbed out their misery. Charles looked on as he wrung his hands.

The dogs howled and circled the two wailing women, who ignored them.

"We need a drink, Charles. A stiff one. I think you need one, too, so you can think about your memoirs and how you're going to make your life interesting," Annie said as she led Myra into the living room, where a fire blazed and the Christmas tree sparkled.

"I wasn't expecting that, Annie. The worst part is, I can't blame them. They're young. They deserve to get on with their lives. I guess I even knew it was coming. I just didn't expect it to be this soon. Did you? What's taking Charles so long with our drinks?"

"I think he's picking up your pearls. You really made a statement, Myra, when you snatched those pearls and flung them across the room. Did that help? Do you feel better yet, Myra?"

"About as good as you felt that day you got your ass tattooed. You weren't expecting the pain, and I sure as hell wasn't. You're right, Annie. This really, really sucks."

"There is a bright spot. Yoko is going to have a baby, and I do think Nikki and Jack will follow through and adopt. Lizzie, Cosmo, and Little Jack are coming for Christmas, so we have that to look forward to."

Myra sniffled. "It's not the same thing, and you damn well know it, Annie. I must say you are taking this rather well."

"We don't have a choice, Myra. If we try to interfere, try to coax them to stay, they'll end up hating us. You like to knit. I'm sure we'll find some other interests to take up our time."

"Liar, liar, pants on fire!" Myra blubbered.

"Oh, good, here's Charles with our drinks. What should we drink to, Myra?"

"Our new lives!" Myra wailed.

Charles set the drinks down on the coffee table and ran from the room. He was so choked up, he was afraid that he was going to burst into tears himself. He must really be getting old, or else he just didn't realize how stupid he was. In a million years he never thought his chicks would fold and move on. Never. Ever.

A lone tear rolled down his cheek, then another one, until he was blinded with his own unhappiness.

Chapter 26

They were in place. The six-room apartment on Kilbourne Place was in lockdown mode.

Isabelle turned on the big-screen TV. "What will it be, girls? The Cooking Channel, the Shopping Channel, or *The Ellen Show?*"

"What are they cooking?" Kathryn asked.

Isabelle clicked on the Cooking Channel. "Some kind of fish with the head still on it. They're going to stuff it. Yuck! They're selling handbags on the Shopping Channel. Made out of candy wrappers. You wanna watch that?"

"Why not? A girl can always use another handbag," Alexis said as she peered at the colorful bags lacquered to a high shine.

The truth was, no one was the least bit interested in what was on the big screen. They were just yakking to pass the time until they got the call from Avery that Mr. OO was on the way.

"The roads are pretty good, and it finally stopped snowing. Maybe our guy will leave early today to beat traffic," Annie said.

"You wish," Myra said as she reached for the pearls that were no longer around her neck.

"The minute Avery calls, we have to go dark, and that means turning off the television," Nikki said. "I wonder how Jack and the others are making out with Jason Parker. No one said what *their* game plan was to get him here."

Yoko laughed. "Harry will simply put him to sleep, and they'll carry him in. Harry has no patience."

Myra's and Nikki's phones rang at the same time. Isabelle quickly turned off the TV. Her hand was on the light switch to darken the apartment when Nikki held up her hand, a signal to wait. Both women listened to the voices on the other end of their phones. Nikki spoke first. "Yoko was right. Parker is asleep in the back of Ted's car. They should be here in fifteen minutes. They cleaned out his office. They're bringing all his files, his client list, his personal laptop, and all the computers his people use.

"Parker Investments is no longer in business. They even put a sign on the door to that effect. It's a good thing that Avery's people cleared the street and put up those NO PARKING signs so we would all have parking spaces. That yellow tape is like magic. People actually respect it."

"Mr. OO's ETA is in twenty-five minutes, according to Avery. He's driving in front of him, and two of his people are behind him in case he makes a stop along the way. We'll be cutting it close if Jack and the boys are running late. Avery did say the roads are starting to ice up, so driving is hazardous," Myra said.

"So we sit and wait. Ten more minutes of light, then we cut it off," Nikki said.

"Are we going to shout 'Surprise!'" Kathryn asked. "Do any of you think he's going to put up a fight?"

"If you want to, dear. Cornered rats usually either spring at their tormentor or scurry off into the dark. By the way, have you all noticed that the man doesn't even have an artificial Christmas tree? There are no signs anywhere that a holiday is approaching," Annie said.

"And this means . . . what?" Yoko asked.

Annie shrugged. "Men aren't like women when it comes to holidays and sentiment. I read that somewhere. You can't just ignore Christmas," Annie said fretfully.

"Don't worry, dear. We'll make sure Mr. OO knows it is the holiday season," Myra said grimly.

The room went silent. Kathryn and Isabelle moved to the front window so they could report what was happening. Avery Snowden and Jack were reporting in every five minutes with progress updates.

"Douse the lights. A car is coming down the street very slowly. I think it's Jack. Yes, it's Jack, and Ted is right behind him. I wish we'd had the foresight to knock out that streetlight two doors up. No one is on the street, though, that I can see," Kathryn said.

"Okay, they're parking now. Doors are opening. Mr. OO is going to have to park behind him. I hope that doesn't make him suspicious that his parking space has been taken by a strange car," Isabelle said. "Ted has Parker on his shoulder. Okay, they're coming up the steps now. Door is opening downstairs. Someone needs to show them the way with the flashlight."

Nikki ran out to the hall with her Maglite.

Myra clicked on her phone, listened, and powered down. "Avery said ten more minutes, nine if they make the next traffic light."

A commotion ensued as the boys, in a change of plans, dumped Jason Parker on Mr. OO's bed, then duct-taped him to the bedpost. Jack's arms were full of files and laptops, as were everyone else's. He dumped everything un-ceremoniously on the floor.

Nikki handed Jack a flashlight. "You guys stay in here until we call you, okay? How long is he going to be out for?"

"How long do you want him out?" Harry asked.

"At least twenty minutes," Nikki responded.

"Your wish is my command," Harry said, walking over to the sleeping man. He bent down, touched his neck, and smiled at the little group. "Done."

"Jack, the minute Orzell reaches the top of the steps and opens the door to the apartment, you and Bert hit the hall-way in case he backs out and tries to run," Nikki said.

"Gotcha."

Kathryn shouted from down the hall. "He's here. At least I think it's him. He must have made the traffic light. Yep, it's him. Avery is right in front of him and parking farther down the street. Okay, he's out of the car and walking toward the steps. Everyone in position now."

No one breathed as they waited for the door to open. The minute it opened and Mr. OO stepped into the room, Annie turned on the overhead light. "Surprise! Surprise!" they all shouted.

Owen Orzell froze in place, a look of pure horror on his face. "Who are you? How did you get in here?"

"You have to guess who we are. And we came down the chimney like good old St. Nick," Myra said.

"Oh, sweet Jesus, you're the vigilantes. I recognize you. I don't have a chimney or a fireplace."

"There you go!" Kathryn said, giving him a push that sent him flying across the room.

Alexis picked him up and set him on one of the dining-room chairs they'd brought into the living room. "*Sit!*" she said.

Orzell sat, his face mottled with fear.

Annie moved across the room to stand in front of their captive. "Now, listen to me very carefully, Mr. Orzell, because I will repeat nothing. We're going to ask you some questions, and if you answer them quickly and truthfully, we will not peel the skin off your face and pour vinegar on said face. We might or might not push your ugly face into a salt box. After we give you your facial peel."

"Please don't hurt me. I'll tell you anything you want to know. I knew this day was coming. Span said it would never happen, but I knew he was lying."

The Sisters stared at the man in disbelief. "I can tell, this is not going to be any fun," Kathryn muttered.

"Talk!" Myra said.

"Promise you won't hurt me. I can't stand pain. Blood either. I get sick. You were joking about . . . about peeling the skin off my face, weren't you?"

"No promises. We do not give a good rat's ass if you can't stand pain or blood or if you get sick. We were more than serious about your facial skin," Alexis said, pulling out a KA-BAR knife and a bottle of white vinegar from her red bag.

Annie looked over at Myra and hissed, "So much for going out in a blaze of glory. This looks to me like a shoo-in. I was hoping for some fireworks."

"I know, dear, but we have to play the cards we're dealt. The evening isn't over yet."

"We're waiting," Nikki said. "How about this for a jumping-off spot? Tell us how a dead man can be living upstairs on the third floor?"

"You know about Joel?" Orzell said.

"And the staircase leading to the third floor. We also know about Jason Parker. Actually, Mr. Parker is snoozing on your bed as we speak," Nikki said.

Something sparked defiantly in Orzell's eyes. "Well, if you know all that, then why are you asking me?"

"Confirmation. Do not make the mistake of lying to us, and while you're at it, wipe that smirk off your face," Alexis snarled as she advanced with the fighting knife.

Annie perked up. Maybe that blaze of glory was going to happen, after all. She deflated like a pricked balloon when Orzell said, "Oh, God, please don't hurt me."

"Talk fast," Kathryn said as she bent over until she was a mere inch from Orzell's face.

"It was Span. He had a gambling problem. He was really good at ferreting out other people's weaknesses and making those weaknesses work for him. I like to gamble, too. He saw me in Las Vegas once, and that's how it all started. He lost over two hundred thousand dollars that night. Even if I was stupid, which I'm not, that put up a red flag to me. A director of the CIA does not make the kind of money where he can lose that much money in one night and not break a sweat.

"Eight years ago, about a year after Joel died, Span came to me, since I am the guardian of the CIA fund, and gave me a pitch about God and country and how this guy Jellicoe was going to single-handedly make the world a better place. It was a crock, but I went along with it. I was pretty down at the time because of my best friend's death, but I know that's no excuse. Jellicoe charged outrageous sums of money for his government contracts, which were numerous, but there were caps on those contracts. Span made up the difference from the fund I control."

"Where does Jason Parker come into all of this?" Nikki asked.

"The monies in the fund just sit there. They are never invested. It's like a never-ending source of money flowing in from drug deals abroad, auctions. It just never stopped.

Span suggested we take some of it and invest it, and the two of us would keep the earnings. He found Parker. We had a meeting, and I pretended to be Joel Jessup because, for obvious reasons, I couldn't use my real name. I was the client. My fund's money is what put Parker in business, but it was all a scam. He was just like that guy Bernie Madoff. But I have to say, he paid me off. The last two months the earnings went down, but not enough to alarm either Span or me. The economy," he said, as if that explained everything.

"How much money did you two skim off?" Annie asked, a dangerous glint in her eye.

Orzell licked at his lips. "A lot."

Alexis advanced with the KA-BAR in one hand and the vinegar bottle in the other.

"Upward of a hundred million."

"Dollars?" Myra squawked.

"Where is it?" Nikki demanded.

"Mine is offshore, what I didn't gamble away. I honest to God don't know where Span's is. He went nuts when Jellicoe was arrested, and he got fired. In case you don't know this, Span was found dead this morning. I heard the news at the Pentagon. He was shoveling snow and keeled over. He knew better than to shovel snow after his open-heart surgery a few years ago, but he went ahead and did it, anyway. I think he had a death wish. That means he's off the hook, and I take the fall for all of it, right?"

Annie blinked. The blaze of glory looked like nothing but smoke just then. "Right," she said through clenched teeth.

"How much did you filter?" Myra asked.

"Millions and millions," was the response. "It's all in the computer."

"Give me your password," Nikki demanded. "If you

don't, I have a program that will crack it. But if we do that, you'll be in pain a lot longer."

Alexis waved the wicked-looking knife in front of Orzell's face.

"That won't be necessary. My password is Yenom. It's *money* spelled backward."

"How much of the fund's money is still in Jason Parker's hands?" Myra asked.

"Tens of millions."

"We want it. We want yours, too." Kathryn whistled sharply, and Bert poked his head in the door. "Showtime. Wake him up and bring him and his personal laptop in here!"

"Okay, honey."

Kathryn blushed, and then she shrugged.

"Who else knows about all this?" Yoko asked.

"How should I know?" When the knife was a millimeter away from his hairline, Orzell said, "The president. At least I think she knows. She wanted to make a substantial transfer, but I stalled her. She wasn't even supposed to know about this special fund so she could plead plausible deniability. When I told Span, he said she was chasing ghosts and trying to scare me, and I should just hold tight."

"We need to huddle," Nikki whispered to the others.

Kathryn looked down at Orzell. "You so much as twitch, and we'll peel the skin off your ass and . . . assorted other places."

"Please don't hurt me. I won't move. I swear I won't twitch or blink."

Kathryn laughed, a truly evil sound.

"I think he's telling the truth," Myra whispered. "We'll know for sure when Nikki logs on to his and Parker's computers."

Bert and Harry took that moment to lead a groggy

Jason Parker into the room. Jack dragged another chair from the dining room and set it next to where Owen Orzell was sitting.

Parker was a little braver than Orzell. "I know who you are, and you're breaking the law because you were pardoned, and here you all are, up to the same old tricks. You kidnapped me. That's against the law. I demand that you release me right now."

"Shut up!" Alexis said.

"Don't tell me to shut up. I'm on a first-name basis with the president of the United States."

"A pity she doesn't know that. Now, sit down and listen to what I am going to tell you. Either you give us the information we want, or we will simply peel the skin off your face and then pour vinegar all over it, after which we will roll that same face in a bucket of salt," Alexis said.

Parker's eyes rolled back in his head. Jack jerked him upright.

"Tell them what they want to know, Parker. They're going to find out, anyway," Orzell said.

"What did you tell them, you weasel?"

"Don't call me a weasel, you slimeball. I told them everything. Don't try playing innocent, because I know Span told you everything. These women are the vigilantes, and they don't take prisoners. Everyone in the damn world knows that."

Nikki had the two laptops open and was typing furiously. She looked up a moment later and confirmed, "He was telling the truth about his password."

"Must be your lucky day, you piece of crap," Alexis said, lowering the KA-BAR to her side. "Okay, Mr. Parker, you're up. Give us your password, and I won't peel the skin off your face. They say vinegar burns like hell."

"No way am I giving you my password! If you're so damn smart, figure it out."

"Now you see, there's a problem there. We really don't have time for fun and games. Either you give it up now, or you both get a facial peel. Your choice," Isabelle said.

Alexis looked over at Orzell. "This might be a good time for you to tell your buddy here that the game is over, and if he doesn't cough up the password, you both get the peel, and he goes first."

"Parker, give it up, for God's sake. There's no way either one of us can win this. Besides, you're a damn crook, bilking people out of money just like that scum Madoff."

"And aren't you the lily-white little weasel."

"No, I'm not a lily-white weasel. I'm guilty just the way you're guilty. At least I had the good sense to own up to it. Look at them, for Christ's sake. They have blood in their eyes. They won't blink if they start skinning you. The president pardoned them, and here they are, doing what they did before the pardon, so that means the president knows about it. She's looking the other way, you stupid clod."

For the first time, Parker looked unsure of himself. "Okay, let's cut a deal here. I tell you the password, and you let me walk out of here."

The women doubled over laughing. "Sweetie, you aren't going anywhere except where we send you. We closed up your office. You are officially out of business and have left the country. We're going to give your clients back all their money, plus a little extra for being stupid enough to get involved with you," Annie said.

Alexis walked behind Parker's chair, grabbed a handful of hair, and yanked his head back. "On the count of three, I'm going to slice off the top of your scalp, roots, skin, and all, if you don't give up the password. One! Two!"

"Okay, okay! It's Rich."

Nikki looked up. "That's stupid. I would have guessed that right away. What's the password for your client list?"

Alexis gave Parker's head another jerk backward, the tip of the KA-BAR digging into his skull. "Fools. As in plural."

"Look who's the fool now," Nikki said as she typed in the passwords. "Well, lookie here! This sure is a lot of money just sitting there. Let's see, how should I divert it? I think I'm going to need more time to decide what I want to do with it. You, too, Orzell. Now tell me where that really big fund is, Mr. Orzell, and the name of it and how you work it."

"It's all in a file named Rose of Sharon. It was my mother's favorite flower. Everything is in the file, the brokerage houses, the account numbers, the offshore money, all of it. You aren't going to take my personal money, are you? My parents and my friend Joel left me an inheritance. You can't take that!"

"Oh, you silly, silly man, of course we're going to take it. Where you're going, you aren't going to need money. I'm going to print out some quitclaim deeds you're going to sign so your properties become ours. We are going to have such a good time spending your money. Yours, too, Parker," Nikki said.

Nikki turned to Jack and said, "Go into his office and hook up his printer. I'm going to download the deeds. Alexis is a notary, and I'm sure she has her seal in her red bag."

"You're thieves!" Parker spat.

"Yes, we are," Nikki said agreeably. "Rich thieves," she clarified.

Jason Parker sprang off his chair and lunged at Nikki.

Harry moved quicker than lightning, and the next thing they knew, Jason Parker was out cold across the room.

Owen Orzell started to cry.

"Will you just shut up already? It is so unmanly to snivel like that," Kathryn barked.

"Did you really think you were going to get away with this?" Myra asked in a tone that she would use to discuss the weather with a friend.

"At first I did. Then, when Span started gambling more and more and demanded more money, I knew it was just a matter of time. Will it do any good to say I'm sorry? It's all drug money, anyway, from around the world that found its way into the CIA coffers."

"Where did you lose all that money, Mr. Orzell?" Annie asked.

"Vegas. I'm a gambling addict, but not as bad as Span was. I knew when to hold and when to fold. He didn't."

"Which casino did you lose all that money in?" Annie asked.

"That big one, Babylon."

"Really!" Annie trilled. "Span, too?"

"That was his favorite casino. And now he's dead."

"That is just too interesting. I don't suppose you have his bank account numbers, or do you?" Annie asked, a decided gleam in her eye.

"Stop thinking I'm some dumb schmuck. Of course I have his account numbers. How else do you think he got the money? Do you think I met him in some dark alley and handed over a check? I don't think so! I wired the money to his banks. It's in the file under his name. If you plan on taking it, you'd better do it quick, before a couple of his ex-wives go after it."

"Why, Mr. Orzell, thank you for that valuable information," Nikki said. The Sisters watched as she tapped at the keys. A blizzard of numbers rushed across the screen. "It's all ours now!"

"I cooperated. Please let me go. I'll quit gambling. I'll get a job working at some fast-food joint. I'll stay on the straight and narrow. I swear, I promise never to gamble again. I helped you. Please!" Orzell wailed.

"You need to shut up, or I'm going to knock your teeth out and stuff them down your throat. You are a gutless wonder, and we are not going to let you go. That's the bottom line," Yoko said sweetly.

Orzell howled his misery just as Jack returned with the quitclaim deeds. "Sign on the dotted line." Orzell signed, his hand shaking so badly Kathryn had to threaten him again.

"You're up, Parker! Sign here!" Kathryn said as Ted and Espinosa dragged a sputtering, kicking, panic-stricken man over to the pool of light in the living room. "Sign your name and be quick about it."

With no other recourse available to him, Jason Parker signed his name on every piece of paper Jack handed him. Alexis squatted down and dug her notary seal out of her red bag but not before she handed the KA-BAR to Kathryn, who waved it about like a sword.

"Well, I think our work here is done," Annie said.

"And we didn't spill a drop of blood. We didn't do anything violent. We acted like the civilized women we are," Myra said. "I'm very proud of all of us tonight."

"I really hate to bring this up, Myra, but I wanted us to go out in a blaze of glory. I really did. We didn't even make a puff of smoke."

Myra patted Annie's hand. "I know, dear. Sometimes things just don't work out the way we plan for them to. But we accomplished what we set out to do. Nikki and the girls will make all that money go where it belongs. The president will be happy that we kept our bargain."

"I wanted that blaze of glory, Myra," Annie said stubbornly.

"Yes, well, I want my pearls back, too, but that isn't going to happen, since the dogs ate them. Be happy we're all walking away in one piece, that justice is done, and we have our lives back. I have to call Mr. Snowden now to have him pick up these two men. I don't think we should ask what's going to happen to them. I, for one, really do not want to know."

The Sisters agreed with that sentiment entirely.

When the downstairs door closed behind Avery Snowden and his men, the Sisters looked at one another. No one said a word as they gathered up their belongings while the boys carted all the computers out to the cars.

"We'll have to send a letter to the tenants downstairs, telling them they have to relocate," Isabelle said.

Nikki nodded.

"Then I guess there's nothing more to do here. We close up shop and . . ."

"Go home," Annie said flatly.

"Yes, dear, we're going home," Myra said. "Fergus is waiting for you, just the way Charles is waiting for me." Myra turned and whispered to Annie, "Did you ask him?"

"Good Lord, no. In all the excitement, I forgot. I'll do it right now. Ted! Can I talk to you a moment?"

"Sure, Annie. What's up?"

"How would you like to be the new editor in chief of the *Post?* Maggie will be leaving after the first of the year. She suggested you take her place. She said you would do as good a job as she did. You don't have to tell me right now. There is a considerable increase in pay and some handsome perks. You can hire Joseph as your right hand if you like, and he, too, will receive a considerable pay increase. Can you let me know by January first?"

"I'll take it. I don't have to wait till January first. Joe will come on board. Did Maggie really say that?"

"She did, plus a lot more. All of it good."

"Well, damn," was all Ted could think of to say.

Annie smiled as she linked her arm with Myra's and followed the rest of the Sisters out the door, down the steps, and outside.

"I'm okay, Myra. I was just a little miffed back there. We'll always be friends, right? By the way, I'm going to give all the girls an interest in Big Pine Mountain for Christmas. I already have a mountain. I don't need another one. Lizzie is going to do the deeds and have them all ready for Christmas. This way, the girls can take their families and all the animals there whenever they want. If we're lucky, they might even invite us from time to time."

"Annie, don't you dare ever change."

"Okay, Myra, I won't. You either."

"Never," Myra said.

Epilogue

Thirteen months later

Not much had changed at Pinewood or in the Sisters' lives. Life was leisurely for Myra, Annie, Charles, and Fergus. Myra and Annie visited almost daily, weather permitting. Charles worked down in the war room, compiling what he was fond of saying were his boring memoirs. Fergus Duffy worked at his new job heading up security at Myra's candy plant, a job he professed to love.

The younger Sisters called Pinewood on a daily basis to check in, and every Sunday they and Maggie and the guys made it over to have one of Charles's home-cooked dinners and catch up on each other's lives.

They always had presents for Yoko and Harry's baby girl, because that was what seven godmothers did. Little Lotus Lily Wong was spoiled to the nth degree. Maggie and Gus had gotten married in June, only weeks after he was able to walk down the aisle. Maggie had asked Charles to give her away, and after their honeymoon, they had bought a farm property outside Richmond, where Gus was busy breeding dogs. They kept threatening to bring a puppy to give to little Lotus Lily, but so far Yoko had managed to head them off.

The weather hadn't changed much, either. It was still snowing, just the way it had snowed a year ago to the day.

Myra stood at the back door, watching the snow fall. It was quiet outside, but not as quiet as it was in the house. It did smell good, though. Charles had prepared a huge pot of chicken noodle soup, and it was simmering and throwing off tantalizing aromas. Two large chickens complete with stuffing were roasting in the oven.

"You're bored, aren't you, Mom?"

Suddenly the kitchen was filled with a blinding white light. Myra whirled, her hands going to her throat for the pearls that no longer graced her neck. Standing by the table was her beloved daughter. "Dear God," she whispered in a strangled voice. She wanted to move, but her feet were rooted to the tile floor. "Darling girl!"

"Mummy, don't be sad. I worry about you."

Myra reached for the edge of the counter. "You look so beautiful. I remember the day I bought you that red sweater, and you said you loved it. Why in the world would you worry about me?"

"I loved everything you ever gave me, Mom. I don't want you to be sad. Don't tell anyone I told you this, but Nik and Jack are going to be getting their new baby any day now. I am so happy for her. I stopped by her office for a chat before I came here, and she told me. She wants to tell everyone, to shout it from the rooftops, but she's afraid she'll jinx the adoption. But the real reason I stopped by was to give her Willie. She cried, Mom. She said her new baby was going to love Willie as much as I do."

Myra did her best to absorb what she was hearing. "That . . . that's wonderful. I won't say a word, and I'll act surprised. God in heaven, I miss you, Barbara."

"I know. I miss you, too. You're doing the right thing, you know. That's what I came to tell you. I know how

worried you are, but don't be. It smells good in here. Charles was always the best cook. If I try, I can almost taste those brownies cooling on the counter."

Tears rolled down Myra's cheeks as she walked toward the bright light and the beautiful girl in the red sweater. "I need to touch you, honey. I need to feel you. Can I do that?"

"Let's try, Mummy. Let's both try real hard."

Her arms outstretched, Myra waited until the girl in the red sweater moved. She heard the endearing words, *"Oh, Mummy, Mummy, you feel so good, so warm, so soft, so motherly."*

"Oh, God, oh, God, you feel just the way you felt the day I held you in my arms for the first time. I can feel you. I can really feel you. I want to hold you forever, never let you go," Myra sobbed.

The blinding white light waned, and Myra was left standing with her arms outstretched, tears rivering down her cheeks. The last words she thought she heard ricocheted inside her head. They were words Annie was fond of saying to her and they now were the words her spirit daughter was whispering. *"You rock, Mummy."*

Myra sat down on the kitchen chair where her spirit daughter had been sitting. Was it her imagination, or did the seat still feel warm? She smiled as she wiped at her tears. Well, if she even had one doubt about what she was planning, that doubt was now gone.

Off in the distance, Myra heard the sound of a horn, then a second one.

Time to get moving.

Fifteen minutes later Myra and her entourage descended the steps leading to the war room, where Charles stood waiting. The large-screen TV was on so Lady Justice could preside over the meeting and the people seated at the table.

In the middle of the table was a package wrapped in brown paper and sealing tape.

All the chairs were full.

Charles descended the two steps from his dais and stood behind Myra's chair. "Before we begin, I would like each of you to affirm that you will swear your loyalty to this little group. As I call your name, say aye or nay.

"Annie de Silva?"

"Aye."

"Fergus Duffy?"

"Aye."

"Nellie Easter Cummings?"

"Aye."

"Elias Cummings?"

"Aye."

"Pearl Barnes?"

"Aye."

"Myra Rutledge Martin?"

"Aye."

"Martine Connor?"

"Aye."

"Since we're all in agreement, let's begin our meeting. Myra, open the box."

Myra ripped at the wrapping and held up the box for everyone to see. She turned to Martine Connor and said, "I think you should do the honors."

Martine Connor opened the box and withdrew a gold shield and held it up for everyone to see. "It's the only thing I took with me when I left the Oval Office. I have one for each of you and one for myself."

"Then, ladies and gentlemen, I think we are good to go," Charles said happily. "That's another way of saying, we are indeed back in business, and I, for one, couldn't be happier."